WHAT SEEMS TRUE

a novel

"What seems true depends on who you are, where you stand, and what you want—and sometimes you're wrong."

JAMES GARRISON

Relax. Read. Repeat.

WHAT SEEMS TRUE
By James Garrison
Published by TouchPoint Press
Brookland, AR 72417
www.touchpointpress.com

Copyright © 2021 James Garrison
All rights reserved.

ISBN-13: 978-1-952816-56-7

This is a work of fiction. Names, places, characters, and events are fictitious. Any similarities to actual events and persons, living or dead, are purely coincidental. Any trademarks, service marks, product names, or named features are assumed to be the property of their respective owners and are used only for reference. If any of these terms are used, no endorsement is implied. Except for review purposes, the reproduction of this book, in whole or part, electronically or mechanically, constitutes a copyright violation. Address permissions and review inquiries to media@touchpointpress.com.

Editor: Kimberly Coghlan
Cover Design: Colbie Myles
Front Cover Image: Geoffrey Garrison

Visit the author's website at https://jamesgarrison-author.com/

First Edition

Printed in the United States of America.

For my wife, June, who always has my back
and usually keeps me out of trouble.

"For now we see through a glass, darkly; but then face to face: now I know in part; but then shall I know even as also I am known. And now abideth faith, hope, charity, these three; but the greatest of these *is* charity."

—1 Corinthians 13:12-13, KJV

Part I

Chapter One—One Ranger

THE DAY AFTER THEY FOUND Billy Graham's body out behind the old StarLite Drive-in Theater, a Texas Ranger came down to the refinery to investigate. I was there since I had just driven over from Houston that morning to meet with Perry Comeau, the HR Manager. Instead of discussing his troubles with the union, we spent my first cup of coffee and two doughnuts rehashing what he'd heard about the murder.

From Perry's office, I could see the stairs leading up from the ground floor of the administration building. It was a hot October day on the Texas Gulf Coast, and his hall-door was wide open to let in some fresh air, or as fresh as it gets less than a hundred yards from the refinery's hydrocracking unit.

Only halfway listening to Perry, I watched as the head and shoulders of a big man hove into view in the dim stairwell like a submarine from the deep. First came a white Stetson, then a camel-hair sports coat and white shirt with a bolo tie, followed by creased blue jeans tucked into a handsome pair of tan cowboy boots.

We knew he was coming. This being the South in the waning days of Jimmy Carter and the Klan still holding sway in this neck of the woods, a lot of people were interested in how and why the refinery's first black supervisor had met his end. And who killed him. The Port Oso police were investigating, as was the Jefferson County Sheriff's Department. Even the FBI was nosing around, although they hadn't offered to send an agent. But Derek Frazier, the Port Oso Plant Manager, had demanded that the state police get involved—and not just any run-of-the-mill DPS officer. He wanted the Texas Rangers. And lo, here within hours, was a Ranger.

He was unlike any I had ever read about or seen in the movies or in real-life photographs. Gaunt with sunbaked, leathery skin, mustachioed cavaliers? Such as this, the man was not.

With a wheeze, he came to a halt on the landing and leaned with one hand on the railing. He was built like a bull and wide as a pickup truck. An expanse of white shirt bulged over a finely worked leather belt and a shiny brass buckle big enough to hold up the prodigious belly above it. His coat flapped open and I caught a glimpse of a long-barrel, silver pistol in a leather holster tied down to his thigh, just like he was John Wayne.

Merely an unlearned immigrant to the state, I wasn't sure that real Texas Rangers still existed. But here was the living proof—even if the legendary mold formed by years of riding horseback through chaparral and arroyos in west Texas in pursuit of Comanches, cattle thieves, and train robbers had been shattered and recast by long automobile rides over ranch-to-market roads and platters of chicken-fried steak and mashed potatoes in small-town cafes.

Perry and I hurried out to greet him, and a large paw engulfed my stubby hand, accompanied by, "Howdy," in bass. He took a deep breath.

"Name's Rogers. Leroy R. Rogers, but everybody calls me Roy."

"Dan Esperson," I said, struggling not to cringe at his grip. "I'm a company lawyer."

Releasing my hand and removing his hat, he wiped beads of sweat from his forehead with a white handkerchief that appeared out of nowhere.

"Pretty lady downstairs said you'd be employee relations." Whisking the handkerchief back into a pocket, he took Perry's hand and pumped it. Perry's round head and shoulders bobbed up and down.

"Yes sir, that's me. Human Resources is what we call it these days. I'm John Comeau, 'cept they call me Perry, like they call you Roy."

The Ranger gave him a quizzical look as he dropped Perry's hand.

"He means Perry Como, the singer," I said.

"Oh, ho." The Ranger chuckled and looked truly amused.

"Come on in," Perry said and started back through the open door of his office, then detoured a little to the right and yelled into another door just down the hall. "Hey, Sheila, bring us a jug of coffee and another cup. And bring the rest of them doughnuts." He twisted back to the Ranger. "You'd like a doughnut, wouldn't you?"

"Thank you, sir, but no thank you. I'm on a diet." The Ranger patted his stomach on the side away from his six-shooter, or whatever it was. I'm no expert on guns.

Once in his office, Perry motioned toward his conference table, a rectangular piece of solid-maple furniture that projected at a ninety-degree angle out from the front of his desk. The desk, table, and chairs were far older than I was, but in better shape—sturdy and polished to a dark gloss with only a few scratches here and there.

The office wasn't large, with one window behind Perry's desk and two doors, one to the hallway and one to the small anteroom where Perry's secretary and assistant kept watch for him. The office's white stucco walls were adorned with HR plaques and awards and a single 24-by-12-inch color photograph showing two men in hardhats, one of them Perry pointing down at something on the ground, the refinery cracking towers looming behind them. A pair of endangered shorebirds had taken up residence at a wastewater pond, Perry had told me, and he found a clutch of eggs in their nest.

The Ranger pulled out a chair and sat, shifting his buttocks to one side to make room for his gun inside the chair arm. Perry and I took the chairs across the table from him. Looking out the window past Perry's head, I could see a tangle of silver-and-gray metal piping and spindly towers giving off clouds of steam. Beyond the hot white vapor, the ghostly fabric of the refinery stretched out to the coastal marshland where it met a pastel blue sky.

"So, tell me about this boy of yours who got himself kilt the other night," the Ranger said. "Maybe we can figure out what happened and get this thing wrapped up by lunch."

"Know just the place," Perry said. He leaned forward in his chair. Lunch was always a priority for Perry when he had visitors. "Great little Mexican restaurant." His grin quickly faded at the Ranger's lack of expression.

"Gotta be downtown by two…" The Ranger's face brightened. "But we'll see how it goes." He reached up to his hat, and I saw why his face had lit up all of a sudden.

Sheila had appeared in the connecting doorway to the outer office. She was carrying a tray with a silver thermos of coffee, an orphan mug from the Texas State Fair, and loose packets of creamer and sugar. The Ranger struggled to his feet and tipped his hat to her. Shorter than the Ranger but tall for a woman, Sheila displayed a limber, athletic physique. She was dressed in light gray slacks fitted snugly across her hips and a thin pink sweater stretched tautly across her chest.

"Sheila Mills, my administrative assistant," Perry said, also rising. "We don't have secretaries anymore." As we all knew, the change was only in name.

"Pleased to meet you, ma'am," said the Ranger. "Roy Rogers." He held out his hand to her. Sheila hesitated, then timidly poked her hand forward.

"Are you really a Texas Ranger?" she asked, her eyes wide. They darted over at me and I smiled at her. I always made sure to get to know the secretaries, whatever they were called, and Sheila was one of the more pleasurable ones to know.

"Been a ranger thirty-five years." Placing his hat on the table, the Ranger pulled his coat aside to display a round, silver badge with a star. He ran a thick index finger along the bottom of the circle and the words "Texas Ranger."

"Same badge since the beginning of time, 'cept now we're part of the Department of Public Safety. Only about a hundert and thirty of us for the whole dang state, but we still handle the tough stuff."

Smiling broadly at her, he let the coat fall back into place over his big chest and stomach. "The whole dang state," he said again. Still smiling and looking around, as if in a room full of people, he settled his bulk and the pistol back into the chair.

Sheila, who seemed as nervous as a star-struck teenager, removed the fresh mug from the tray and began pouring coffee into it. Her hand was shaking, and coffee sloshed over the side as the Ranger reached for the mug. I jumped up, thinking that the poor woman was overawed by this Texas legend.

"Here, let me get a paper towel for that." I started for the door.

"Oh, thank you, Dan," Sheila said. She looked at me with her wide blue eyes, the palest blue I'd ever seen. I nodded and smiled back, then left for the paper towels.

When I returned, Sheila had gone back to her office. Both the door to it and the hall were closed, and Perry and the Ranger sat across from each other, the Ranger leaning back in his chair with one arm draped over the back and his Stetson resting top down on the table. I quickly wiped up the spill and threw the paper towel in the metal trashcan by Perry's desk.

"What I need from you folks," the Ranger was saying, "is to know all about this fellow. What he was like, who his friends were, his enemies"

"Billy didn't have enemies," Perry said, shaking his head.

"Must've had at least one. A friend wouldn'ta shot him so many times."

Perry blinked his eyes as he did when he was flummoxed. "Everybody liked Billy. I never heard an unkind word about him."

"Even from those in the Klan?"

"We don't have any of them in here." Perry shifted uneasily in his seat and raised his eyebrows in a surprised look, like, who would ever imagine a thing like that. I knew he knew better.

The Ranger leaned farther back in his chair and fixed Perry with hard gimlet eyes, a flinty green.

"They wouldn't tell you if they were," he said. "Not these days."

"Well, I know the people in this plant. All that Klan stuff's in the past."

The Ranger gave a snort and picked up the coffee mug while he kept Perry pinned with his skeptical gaze. Perry was a rotund, amiable man with a fringe of pure white hair on three sides of his baldpate, reminding me of a white marble bust of a garlanded Roman emperor I had seen somewhere.

"Billy was friendly with everybody," Perry said, darting his eyes over at me, as if seeking help, or at least some confirmation. I only shrugged, so Perry charged ahead. "He was easy goin', bit of a smooth talker maybe ... maybe not firm enough with the people who reported to him." Perry fidgeted and twisted his coffee mug back and forth on the table without lifting it. "Now Eddie Sykes, I wouldn't be surprised at all if somebody shot that sucker. He was the next black we promoted, and he turned into a regular drill sergeant, drove his men 'til they sent the union rep up here to complain. But not Billy. No sir. He worked at being one of the boys, er ... guys." Perry raised his hands at the Ranger's unblinking stare. "You may think that'd cause some problems out there, familiarity and all that, but his people respected him. And he was goin' back to school at Lamar nights, Port Arthur campus and—"

"Okay, okay." The Ranger patted his stomach and sat forward in his chair, moving his hat to one side and resting his elbows on the table. "Was there anybody with a reason to kill him? He diddlin' somebody's wife or something like that?"

"Oh no, not Billy. He was a strong Baptist. Of course, in the black church. Married and kids and all. Even a lay minister. Maybe it was a robbery."

"Don't add up. Out there behind that old drive-in theater in the middle of the night and a second set of tire prints almost on top of his'n. Shot five times or more, front and back and one in the face, the coroner tells me. Robber only needs one shot, maybe two."

The Ranger rubbed his cheek with a large hand and stretched up in the chair. "Wallet was gone, though," he said, like he was thinking out loud. Settling back, he shook his head and picked up his coffee mug again.

"But I don't reckon it was a robbery. Had to be some hate and meanness in what they done to him. Only thing that'd add up to that kind of killin', least in my experience, would be a woman." He drank from his mug. "Or just 'cause they thought he was a smart-ass nigger."

He looked over at me and I grimaced at him. The words might be crude, but that sounded about right for some white folks in this part of the country. Perry was silent.

The Ranger picked up his hat off the table. "Now let me give you the program," he said, slowly rotating the hat by the brim in front of him. "First you tell me who all Mr. Graham worked with and who he palled around—"

"Got an org chart right here," Perry said, pushing back his chair and starting to go behind his desk. "And his pals—"

"Hold on and let me finish." The Ranger held up one hand and leaned back in his chair with his hat resting on his stomach. "I want your employee files—I'll tell you which ones—and I plan to interview a few people."

"Conference room across the hall would be good for that," Perry said and gestured toward the outer door. By now, he was behind the desk, digging in a drawer for the organization charts.

The Ranger's mouth bent down at the corners, and he looked around the office, first at the ceiling and the window, last at Perry's high-backed leather chair. Then he nodded slowly, both head and shoulders.

"I'll be fine in here. A little more in-ti-mate than a big ol' conference room. I want to get the feel of the man I'm talking to, how he looks and smells close up. Or she, if it's a she." He grinned at me, then at Perry. "Only takes about five minutes with most people and I can tell if they know somethin'." He nodded again and spun his hat around. "I'm thinkin' we'll be all through here by lunchtime."

It occurred to me later, much later, that we, especially Perry and I, had been rather cavalier in talking about Billy Graham. And his murder. Maybe even disrespectful. We weren't considering him as a fellow human being who had suffered a terrible fate, but merely as an object of interest—a cipher, a problem to be solved, or at least dealt with in our little frame of reference. At worst, we were just rubberneckers on the highway of life, gaping at an accident and a covered body in the grass.

Chapter Two—The Interviews

WHILE ROY THE RANGER reviewed the employee files, Perry hauled me down to Derek Frazier's office to report on what was going on. First, though, he had to pull out his organization charts and seniority lists and explain them to the Ranger; then he dispatched Sheila for the files, almost twenty of them, on people the Ranger ticked off from a list he had been making in a small pocket diary. Perry left Sheila with instructions to summon everyone the Ranger wanted to interview and have them wait in the hallway outside Perry's office.

Derek Frazier was a tall skeletal man with a thin, craggy face and a thick crop of dark brown hair I greatly envied, even if it was dyed. He had been a tank commander in Patton's army and he still had the carriage of an officer—one in the British Raj.

Perry reported in the hurried, clipped way he got when he was excited, dropping words and cutting off the ends of sentences, while the plant manager paced from behind his desk to the window looking out over the plant. Derek was left-handed, and in his left hand, he held a short stick with a leather grip—a riding crop or swagger stick of sorts, which he tapped in the palm of his right hand. When he didn't dangle it behind him as he paced.

"Who does he want to talk to?" Derek asked, his back to us as he stared out the window.

"Don't know, boss," Perry said with a negative wag of his shoulders. "He was still looking through ... He seems to think it has to do with race or sex or—"

"Why would he think that? The man was robbed."

"Well, sir, he says based on his experience—"

"Counselor, does he have a right to see the employee files?" Derek turned and paced back to the front of the desk, to stand a few feet from me. He popped the palm of his hand with the riding crop.

I leaned away in my chair and looked up at him. To have adopted such a swashbuckling, hard-nosed persona, Derek was one of the most cautious refinery managers I had to deal with. Normally, that made my life easier, but not always.

"We could stand on the formalities," I said, "but it *is* a murder investigation, and one of our employees. If it were my plant, I'd let him have what he wants."

Derek gave me a sideways look that I took for skepticism, then paced back around to the other side of the desk.

The desk was completely bare, as was the credenza behind it. Not a picture, not a paper or any of those usual froufrous you see in a manager's office, awards and such. The only decorations on the wall were photographs of the refinery units. Well, there was one personal item: an enlarged frame from the Patton movie, George C. Scott in front of an American flag.

"I agree with Dan. I..." Perry started.

"Do you know what he's after, Dan?" Derek pivoted about and headed to the window again.

"Best I can tell he just wants to take the measure of the people around Graham. See if he can stir something up. He sure doesn't have much time to do a real investigation."

"Okay, keep me posted ... Perry, I need to talk with you. And get Layton Van Horn in here.... Thank you, Dan." Derek was back behind his desk, and I had been dismissed.

RANGER ROY had taken over Perry's office and the door was shut tight. I sat outside in the anteroom and pretended to review a notebook on contract negotiations with the union. The anteroom was smaller than Perry's office, windowless with the same white stucco walls, except for two large, glossy photographs: an offshore rig at sunset and a brightly lit Texaco station at night. A wooden railing divided the work area—with its filing cabinets and a couple of desks, one occupied by Sheila and the other empty—from the waiting area with its two worn leather chairs. I took the chair next to the railing so that I faced the door to Perry's office.

What I really wanted from this vantage point was to observe the Ranger's subjects as they came and went. And to have an opportunity to chat with Sheila and observe her as she typed and did some sporadic filing.

Sheila had started as a laborer in the plant, like all new blue-collar workers, and moved up to light-equipment operator and then to truck driver. Along the way she had managed to get an associate's degree, and this last July, she made her way into the administrative job with Perry. At the time, Perry, chuckling on the phone, had told me she had nice tits, which caused me to cringe, mainly because Perry never talked like that. And he *was* the HR Manager.

Out of the corner of my eye, I watched Sheila pull open a desk drawer and take out a small bottle. Removing the cap, she squeezed a white lotion into her palm and began applying it, first on the backs of her hands and her fingers, then rubbing her hands together, and finally massaging the back of each hand. Her fingers were long, almost elegant. It was hard to imagine those fingers sheathed in heavy work gloves. But unlike her smooth, fair face, her hands were ruddy and rough. As she finished and screwed the top back on the bottle, I resumed skimming the contract guide—but not for long.

"Who all's been in there?" I asked, stretching out my legs and settling my feet against the bottom of the railing.

"Only the crew on his unit and a couple of supervisors." She flipped through a stack of papers on her desk and slid another form and two carbons into her typewriter. "They only stay a few minutes, then they're out. He gets me to call five at a time. They sit out in the hall until the one before leaves."

"Yeah, I saw 'em when I came back from Mr. Frazier's office. Isn't that your husband at the end of the row?"

Back when Sheila first started, Perry had pointed him out to me. He was as dark as Sheila was fair, but ruggedly handsome: swarthy complexion, coarse black hair combed down over a low forehead, thick black eyebrows, broad shoulders, and a narrow waist. A slightly crooked nose, broken, Perry said, in a fight as a kid. He was a high school baseball star who hadn't made it on a farm team, so he'd come back to work in the refinery, like his daddy before him.

"Zack's on the list," Sheila said. Clickety, clickety, click went the typewriter.

"Why's that? Isn't he in maintenance?"

"He worked with Billy on a turnaround—he's a pipefitter. Back in the summer." She pulled out one set of forms and inserted another. "Looks like he's jumping around different areas now. But he doesn't take any time with most." She stopped typing and sat looking at the machine. "Except old leather face and Levi Lemieux. They stayed in there maybe ten minutes or so."

"Old leather face?"

"He's a supervisor." She was typing away again, filling in a line, shifting the carriage, then looking at a page of handwritten notes beside the typewriter and typing another line. "Jack Boudreaux. He's been here thirty years."

"He work with Graham?"

"Not really ... They would've crossed paths, though. He's never made it any secret that he doesn't like blacks on the units. Or women. He started before there were any women out there. Blacks only worked in the labor gang."

"He live in Vidor?"

The typing stopped. "What's that got to do with it?"

"I heard no black man would ever dare show his face there after sundown."

The carriage on the typewriter whipped to the side with a ka-chunk that was harder than before. She turned toward me, a pained expression on her face, her mouth taut. Without the corners turned up in a smile, she looked almost plain—but not quite.

"Look, I used to live in Vidor. It's not like that. 'Least not anymore."

"Sorry." I held up my hands, leaving the notebook resting in my lap. "I was just repeating what I heard."

She wasn't in a mood for teasing, I could tell—though she never spared me. When I bought a new cowboy hat and wore it to go with Perry to see Reagan at the Beaumont airport, she'd patted the front of my plaid shirt and asked if I'd gone cowboy; I'd be joining Ronnie's posse soon. That gave me a thrill—not seeing Reagan, her patting me on the chest. Later, when I thought back on it, I remembered she'd often edge close to talk, touching my hand, my arm, and that one time my chest, almost like a cat rubbing against your leg.

Today she gave me only a wan smile and turned back to her work. "Well, we don't like hearing that. Vidor always gets a bad rap."

"So where does old leather face live?"

"Vidor."

"And the lone ranger in there is checking out the racial angle?" I regretted the sarcasm even as I said it.

"Levi Lemieux stayed longer, and he's black as the ace of spades."

Ka-chunk went the typewriter again. I studied her profile. Pale yellow bangs low on her forehead, straight nose, high cheekbones, and wide mouth. Just a few freckles under her eyes. Her hair was cut in a shag that was almost boyish, thick and shaped over her ears and draped halfway down her neck. The ends swung forward when she tilted her head to look at the paper. Not so much pretty, as alluring. A nice shape, down to her waist and hands on the

13

typewriter keys, all I could see over the railing.

I flipped a page or two in the notebook and stared at the union demands. Not likely to receive much attention in these tough times. I tapped my finger on the edge of the binder.

"That's his female angle," I said.

"What?" She stopped typing.

"The black guy ... Lemieux. Graham was killed over a woman."

She turned her head and gave me a sharp look, her brow knitted. Her fingers remained poised over the keys.

"What do you mean by that?"

"Roy Rogers in there," I pointed toward the door to Perry's office, "says it wasn't robbery—too much hate in the killing—so it had to be race or sex."

Looking down at her hands, she was silent for a moment, then she resumed typing. An interviewee opened the office door and came out. A muscular black man with a lined, weary face. Without speaking to us, he exited to the hallway. After a moment, a tall white woman entered and said hello to Sheila. She gave me only a glance as she brushed past then disappeared into the Ranger's lair.

"Who are they?" I asked.

"The man's Billy's brother. George Graham. He heard the Ranger was here and came in on his own. The woman's no one you'd be interested in."

"Boy is she tall. Kinda nice lookin' in a tall woman's way." I wagged my eyebrows, curious to see Sheila's reaction. She gave me a thin smile.

"They call her Too-tall Jones."

"Why's she called too-tall?"

"You'll have to ask that bunch of horny toads out there. They all want to get in her coveralls, but she's not really interested in men." Sheila shrugged and pulled the form out of the typewriter and inserted another.

Too-tall Jones was in and out of Perry's office in no time at all, certainly less than five minutes. She spoke briefly to Sheila, asking how the house was coming along, and ignored me. Plopping her green hardhat on top of her short red curls, she left to be replaced by a black employee Sheila said was Larry Phipps. He stayed inside a good ten minutes, and after him came Joey Hernandez. Sheila said he was also known as the Cisco Kid, although he was more Cajun than Mexican. He and Graham supposedly had an argument over a car Graham sold him, Sheila said. The Cisco Kid stayed inside a while, and I left to stretch my legs and answer the call of nature.

When I returned, there was only one man—white, with the smudged face and dirty blue coveralls of a maintenance worker—remaining out in the hall. As I entered the outer office, Sheila's husband Zack was leaning over the railing, whispering to her, or more like, *at* her. The door to Perry's office was shut tight.

I hesitated in the doorway, not wanting to interrupt the family tête-à-tête, and as I did, Zack reached out and grabbed Sheila's raised arm by the wrist. He hissed something I couldn't quite make out except for the words, "don't you." Her eyes met mine with a look like I'd caught them *in flagrante delicto*. Turning quickly, Zack released her arm—more like he cast it away from him.

He gave me a sour glance, his eyes narrowed under his black eyebrows, and then stalked out past me. His work boots echoed in the hallway, then stopped.

Sideways to her typewriter, Sheila remained staring out the door, her hands in her lap. I resumed my post by the railing across from her.

"Zack see the man?" I knew they had been arguing, and I was curious why, but I couldn't just come out and ask.

She didn't answer at first, and then she looked at me with vacant eyes, as if staring right through me. "Yeah, he saw the man." She swung around to the typewriter and fiddled with the paper sticking out the top.

"So how long was he in there?"

"Not long."

The smudged-face worker from the hallway sidled in slow and confident. Outside, Zack's boots tramped down the stairs. The worker grinned at Sheila as she rose from the desk and started toward the file cabinet to one side.

"Hiya, babe. You enjoyin' the little parade?"

"No," she said, "I can't get any work done with all this...." She swung her arm around toward the closed door to Perry's office. And me.

"Zack sounded pissed when he came out."

Sheila shrugged and opened the filing cabinet. She extracted a file.

"Said he's goin' huntin'," the man said. He held onto his cockeyed grin. Shorter than me and wiry, he had a surfer's golden tan, under the smudges, and bleached blond hair with a cowlick that flipped a long strand almost down to one eyebrow. As he talked, he bounced on the balls of his feet and tapped his thigh with his hardhat.

"He does what he wants," Sheila said, "and he's got the days comin' to him." Headed back to her desk, she kept her eyes lowered, not looking at the worker.

"You almost finished up with the house now?"

She dropped the file on top of the papers beside the typewriter. "They're layin' the carpets tomorrow." She didn't sound too enthusiastic about it.

Leaning against the railing, the man ran his fingers along it, watching her as she went around the desk and sat down. I was watching her, too. Her movements were liquid and smooth, like oil being poured slowly out of a bottle. She knew how to hold her body so that men liked to watch her. At least I did, and I could tell this guy did, too.

The door to Perry's office swung open, and the Ranger's head of white hair popped out, followed by one arm of his camel hair coat.

"Where's the next 'un?" he asked in a gruff voice. "I don't have all day."

"That'd be me," said the worker. "Reckon I'm the last." He glanced back at Sheila. She was staring past him at the Ranger.

"You be sure to invite me to the housewarming," the worker said and strutted off toward the Ranger, who backed into the office ahead of him. The door closed behind them.

"Cocky fu-u ... joker," I said. "Who's he?"

"J.C. Ledbetter. One of Zack's friends."

"Not one of yours?"

"He's okay." She opened the file she'd retrieved and pulled out a sheet of paper. We were silent, and I opened my notebook again.

"So, what's the man in there asking everyone?" I asked after a minute or so, while checking the clock on the wall. Eleven-thirty. Lunchtime.

"I don't get much chance to ask 'em." She was studying the paper she'd taken out of the file.

"No one mention anything?"

She dropped the paper on top of the file and rolled another form into the typewriter. Her fingers resting on the keys, she turned her head to look at me.

"Old leather face told me he asked a few oddball questions, then asked if *he* knew who killed Earl Graham, and when he said no, he didn't, the Ranger just sat there and stared at him a long while ... then told him he could go." She turned away and the keys started going clickety-click almost before she'd finished talking.

"And Zack," I said. "What'd the man ask him?"

The keys stopped. "Where he was night before last."

"And where was he?"

"Home, of course." The carriage ratcheted back to the next line. "Where do you think he was?"

The door to Perry's office opened, and J.C. Ledbetter exited, looking solemn and less cocky than when he went in. He pulled the

17

door to behind him, softly not hard like I expected. Ignoring me, he gave Sheila a shrug and half-smile, almost as if he were apologizing for something. He slapped his hard hat against his thigh.

"I don't like that guy," he said. Sheila had stopped typing. He tapped the hard hat with the knuckles of his other hand. "Tell Zack I'll be in touch."

"He's leaving right after shift change," Sheila said, her mouth in a tight line. "You can tell him yourself."

Ledbetter nodded and left. Sheila glanced at me, then started typing again.

"When are they gonna get you one of those new electric jobs?" I asked. "Perry trying to keep you in the dark ages here?"

"This one's best for forms."

The door to Perry's office opened, and the Ranger peered out again.

"Mrs. Mills, would you be so kind as to step in here and speak with me now?"

Sheila gave a start and stared blankly at me, her face pale. She pushed back from the desk and turned toward the Ranger.

"I don't know how I can help you any," she said, shaking her head. She stood slowly, one hand on the stack of files and loose papers beside the typewriter, like she was pushing herself up. She smoothed down the side of her grey pants.

"In my business, you never can tell what'll help." As he spoke, the Ranger's drawl seemed to deepen, as if he were enjoying the part he was playing. He stood aside and held the door open wide for Sheila to go inside, past him.

Chapter Three—Mi Casita Bonita

"**Why'd you want to** talk to Sheila Mills?" I asked, placing the red plastic cup back on the table. The Coca-Cola was watery, as usual. Across from me, the Texas Ranger was quickly dipping one tortilla chip after another into the red sauce. Perry sat to one side, concentrating on getting his share of the dip.

We had driven the straight road down the refinery fence line, past the tank farm with its white, monster storage tanks, across the canal and the main road to the Mi Casita Bonita Restaurant at the far corner. It was a low concrete-block building, formerly part of a strip mall that had shriveled up and died a slow death from cash starvation. The restaurant was the only building with any life left in it. The interior was dark and somewhat dingy: dim fluorescent lights in a black ceiling, red carpeting speckled with lint and broken tortilla chips, aluminum chairs with red plastic backs and seats, and red tablecloths. And red plastic cups. The bowls for the red sauce and the plates piled with food the waiters ferried past were a gleaming white.

An odor of mildew—not unusual in low-lying buildings in this climate—mingled with the kitchen smells of Mexican food and hot grease. And a cleaning agent, Lysol or something, wafted under the door of the men's room behind me. Perry, a frequent patron, had grabbed the choicest seat, away from the restrooms and facing the other tables and the entrance.

The Ranger didn't answer right away, my question about Sheila. He took the time to look around the windowless room, pausing to stare at the far wall and its floor-length images of old Mexico: a vaquero with a lariat, a twirling dancer in a white blouse and billowing red skirt, a mariachi band in tight gray pants.

"She was out sick yesterday," said Perry, taking up the slack through a crunch of tortilla chips. "Stomach bug or somethin'. And she wasn't feelin' so good this morning. I sent her home right after she talked to you."

She had reappeared from her interview just as Perry returned from Derek's office. "Why'd he want to see *me*?" she asked, looking vaguely in my direction, then at Perry. She was leaning with one hand on the railing and shaking her head.

"I wouldn't know," Perry said. He shrugged and made a face. "You worked out there with him a while. And you know—"

"Well, I don't know a thing about *this*." She went inside the railing to her desk and sat down heavily in the chair.

"What did he want to know?" I asked. I was out of my chair and ready to leave for lunch.

"Not much," she said. Then to Perry, "Okay if I take the rest of the day off? I'm still a little under the weather." And of course, Perry agreed.

The Ranger tapped his red plastic cup with a sausage-like finger. "Just checkin' out some leads," he said, back to my question about Sheila. He smiled over at me. "She's a pretty lady, ain't she? Saw you lookin' at her this morning."

I gave a hearty laugh, a bit forced. "She *is* nice to look at." Bet you were looking, too, I thought.

"And a pleasure to talk to." The Ranger nodded, the corners of his mouth turned up, but not exactly in a smile. "It was a good morning ... A very good morning. Got the lay of the land, how everybody gets along out there. I pur-ty much know the dynamics around your man Graham now."

My surprise at the word "dynamics" must have shown. He grinned at me and added, "Not only do I have more'n thirty years of experience, I also have a master's degree in criminal justice. I do field investigations 'cause I like it—and I'm good at it."

Perry and I both nodded. The man had a brain in his big head.

"Most of all," he said, "I'm a good judge of people—men *and* women." He grinned over at Perry, then back at me.

I didn't say anything. I used to think I was a good judge of people, too, but I was beginning to wonder. I couldn't even figure out my own wife these days, and I'd been living with her for more than twenty years. Maybe that was just the nature of marriage.

The Ranger abruptly changed the subject. "You folks expectin' a strike?"

"Yep," said Perry.

A waiter dressed in an embroidered black vest and white shirt appeared with a tray of food. Steaming plates of fajitas, chili rellenos, and enchiladas, all with sides of refried beans, yellow Spanish rice, *pico de gallo*, and guacamole.

"First strike in six years," Perry said, leaning back so that the waiter, holding a plate with a white napkin, could reach past him.

"Plate is hot, *señor*." The waiter deposited the plate in front of Perry. "*Cuidado*."

Perry grabbed it anyway and quickly jerked his hand away. "It's the work changes and staffing cuts that'll do it," he said, shaking his hand, then blowing on his fingers.

"Cutting back on medical won't help," I said, poking at my enchiladas to see how much chicken was in them.

"We ca-can't keep absorbing all the cost," Perry said. "Medical care keeps skyrocketing and they have to understand it ain't free." Now he was in his element, with both Mexican food and subject. "But it's *tech*-nology that'll change everything. Next five years ... we'll have computers in *all* the control rooms. Union sees that as a threat..." He waved a fork with a chunk of meat on it. "And they're right. New control systems, maintenance changes, we'll operate this plant with a third the people we have now." He popped the chunk

21

into his mouth. "But the company's gotta have the flexibility ... you know, in the contract."

We were plowing through the food, the Ranger especially quick at it, sheering off section after section of a bulging tortilla, squeezing out stray bits onto his plate with each bite. He and I ate in silence while Perry described the company and union positions in the contract negotiations, something that was clearly on his mind, and then what he was doing to prepare for a strike.

"Got a caterer comin' in," he said. "Full kitchen and everything ... eggs to sandwiches and steaks. Hired additional security; bought two-way radios, razor wire for the fence line, high-powered lighting, and high-resolution cameras with monitors for all the gates." He gestured toward me. "That's what the lawyers wanted, so we have ir-re-futable evidence when we go to court."

"For an injunction," I said, "if there's violence or mass picketing."

"We're the good guys," Perry said. "We'll even run a line out to the union's picket shack so they can have lights and heat." He grinned at the Ranger. "We try to keep it as civil as possible."

"We don't want anybody, even if he's union, overcome by fumes from a gas heater," I said. "It's happened ... one of the other refineries."

The Ranger was mopping up the last of his fajitas, and he chewed slowly as Perry laid out his contacts with local law enforcement. "I even have the sheriff's and the Port Oso's police chief's home numbers on autodial."

"Things must be pretty tense out there in the plant," the Ranger said.

Perry's white-fringed head jumped around like a bobble-head doll's. "Could be, could be. But we can always hope the union'll see we don't have any other choice. Once a strike starts, it's hard to end." He was getting revved up now, his shoulders hunched forward over his empty plate. "People get set in concrete. Get mad at each other.

Brother against brother. Sons against fathers. There's families that still aren't talking to each other from the last big strike, and that's been over twenty years. Funds start running low, and those that are working are buying new cars and boats. A few cross the picket line, and the war's on—if it wasn't before. Bricks and bottles fly. One strikebreaker over at Fina got shot a half-dozen times. He lived, but no one was ever arrested. Some say the union put their people up to it, 'least agitated against him til someone went out and did what they all were talking about ... Always a threat of violence—that's why we have Dan here. He'll go get an order for 'em not to do that kind of stuff."

As if it worked, I thought. "We get a court order," I said, "then we try to hold the union and its leadership, or whoever the goons are, in contempt for violating it. They'll sue us, too, or go to the NLRB. Stir up the local media."

"Sounds like you boys'll be havin' a good ol' time come January." The Ranger patted his coat pocket, then leaned forward and took a couple of toothpicks out of a holder beside the napkin dispenser in the center of the table. "So, what you're tellin' me *is* that supervisors like Mr. Graham will keep on workin', maybe doublin' their pay, while fellas like Mills and Ledbetter'll be strugglin' and maybe on short rations. Then when it's over, they may lose their jobs altogether."

"Are you thinking that may have something to do with him getting killed?" I asked.

"No. Not likely. He was killed for a different reason. But it may have somethin' to do with the enthusiasm that went into it."

"Well," Perry said, taking the check from the waiter, "usually people don't get mad enough to kill each other until a couple of months into the strike." He pulled out a company credit card and handed it to the waiter.

"Hold on," said the Ranger. "I need to pay for mine. Department rules." He gave an exaggerated smile at Perry and extracted a money clip from his jeans and a twenty from the clip. "I need a receipt," he told the waiter.

The waiter left and Perry continued. "Even the supervisors start going stir-crazy at the twelve-hour days, week after week. Some've even come unhinged. More'n a few divorces. My secretary—one long before Sheila—got her a boyfriend during a strike. Divorced her husband 'fore it was over."

The Ranger looked at me. "You stay over here during all this?"

"Depends. I'll be here some ... all the time for the first month or so—*if* there are problems." I looked off toward the far wall. "But I don't mind. The food's good and I get to move around, not like the guys inside all the time."

"Not if we have to lock down the plant," Perry said. "Out in L.A., we slept inside for three months. Choppers brought in supplies—"

"Shit, I hope it's not like that," I said. "But I don't have much to keep me in Houston. It'll be better than staying in the office."

"I wouldn't bet on it," Perry said. "You just wait."

"You married?" the Ranger asked, looking at me.

"Sort of." That's how I felt at the moment. Dana and I were arguing all the time now, something we'd never done before. Well, not as often. I was ready to get away for a while, and I felt like she was ready for me to be gone.

"That's a funny way to be married," the Ranger said. He gave me a questioning look. "But I know what you mean. My old lady left me ten years ago, and I ain't never regretted it a moment. Best to have one to squeeze ever now and then and move on before they do."

I was wondering if he had trouble finding a woman to squeeze, given his substantial girth and red face. Yet, with that mane of white hair, he wasn't a bad-looking man, once you got past the belly.

Perry must've had even less generous thoughts because he smothered a laugh with something close to a snort. "From what I've seen," he said, "the problem usually ain't the woman so much as the man who doesn't understand her. I've been married thirty years, three kids, and never regretted a moment of it."

The Ranger's face turned redder than before. He shook a finger across the table. "I tell you, you can't trust any of 'em. Eve deceived Adam in the Garden of Eden and the female sex ain't changed a bit since."

Perry shrugged and concentrated on adding a tip to the credit card charge the waiter had placed on the table in front of him. The Ranger sorted out two dollar bills of his change from the twenty, pushed them to the middle of the table, and pocketed the rest along with his receipt. Our discussion of women was over, but it had me thinking about Dana.

Something was bothering her. I knew she wanted to change her life, what she was doing, and she wanted us both to go for counseling, but she wouldn't—or couldn't—explain why. She just did. I felt it was a waste of time. But maybe not. Maybe I should give it a try.

Chapter Four—A Small Matter of Malingering

THE RANGER WENT HIS WAY and we went ours, back to the plant for a meeting with Derek. The day had turned gray and blustery, a strong wind blowing steadily from across the marshlands to the northwest. The temperature had already dropped ten degrees. By evening it would be thirty degrees lower and I'd be shivering in my shirtsleeves.

From the road leading into the tank farm, the old refinery looked more dismal to me than ever. A skeletal array of silver and gray pipes and towers, low boxy control buildings and maintenance sheds, a row of red brick kilns from the nineteen-twenties, and above it all, the rising clouds of white steam. From the mouth of the tallest flare shot a giant yellow flame, like a Precambrian volcanic eruption that seemed eternal. Its fiery cone yielded up a column of black smoke that boiled off to the southeast beneath the lowering clouds.

In front of it all, less than a hundred yards from the channel that bore mammoth oil tankers to and from the Gulf of Mexico, was the main administration building from which Derek Frazier and his court ruled this essential netherworld of the American economy. Two rectilinear floors high, the building was an adobe-colored fortress with tall dark windows that rattled and moaned in the gales out of the Gulf or the blue-northers off the plains. Like the one today.

A verdant park—lush green grass, tall palm trees, and oleanders—filled the acre or so between the road in front of the building and the ship channel. In the middle was a yellow Victorian house with white gingerbread trim, a shaded front porch, and flowerbeds that were tended by the plant labor gang.

The house was empty. At one time the plant manager's residence, it had gone unused for years. Even if Derek had wanted to live there, he could not, for the powers in New York had decreed that it remain vacant—like some bizarre shrine to the plant manager and his wife who had died there. From multiple gunshot wounds.

Perry waved his ID at the guard and we drove through the main gate and down the asphalt road and into the parking lot behind the Admin building. When we got out of the car, he left the keys in the ignition and the car unlocked in case someone had to move it, and fast. It was only a company car; no one would have mourned its loss; but in the event of a general conflagration, it would be both obstacle and fuel. My own pool car, an old Plymouth parked out front in the visitor's lot, was similar to Perry's but in far worse shape. The front seat sloped forward and the interior stank from the astringent deodorant in which it had been bathed to counter the odor of stale cigarettes. By contrast, the plant odors of boiling crude, sulfur, and asphalt had seemed almost pleasant when I arrived that morning. Almost, but not quite.

"I need your help with Derek on this thing with Gene Jarvis," Perry was saying as we crossed the parking lot, interrupting my thoughts. I was staring back over my shoulder at the flare's surging yellow flame and roiling black smoke and feeling thankful I wasn't the one who had to explain *that* fiasco to the EPA.

"Uh, how's that?" I sensed a problem of my own brewing. Gene Jarvis was the plant's most diligent malingerer, according to Perry.

"Now he's claiming he can't work 'cause he got a whiff of benzene over at the terminal and all the fumes make him sick ever' time he comes in the gate."

Sniffing, I thought I caught a whiff of rotten eggs and was tempted to say that the fumes made me sick, too, but that wasn't really true—they only irritated my senses, though I didn't have any idea what they were doing to my lungs. Besides, any show of sympathy for Jarvis would likely weigh against my advice.

"Hmm," was all I said as we climbed the steps into the building.

"He came back for a few days last week." Perry turned toward me. "Wearing that damned insurance collar. You know, the thing the lawyers get 'em to wear. And he got that quack doctor to restrict his lifting to fifteen pounds. Fifteen pounds! ... His damn back. That was before the benzene." Perry was gesturing out to the sides and I had to stay a step or two behind him going up the inside stairway.

"You know what I caught him doing?" Both arms went up. "He was goin' down the hall with that collar on, lookin' in ever' door that was open." We were upstairs now, and Perry twisted his Roman-bust of a head up and to the right, then to the left, several times, to illustrate Jarvis' passage down the hall. "When he went by Sheila's door, I thought the ol' boy was gonna jerk his neck plumb outta joint—and for real." Perry grabbed my arm. "I was just comin' out of my office when I saw him."

"So, he's back now?"

"Hell, no. That's what I'm tellin' you. He called in sick yesterday. Claims he can't be around chemical fumes and that it was caused by the benzene spill. Even had that damn doctor give him a restriction for it." Perry swung his arm out and hit me in the shoulder. "How the hell can you work in a refinery if you can't ... you aren't allowed to smell any chemicals?"

"Have him wear a respirator."

Perry stopped at his door and stared at me. "Really? You think that would work?"

"No, but might be a quick cure if you told him that."

"Well, Derek and Layton want to fire his ass."

Derek and Layton Van Horn, his assistant manager, did indeed want to fire Gene Jarvis. Especially Layton.

Of average height and sturdy build, Layton exhibited all the humanity of a Rottweiler. A broad forehead and heavy eyebrows overshadowed a pair of dark, intelligent eyes, and he never seemed to smile. His overall demeanor gave him an air of menace, especially to me, since it had been evident from our first meeting that he hated lawyers. When he spoke, his voice was low and gruff, a no-nonsense tone that, with the freight of his words, was designed to brook no disagreement.

"Are you telling me we can't *fire* the bastard after this ridiculous claim?" Layton sat in a chair by the window, to one side of Derek's desk. Per usual, the hired help was in the hot seats to the front.

"No, I'm just saying—"

"He's missed half the year, and we've given him two warnings already." Layton shook his finger at me. "That's all the absence program calls for. He should've been gone before this."

"All I'm saying is that your policy up to now has been *not* to count absences due to work-related injuries." I tried to keep from glaring at him.

"How the hell can this be a work-related injury? The son-of-a-bitch is nothing but a fraud."

"What've you got to prove it? There was a benzene spill, even if it was small. He has a doctor who says he's suffering dizziness and headaches and attributes it to the benzene. Even if we win a medical arbitration, you'll have a lawsuit for worker's comp retaliation." I tried not to smirk at him—without success. "Tony Joplin would love to get you in front of a jury up in Beaumont."

Antoine Joplin was the plaintiff's lawyer to whom the union steered its members. He was also the lawyer for the union.

"We've got to do something about this man," Derek said. He had been fidgeting in his chair and not saying anything. He tapped the end of his swagger stick, or whatever it was, on the desk, then rolled his chair back and stood. "We lose credibility if we don't nip this kind of thing..."

Pacing, he trailed off as he reached the window beside Layton and stopped to look out. I figured he didn't say "in the bud" because Jarvis had long been in full flower.

"Give the union an inch and next thing you know, they'll run right over us," he said after a moment staring out the window. He clasped his hands behind him and almost hit Layton with the swagger stick.

Even though this was Perry's bailiwick, he was laying low in the grass, so I had to say something. "He's not exactly the union, sir."

One of my basic rules: always show deference and respect to a plant manager. Even to his back. I resisted meeting Layton's hostile glare.

"Well, they always go to bat for him," Derek said to the window.

"They have to." Perry finally spoke up from his chair close to my left arm. "They have a duty to represent him, boss."

"They represent every goddamn creep that comes along," said Layton. "Doesn't matter what kind of shit they claim ... That's why we can't work with 'em." He leaned forward and shook a finger at me again. "Why the hell can't you get rid of those bastards? You're a labor lawyer, aren't you?"

On the other side of Perry, I could hear his assistant, Hank Greenberg, clear his throat, as if he wanted to say something. Being an outsider—but probably smarter than anyone else in the room—he'd hold his tongue. New York HR had hired him straight out of Cornell, then shipped him south for hands-on training in a real industrial relations setting, with a real union and real management. From my chats with Hank, I knew he'd been traumatized by the culture shock: his grandfather was a labor organizer and his father a union lawyer and now he had to deal with Layton Van Horn.

"There's got to be an employee movement to decertify 'em," Perry said.

"We put our fingerprints on it," I said, "we'll have nothing to show for it but a lot of wasted time." What I didn't say was that the union had more support than ever, given the rumors about work changes and a layoff.

"Why don't we do the usual?" Perry said, back to Jarvis. "Send him to an outside doctor and get a third opinion."

The second opinion, from our company doctor, was as predictable as that of Jarvis' doctor, whom the union kept stabled in Antoine Joplin's office building, the local skyscraper.

"Shit," said Layton. "When have we ever gotten anything useful out of the quacks over here?"

"We could hire an investigator." Hank Greenberg had finally spoken. A safe subject.

"What?" said Derek, by the window again. He turned to look at Hank.

"If we think Jarvis' injuries are faked, or exaggerated," Hank said, "we could hire an investigator to watch him, maybe even make a movie of him working, or lifting something. One of the guys on his old unit told me he drives to Houston to do electrical work on new construction."

Everyone was looking at Hank. A thin young man with angular features: narrow forehead, nose, and chin, prominent cheekbones. Thick black hair combed neatly to one side. White buttoned-down shirt and dark tie. Fresh-faced, idealistic, and eager to please, but a little too understanding of the union sometimes. I'd once been that way, but I'd gotten over it.

"Why would he tell you that?" Derek asked. The man on Jarvis' unit.

Hank shrugged. "I have to be out in the plant a lot, so I occasionally stop by and have lunch with the men on the units. And the women," he added. "It's interesting what they'll tell you sometimes. And it's often not an accident when things slip out."

"Perry, you ever do that?" Derek asked, staring at Perry now.

"Do what, boss?" Perry shifted in his seat and glanced toward Hank, then back to Derek. I smiled to myself. Perry spent most of his days in here, protecting his backside.

"Go out in the plant and talk to the men?"

"I ... I don't have a lot of time for that, Mr. Frazier. Deal ... dealing with the union and New York and Houston. Then there's the comp program and ... and salaried employees..." Derek waved his hand at him, but Perry kept going. "And I don't have a big staff like the other plants. The supervisors—"

"That's what he has Hank for," I said. "To stay out in the field and keep tabs on what's going on out there."

Of course, Derek never went "out there" either. Although, to his credit, Layton did, and often. What worried me was what Layton was up to when he was roaming around among the hourly workers.

Perry gave me a smile and lifted his eyebrows in appreciation for my save. "That's right," he said. "Hank spends most of his day out with the troops. He's my eyes and ears—"

"Okay, okay," said Derek. "Can we put a tail on this man, counselor, legally I mean?"

I thought about it a moment and decided, why not try it. "Yeah, if you're careful. But you could get in trouble—"

"You have an objection to every damn thing," Layton said. "Just tell us if there's any law against it."

"We did it before," Perry said. "You remember that guy ... you know, Floyd what's-his-name? I took pictures of him movin' furniture."

"That's right!" Derek hit the back of his chair with the swagger stick. "We nailed his butt and the union dropped their grievance when you showed 'em the pictures."

"What I was about to say," I paused to glare at Layton, who returned the favor, "is that you need to hire a professional investigator who knows what he's doing. Just make sure he's licensed and competent."

"Good! Take care of it, Perry," Derek said. "I want Jarvis out of the plant before the union goes on strike." He pulled his chair out to sit. "Is that all?"

"What about that nig—" Layton Van Horn stopped and shifted his eyes from Perry to me. "That Negro supervisor who got shot?"

Derek gave him an icy stare. I couldn't see Hank, but Perry looked down at his hands.

"I saw the Texas Ranger in here this morning," Layton said. "He tell you anything?"

"He just interviewed a few people," Perry said, "then headed downtown to talk with the police. No real leads, 'cept he says it wasn't a robbery ... Though the man's wallet was gone."

"Those people kill each other all the time," Layton said in a low voice.

A disapproving scowl crossed Derek's face, but he wouldn't reproach Layton, not in front of us. Layton was the best engineer in the whole refinery system. Still, there had to be a reason he'd never advanced beyond assistant manager. If he saw Derek's scowl, he gave no indication, nor did he stop.

"If they're not stealing something, they're fighting over a woman or drugs or just trying to prove who's the meanest fucker on the block."

"I don't believe Billy Graham was like that," Perry said. "He was—"

"Only reason he ever got promoted was because he was black, and New York needed to show they were doing their part, keep the liberal press and the Feds off their backs ... Affirmative action. Shit! There's not a black supervisor in the place that would've made it in the old days. The eight of 'em aren't half-educated—"

Derek held up his swagger stick. "Okay, Layton. That's enough on Mr. Graham. He was one of our people and he did a decent job, so I'm told."

"He was almost through college, too," Perry said, nodding his head vigorously. "He'd been going to Lamar, nights, even before he was promoted, and he was gonna get his degree next spring."

Derek's face lit up. "That so?" He held the swagger stick motionless across his chest. "It's nice to hear our people are going back to school." He shook his head. "Too bad when someone with ambition like that..." He didn't finish, but tapped the palm of his hand with his scepter. Layton looked sour and turned to stare out the window.

WHEN WE got back to Perry's office, the union's committee chairman, Frank Landry, and his chief sidekick, Pete Reneau, were waiting in the outer office.

"We need to talk to you," Landry said to Perry, pointing at him with his fat index finger. Landry was a big, beefy man with a big voice and a full head of black hair and a square, red face. Since he had a full-time union position, he wore jeans and a starched blue-plaid shirt that bulged out at the buttons. At the last company picnic, he had won the crawdad-eating contest—and the annual picnic before, and the one before that.

"Let me get a Coke first, will you, Frank? It's been a long day." Perry slipped through the gate in the railing, past Sheila's desk and empty chair, and opened a small refrigerator tucked in the corner. "You like one, too?" he said, bending to reach inside. "And you, Pete? Dan?" He didn't ask Hank Greenberg, who was hanging back in the doorway.

"What I want to know," Landry said, "is why you had Zack and J.C. and the others up here this morning, questioning them about that supervisor—and without a union rep or lawyer."

"Why don't we all go over to the conference room and talk about it?" Perry said. Leaving the refrigerator door open, he held up a Coke can and, giving Frank a questioning look, pulled the tab on it.

"We'll just have coffee," Frank said. "And we're fine right here."

"I'll have a Sprite," said Pete Reneau from behind me. The west side operations steward, Pete seemed to show up on most missions with Landry. He was short and muscular with a dark, smoothly benign face. He was the shrewd one of the pair, to my mind. As usual inside the plant, he wore work clothes, but his neat blue coveralls looked almost pressed and his tan work boots freshly brushed.

"Nothing for me," I said.

"Hank, will you make us a pot of coffee?" Perry said.

Hank nodded and mumbled his assent. He went to the coffee maker and pulled out the pot with the dregs of cold morning brew still in it. As Perry rummaged around in the refrigerator trying to find a Sprite for Pete, I decided to set the ground-rules before Perry became too conciliatory.

"Frank, they didn't have a right to union representation or to have legal counsel present. They weren't under arrest or being subject—"

"Look, I didn't come up here to debate this with a company lawyer. You wanta talk, I can call Tony Joplin and the two of you can jaw at each other all you want."

I grimaced at him. "As you like. But you're wasting your time. A supervisor was killed and a Texas Ranger was here to investigate."

"You should've made him do his investigation away from the plant."

"Come on, Frank," said Perry. "You know Derek's all freaked out over this. And he—"

"The man's always freaked out over something."

Hank had filled the coffee pot with water across the hall, and he made his way between Frank and me to go behind the railing. Perry held the gate open for him.

"After how Clayton was killed, you know he's concerned," Perry said.

"That was an addled-brain fool that shot him."

"An addled-brain fool that was egged on by some people who should've known better." Me talking.

Turning away from Perry, Frank loomed over me like a grizzly bear about to swat an annoying pest. I had touched a sore spot. Joe

35

Clayton had been the plant manager before Derek. A deranged laborer with the IQ of a four-year-old had murdered him. Murdered both him and his wife—Clayton in the bathtub of the plant manager's house across the street and his wife out on the lawn where she'd been chased by the murderer. The man's co-workers had been ragging him about some minor transgression, something to do with the flowerbeds around the house, telling him that the manager was going to fire him.

"Working people have rights in this country," Frank said. "Zack, J.C., the others ... you embarrassed them by making them come up here to the office, on work time, to be grilled by a fucking Texas Ranger."

"You've got to be kidding," I said. "A supervisor's been murdered, and you don't want to help us find the killer?"

"You're twisting my words." He balled up his fist and moved forward, closer to me. Pete Reneau placed a hand on the union chairman's arm.

"It's okay, Frank," Reneau said. "It's nothing but a company lawyer talking. We came to see the man here." He jerked his head toward Perry, who was still standing at the railing, holding a can of soda in each hand.

"They should've talked to us first," Frank said, "before they put Zack and the others through all that." He turned to Perry. "Let's go into your office there and talk. You need to make it clear to everybody, and I mean everybody, that none of these people are suspected of killing that man."

"Well, I don't know..." Perry started.

Frank Landry was already through the door into Perry's office. It seemed to be a favorite spot for everybody. Pete followed, pausing first to lift a soda can out of Perry's hand as he went past.

"See you later," I said and left. Hank Greenberg hesitated, then came after me instead of going inside with Perry.

Chapter Five—Sheila

NOT LONG AFTER I CHECKED into my motel room, the phone rang. It was Sheila Mills, and she wanted to know if I had plans for dinner.

Partially concealed by live oaks and pecan trees, the Drifting Sands Motel was squeezed into a horseshoe alcove off The Groves highway. The company had negotiated a special rate there, so that's where I stayed when I came over to the Golden Triangle to visit the company's refineries and chemical plants. The Golden Triangle was what the local chambers of commerce called this gritty part of Jefferson County, Texas—as in "black gold" rather than anything shiny and bright.

The four lanes in front of the "Sands," as we called it, were always flowing with fast-moving traffic, especially at shift change three times a day. I usually managed to wrangle a room at the back, away from the road, and I turned up the blower on the combination A/C and heater to dull the outside noise. The place had all the amenities of home, and more: a reading light between the double beds, a small table in one corner (if you didn't mind the gale force wind from the wall unit), free soaps and shampoo, and a flyswatter hanging in the closet. The eponymous swatter could also be wielded against king-sized cockroaches that scooted up the walls or sailed over the bed at night and the half-inch silverfish that awaited me in the bathtub shower in the morning. But it was a feeble weapon against creatures that had already outlived the dinosaurs.

The Sands' courtyard held a small, egg-shaped swimming pool.

On my way past, I noticed a large flotsam of dead leaves at one end and a couple of bloated toads drifting belly up in the middle. It was too cool to swim now and it would be until spring, although an engineer working the strike would receive a dunking there that would leave him only marginally better off than the toads.

I was hanging up my suit bag in the closet, next to the flyswatter, when the phone rang. "Dan," came Sheila's voice after I said hello. "I thought you'd be staying there tonight."

"Sheila?"

"You have any plans for dinner?"

WE MET at Caprice's restaurant in Beaumont. Emerging out of the shadows at the far end of the parking lot, away from the cluster of other cars near the building, she approached me like a spy in the night, a trench coat whipping about her in the wind, a scarf pulled tight over her fair hair so that none was exposed. She doffed raincoat and scarf only after we were well ensconced in a booth in the back corner of the restaurant. The place was humming with voices but far from full.

Sheila and I had never met outside the plant before, much less had dinner together. She'd said she wanted to see me, have a chance for us to talk. How could I refuse? While I was curious about why she had invited me to dine with her, I had no illusion that it was because I was an irresistible hunk. Life had disabused me of that notion long ago.

"Zack's gone off with a couple of his friends," she said. "Hunting in the valley." She finished folding her coat into a neat square and placed it on the seat beside her. She hadn't looked at me since we came inside.

"So you told me. You feeling better?"

"Yeah, thanks. Just got a little dizzy." She took off the scarf, a shimmery red silk one, folded it into a smooth triangle and placed it on top of the trench coat. "Kids are at my folks." She gave me a tentative, questioning look. "So, I was kinda at loose ends and thought if you didn't have a meeting or—"

"I'm glad you called. It gets old eating alone."

"You're always so nice to me at the plant, you know, I..." She shrugged and looked down at her hands. I waited, but she didn't continue.

"Well, you seem like a nice person," I said. "I enjoy talking with you."

She raised her eyes. Unblinking, blue even in the subdued lights of the restaurant and the one candle on the table. Her white blouse was open down a couple of buttons below her throat, her skin above the fabric smooth and lustrous in the candlelight. The lines of her cheek, nose, and mouth wavered in the shadows from the flame. Her cheeks were still flushed from the cold, and her glossy pink lipstick seemed to glisten.

My first impression had been wrong. She wasn't uneasy about being here, certainly not as nervous as I was, despite her cloaked identity. Her gaze was level over the cutlery and glasses of water the waiter deposited in front of us, her breathing relaxed and even. I was hoping mine hadn't increased with my heart rate as I stared back at her.

"Zack and I are building a new house," she said. "Over in The Groves." She unfolded her napkin and placed it in her lap.

"That's nice." I remembered her talking about it, with Ledbetter and the tall woman at the plant. I followed suit with the napkin and shifted the fork and knife away from the plate. "When are you moving in?"

"Next month. Just a few more things to finish yet ... You're married, aren't you?" Her gaze was steady, and I met it.

"Yes." I nodded. I must never have said anything to her about Dana.

"My oldest daughter..." She looked down at her hands in her lap.

"She's gone to live with her grandparents now." The waiter appeared with the menus and we looked at them in silence until he returned for our order.

"Zack's got a temper," she said when the waiter had gone. "We have three kids. Esther ... she's the oldest, sixteen going on twenty-five. Zack junior's the youngest ... twelve, and Amy's in between."

I only nodded, trying to figure out why she was telling me this.

"Esther was talking to some people at school Zack didn't like, and he told her to stay away from them. When she talked back, he..." She shrugged.

"That why she's gone to your folks?" I guessed it was Sheila's parents and not Zack's.

"That's part of it." She took a deep breath, looking at me now with solemn unblinking eyes. "You've never said anything about your family."

"Not much to say." It was my turn to shrug. "The usual stuff. Been married twenty years or so, one daughter. She just started college this year. Dana ... my wife's a lawyer with a big firm in Houston, but she wants to be a musician. Her first love." I almost said, true love, but I didn't. "She's good at whatever she does, but she gets frustrated. She's too focused on it—law, music, whatever it is. But we get along okay." Or we had.

"Zack and I were having some problems, but I think we've taken care of them."

"That's good." I nodded. "Al-l-ways good to take care of problems rather than let 'em fester." I was thinking about Dana.

"We were going to counseling. After Esther left." Another shrug. "Zack's not really into that kind of thing."

"Dana's been trying to get me to do that." I shook my head, slowly. "I don't know why. I don't see any problems in our marriage." Well, I did, but I wasn't interested in talking about them with Sheila, and I could tell she wasn't really interested in hearing about my problems.

Sheila cocked her head to one side and her eyes glistened at me in the candlelight. "Do you think that Ranger has any leads?" she asked. She didn't say, "on who killed Billy Graham." Almost like she didn't want to say it.

"I wouldn't know," I said, wondering if this was the reason for dinner. "He didn't share a lot with us—except he believed it had more to do with sex, or race, than anything else. It wasn't a robbery."

"But they took his wallet, didn't they? Couldn't it have been a robbery?"

"Could be someone just wanted it to look like a robbery." The wallet must've been on the news, or Perry let it slip.

Her face screwed up in a perplexed look, and she stared past my shoulder at the mirror on the wall behind me. We had sat so that I faced the front of the restaurant.

"He was actually a nice man, you know," she said after a moment. "I worked for him as a truck driver and I used to see him sometimes over at the school." She looked at me with those clear blue eyes, accentuated by eyeliner and a glossy eye shadow. At that moment, I could've almost fallen into those eyes.

"Just walking to the parking lot and all..."

"I never met him," I said. "But I remember when he was promoted."

"I didn't know him well. He was very private. Couple of kids. But I heard his wife was leaving him ... Or he was leaving her. She's a teacher." Sheila stopped and leaned forward, over the table. "Do you think she could've had something to do with it?"

"No idea. You talked to the Ranger. He tell you anything?"

"No. I don't even know why he wanted to talk to me ... Do you?"

I shook my head. I couldn't help admiring the gold chain around her neck as she leaned over the table. How the chain and the small cross on it gleamed in the candlelight against her pale skin, and the curve of her breast as she shifted to one side and the blouse bulged out at the undone second button.

"Like you said, you worked with Graham." I looked up at her eyes again. "You see a lot of people coming through your office there. Bet you know more about the men in that plant than anybody else in the building."

The food arrived while we talked, shrimp in ginger sauce for Sheila and veal Parmesan for me. I could feel my waistline expanding as we ate.

Sheila finished her final shrimp, leaving everything else on her plate untouched. Pushing the plate aside, she placed her arms on top of the table, one hand grasping the opposite wrist, and rocked forward. She lowered her voice to a husky whisper, even though no one else was near us.

"Dan, I'm afraid they may try to blame Zack ... But he didn't do it."

"Blame Zack?" Stopping my fork halfway to my mouth, I straightened up and stared at her in surprise. "Why the devil would they pick on your husband?"

"The Ranger asked me where Zack was. I told him, he was home ... with me. Then the man just stared at me, and stared, and stared. With those hard little eyes of his."

Her eyes were wide and fixed on mine. I swallowed the last bite of veal almost without chewing it.

"That's what he does," I said, taking a gulp of wine so that I could speak. "He stares at people. Isn't that what they said?"

"Like he's trying to read your mind." She hunched up her shoulders and gave a shiver. Then she leaned over the table again. "Or make you confess to something whether you mean to or not."

"He's a law officer. That's his job."

"He's got a dirty mind. I saw how he looked at me."

I laughed. "I can't imagine you have anything to worry about from him."

She exhaled and bending toward me again, resumed her

whisper. "I'm worried about Zack. He said some things about Billy, out in the plant."

"Like what?" This was deeper than I had thought.

"He called him a nigger and swore some about him."

"Did they have a confrontation?"

"No ... Not that I know about. It was to somebody else ... J.C."

"Did you tell this to the Ranger?"

"He already knew." Sheila drew her lips into a tight line.

"Well, that explains why he'd be interested in where Zack was the other night."

"Zack was in the Klan ... when he was younger."

"What?" I dropped my hands down on the table with a thump. The plates were gone, and all that was left between us was our wine glasses and the candle to one side, still burning brightly. "He was in the Klan? You're kidding me. Is he still?" Now I was leaning forward, and not whispering.

"Oh, no, Dan. That was ten, fifteen years ago. All that stuff's done with these days."

I'd heard that one before. "Well," I said, examining her face, "I guess a lot of people down here were in the Klan at some time or other. Does the Ranger know this?"

"No. But he knows Zack killed a man."

"Huh?" I exhaled involuntarily and my mouth dropped open.

"It was a hunting accident. But still..." she trailed off, and her eyes drifted away from mine. This wasn't looking good for Zack, whom I didn't know from Adam except to see him in passing. And see him grab Sheila's wrist this morning.

"So ... you say it was an accident. When was this? How—?"

"Back about ten years ... He was Zack's best friend." Gripping the table, she looked at me with a sad, earnest face and spilled the words out as if they were burning a hole in her gut. "They were going through a barbwire fence, and Zack's gun got caught in the wire, and it went off. It hit Jesse in the face. The coroner found it was an accident and Zack would've never hurt a hair on Jesse's head. We all go back to high school together and—"

"And Zack was with you the other night—when Graham was killed? All of it?"

"Dan." She reached across the table and grabbed my hand. She squeezed it hard. "Do you think I'd lie to you? Of course, he was with me." The most earnest of looks. "You do believe me, don't you?"

I wanted to believe her; I really did. Even if I didn't know her all that well. I turned my hand over and gave her hand a gentle squeeze in return. Our hands lay there together for a moment, then we each withdrew to our own side of the table.

"Remind me never to go hunting with Zack," I said, trying to smile at her.

"It could've happened to anybody."

That I doubted, but I wasn't going to tell her that.

Her face brightened. "Zack's really good with guns now. One of the conditions of his probation was that he go to classes and then he took up sports shooting"

"Probation?" I may not be the best listener, but eventually the words filter through. "Why was he on probation?"

"They charged him with a misdemeanor ... you know, because Jesse died, but our lawyer got them to put him on probation and then got it all erased."

"Expunged," I said. "What was he charged with?"

"I don't know ... something like negligence with a firearm. But it's all gone off his record now." She paused. "Do you think the Ranger could bring that back up? Jesse's mother got real nasty about it."

I shook my head slowly. "I don't know, Sheila." Then I had an odd thought. "Do you ever go hunting with him?"

"Sometimes. I'm a pretty good shot and I do some skeet shooting myself." She smiled brightly at me. "Won a blue ribbon with my sixteen gauge."

"That's out of my league." I signaled the waiter for the check. "I barely qualified with an M-14. Thought I wouldn't need one, but I did."

We were silent as the waiter handed me the check and I took out my wallet to get a credit card. I changed my mind and pulled out a twenty and a ten. I couldn't put her on my expense account, and it would be easier not to have to explain the credit card slip to Houston.

"Dan, do you think there'll be a strike?" she asked as we waited for my change.

"Your guess is as good as mine." I wasn't about to give her my opinion and have it get out that the company lawyer said there was going to be a strike. Not that I thought she would go blab it around, but she was married to a strong union man, and they were all thicker than thieves in this place, whichever side they were on. Up to the point when some were working and some weren't.

"Don't you have friends who'll tell you what the union's planning to do?"

"They only react to what the company does," she said, picking up her scarf. Looking down at it, she pulled it through her fingers one way, then the other. "I hear Perry and Hank talking and it sounds like there will be."

That's right, I thought. She probably knew more than I did from being around those guys in HR. Along with hearing all the gossip that flew around the Admin building.

I shook my head. "Technology's going to change the way the plant operates, and the union may fight it." Will fight it. With the new control systems and realignment of work, the plant wouldn't need two-thirds of the workers. Maybe not right away, but eventually, in a few years.

"I'm worried what'll happen if there's a strike." She tied the scarf around her hair and reached for her coat. The restaurant was mostly empty now. Holding the coat in her lap, she gave me a forlorn look. "We just finished building that house"

"You'll be all right. You'll still be working and I expect your pay'll just about double in any strike."

She took a deep breath and shook her head. "It's not worth it." She stood abruptly, as if to punctuate her statement.

"It never is," I said. I stood also and removed my sports coat from the back of the chair.

Watching me put it on, she sighed and said, "After they've had their fill of hunting and fishing—the ones that don't pick up a job in Houston or somewhere ... they'll all sit around and drink and stew about it and get madder'n hell, and then when it's over, no one's any better off than before. My daddy was in the big strike back in the fifties, and it wasn't any good for anybody."

"The company's going to get the changes it wants, and Zack and the union need to make the best of it." And it wouldn't hurt for her to pass this on to Zack and his friends.

"There'll be violence."

"We're ready for it."

"And then there'll be layoffs." Her blue eyes took on a steely hardness I'd never seen there before. Perry hadn't addressed layoffs with the union, but it was a safe bet that they'd figured it out. And that Sheila had overheard the discussions Perry had by phone with Houston HR.

I nodded and helped her with her coat. "Maybe. But you can't hold back progress."

I walked her to her car. It was parked away from the tall mercury-vapor lights in the parking lot and in the shadows of a row of oleanders along the property line. Next door there was a dark warehouse with a high brick wall.

She unlocked the car, a late model Oldsmobile Cutlass, then turned toward me. I must have moved closer to pull the car door open for her because she reached one arm around me beneath my outstretched arm.

"I'm afraid, Dan." The edge of the scarf tickled my nose. I

dropped my hand from the door and put my arm around her. There was a catch in her voice. "I'm really afraid ... of what's going to happen."

I thought she meant with the strike, but I was wrong.

"It'll be okay," I said.

She looked up at me. "I better be going," she said.

The lights from across the lot reflected in her eyes and gave her smooth cheeks a sheen of white silk tinged with pink. I was tempted to kiss her, then and there, but I didn't move, just looked down at her face. I thought she wanted me to kiss her or hug her or something; but after a moment, she said goodbye and pulled away and pushed the car door open wide and slipped into the seat. I stood and watched the Cutlass as she drove off—watched it all the way out of the lot, until I couldn't see her anymore.

Chapter Six—What Now?

OVER THE NEXT COUPLE OF months, Sheila and I managed to meet a few more times away from the plant, when I went over to visit Perry Comeau and prepare for union negotiations. Dinner or breakfast, nothing more intimate than that, just an easy diversion from the day-to-day drag of life. This trip, though, would afford no opportunity to see her, at least not outside Perry's office.

It was the end of December, and Liz Johnson and I were on our way to the refinery for a final planning session before the labor contract expired on January 5th. Liz was the new labor relations manager for Texas and a rising star in the Human Resources Department. More than once, I'd helped advance her career, getting her out of a hole she'd dug her way into or just providing sage advice, most of it legal. Somewhere along the way, she had passed me by, and our roles were often reversed now, even though I was a good ten years her senior.

Despite the Ranger's efforts, there had been no arrest for Earl Graham's murder, and the subject had quickly faded from the local papers and television news, written off by those I talked to at the plants—almost all from the white community—as just another black-on-black crime. Oil prices were still sky high, and there were still lines at gas stations, if not as long, and still, there were American hostages in Tehran. Ronald Reagan had been elected president, without my vote, and the nation was about to shift course once again.

My life, too, had shifted course, and not for the better. Dana had packed two large suitcases and left. I hadn't heard from her since Christmas Eve, and I could only speculate where she was. Which I did. Our daughter, Susan, hadn't even bothered to come home for the holidays, saying she'd rather stay in L.A. with friends. So, I had plenty of time to think about what I didn't want to think about. Which made me even happier to get away from my clean, well-kept home with everything in its place and my dingy, unkempt office with stacks of papers everywhere—on my desk, on a long table by the wall, even on the floor. Ten years I had spent in that office—the same old industrial carpet, beaten up wooden desk and credenza, and a swivel chair that tilted back so far I risked catapulting out of it every time I put my feet up. All the new lawyers had updated offices with sturdy new furniture and ergonomic chairs, but I'd refused every offer by the office honchos to upgrade my domain.

I liked my splendid isolation—the quiet and solitude of a back corner on a different floor from almost everybody else, except for my secretary, who sat close by my door, even though she had to tend to two newbie lawyers far down the hall. One thing I'd learned in my twenty years of practice is that your secretary, and maybe your paralegal, are the most important people in your life—outside your family and your girlfriend, if you have one. And I didn't.

That was what I was thinking as I drove the long stretch of I-10 from Houston and tried to avoid the more painful memories. The pool car wobbled and whined on the uneven concrete of the interstate. Not even the deodorizer hanging from the rearview mirror could overwhelm the cigarette smell.

Liz sat beside me and flipped through the negotiations notebook, stopping occasionally to chew on a fingernail completely lacking in polish. Unlike Dana's well-manicured nails. Static finally managed to drown out the timpani in Berlioz's symphony, and Liz switched off the radio.

"Have you hired local counsel?" she asked. Liz had never handled union negotiations before—much less a strike. This was her second trip to the plant since she'd taken her new job, and she tended to worry a lot about whether we'd covered all the contingencies.

"Jim-Bob Lloyd ... like always," I said. Jim-Bob might have a Texas cattle-rancher name and brusque manner but he was one of the shrewdest lawyers I'd ever met. More importantly, he was a Baptist deacon and went to the same church as three of the local judges.

"The union using that ambulance chaser they use for everything else?" She snapped the notebook shut.

"Yep. Antoine Joe-plan."

"Tony Joplin. I've been meaning to ask, is he kin to Janis?"

"All them coon-asses are related, one way or another."

"Don't be so crass."

Glancing at the rearview mirror, I caught only a glimpse of the look she gave me, more tense than disapproving. I was midway around a slow-moving gasoline tank truck, and an eighteen-wheeler was barreling down on my butt. Hitting eighty in the rent-a-wreck, I managed to whip in front of the tank truck just in time to avoid the cowcatcher of the speed demon coming up behind me.

"Well, coon-ass is what they call each other," I said, safely back in the slow lane, doing a mere five miles over the fifty-five limit. "You're dealing with refineries and union workers now, not your prissy ass executives and bean counters who leave their crassness to the second drink."

Despite Mizz Liz's master's degree and experience in human resources, I wondered if she'd gotten this job because she was female. But my thought wasn't that it was a plum promotion. Someone in New York had decided to throw her into one of the most difficult jobs in the company at one of the most difficult times they could find. She would sink or swim, and I suspected the HR

Oberfuhrer, with whom it was rumored she'd had a brief relationship, wanted her to sink fast. These negotiations would be tough even for an old hand at it—but I hadn't shared my thoughts with Liz. Her withering disdain for blockheaded males wouldn't spare me just because I had helped her out in the past. While she wouldn't exactly call me a male chauvinist pig, she would give me the ice treatment for the next month. I'd seen her dispose of an offensive marketing manager once. After a meeting, he had the temerity to suggest they continue their discussion up in his room. She won, he lost, and he was off to Bumfuck, Egypt, or someplace in South Dakota. This was different, but I still didn't feel it'd do any good to tell her she was being set up to fail.

She was saying something to me as I surfaced from my musings. All I caught was, "It struck me wrong."

Well, she wasn't a prude, but she told you what she thought. Sharp handsome features highlighted by a pleasantly aquiline nose, glossy black hair, and olive skin, she looked Italian, which is what she told me her mother was. Liz had once been married and I figured she was between husbands, but taking her time getting to the next one.

"You know," she said, "I'd rather deal with a mob of crotch-scratching, tobacco-chewing coon-asses over here than that bunch of two-faced bastards in New York." For Liz, consistency wasn't a handicap. She twisted toward me.

"What do you think we should tell the union about the end result of our changes?"

"Tell 'em the truth. It'll shock the hell out of 'em, and it's a helluva lot better than making up something and then have Perry garble it across the table. They'll never trust you again, if you don't."

"They never trust what we say anyway."

"You're new."

"Doesn't matter what you tell them."

"They'll listen. And they remember. It's best to shoot straight with 'em."

"Ah, shit ... you know I agree." She sighed and threw her head back on the seat. "But that pompous prick in New York wants us to make like everything will just go on like always—so we can get through this without a strike."

The pompous prick was her boss, the corporate vice president for Human Resources, Jack Dawson. And she was right. He was a pompous prick.

"That dumb bastard," she went on, "is as dumb as kelp and just as slick. He only got the job because he looks like an executive—and kissed every ass that passed in front of him. He never answers a question and he'll never back me up ... or anybody else." She was shaking her finger at me and bobbing her head. "I've learned one fucking thing in this job already: get everything from him in writing. Anything goes wrong and he's approved it, his first reaction is, 'I didn't say that.' Did I tell you—"

"Yeah, you told me. He's a good corporate type. All for one and one for CYA." I'd dealt with Dawson on firing managers and settling the lawsuits that followed.

She stretched back in the passenger seat and tapped the gray roof of the car with her fingers. Her voice was as hard as brass and emphatic.

"We'll do it *my* way if I'm running these negotiations." Good old Liz. Ready for a fight.

We were past the town of Winnie now and off the interstate, sailing between gray checkerboards of watery fields that reached to the horizon. Rice country.

"You'll help me, won't you, Dan?" A slight chink in that armor of self-sufficiency.

"I'll help you." But I had drifted away from the conversation as the gray fields slipped past on either side. I was thinking of my own problems again.

The image of Tim Oakes kissing Dana when he arrived at the Christmas party kept popping into my mind. Everyone else was out on the patio, but I'd been in the kitchen, opening another bottle of wine, and I hurried through the den to the front door when I heard it open. Dana was already there, almost like she had been waiting, and when Tim Oakes came in, he put his arms around her and kissed her, not an air kiss on the cheek, but full on the mouth, and held it. And Dana seemed to lean into him, her one hand reaching around under his arm, to his back. Was it only seconds? More? He saw me watching and they had broken apart, then he gave me one of his limp dead-fish handshakes.

Our row, Dana's and mine, had followed the party, after everyone was gone and our voices could echo through the great room and then fill the master bedroom and bath. My questions and Dana's denials. He was just another musician, a professional she went to see for coaching. All they did when she went to his house was play their violins, or he would give her instructions on playing, and there wasn't anywhere else to meet and his wife was present—when she wasn't working or in the hospital—or their five-year-old—when he wasn't in school or daycare. She had said, in a steady voice, no longer yelling, that she couldn't live with me if I didn't trust her on this.

And I didn't. Not after what I had seen. How she had let him kiss her like that. Then I completely lost it—and hit her. Not a halfhearted sissy-slap either. So, she left. And I hated myself for doing it.

Chapter Seven—A Break in the Case

LIZ AND I NO SOONER REACHED the second-floor hallway across from Perry Comeau's door when he came bounding out and grabbed me by the arm. He ignored Liz.

"You hear what happened?" he said, pulling me down the hall. "We have to see Derek ... deal with it before it gets out in the plant."

"Deal with what?" I said, hitting my knee with my briefcase as I turned to go with him.

"Yeah, deal with what?" An irritated echo from behind us.

"Mornin', Liz," Perry said, only glancing back at her. "Our meeting will have to wait. Got some other business to tend to first." His pace quickened. "You can wait in my office, if you like."

"I'll come with you," Liz said, more like a growl.

I looked over my shoulder. Scowling at Perry's back, Liz was hurrying as fast as she could in her high heels to catch up, briefcase in one hand, purse swinging from a long strap over her shoulder. This wasn't in her schedule, whatever it was, and I knew she didn't like anything not in her schedule. But she also didn't like being left out of anything that might touch on her bailiwick—especially if it involved a cabal of males.

"What is it we're dealing with, Perry?" I asked again as we neared the plant manager's suite.

Perry answered in a hoarse whisper, close to my face. "They arrested Sheila's husband. This morning. They're searching their house—top to bottom. She called me at seven-thirty. She—"

"Whoa." I grabbed Perry's arm and stopped him before we entered the antechamber to Derek's office. "Arrested Sheila's husband?" I wanted to know more before facing Derek. "What for? Why'd they arrest him?"

"Mu ... murdering Billy Graham."

"You gotta be kidding," I said.

Liz pressed up close beside me. "What did you say?" she asked. "Who was arrested?"

"Sheila said they'd already haul ... hauled off two of their shotguns." Perry edged toward the door. "Even seized her car. She ... she couldn't get to work if she wanted to. I told her to take the day off."

"That's your secretary, right?" Liz said.

The three of us managed to squeeze through the door together to face Derek's secretary, a sparrow-like woman who must have been a school librarian in her prior life—gray hair in a tight bun, black skirt, and prim white blouse.

"Helen, is he in there?" Perry asked. "We need to see him right away."

"Layton's in with him. *And* he has a conference call scheduled in a few minutes." She gave Perry a thin smile while casting a disapproving glance past him at Liz. I followed her eyes and saw they were focused on Liz's skirt, which stopped, stylishly, several inches above her knees.

"Hold 'em off, will you?" Perry said. "There's been an arrest in the Graham murder. One of ours."

"The D.A. says *no one* has been arrested. They're just talking to a suspect." Helen pointed to a radio behind her desk. The volume was low, but the faint strains of Montovani filtered out from it.

"Oh ... I didn't know it was on the news."

"Mr. Frazier's on the phone with the D.A. now. I placed the call." Leave it to Derek, I thought, he'll go to the top and they'll talk to him.

"Can we go in?" asked Liz, stepping up to the desk and giving Helen a nice smile, for Liz. In return, she received a stern once-over, then Helen glanced briefly at me and addressed Perry.

"When he's off the phone, I'll buzz him. He may want to wait until after his conference call."

We looked at Perry, and Perry shrugged. Like obedient school children, we sat down, facing Helen's desk, Liz and I on a black leather sofa and Perry in an armchair beside it. The wait was short. Derek did want to see us, although I wasn't so sure that included Liz.

"Nice to see you again, Miss Johnson," Derek said. "I didn't realize we had guests over from Houston—other than our lawyer." He nodded at me as he shook hands with Liz. Layton said hello to her and to me, but didn't offer his hand to either of us. I suspected his dislike for lawyers also extended to highly educated females, whatever their title.

"You heard about Zack Mills?" Perry said as we found seats facing Derek's desk and he assumed the castellan's chair behind it. The swagger stick lay across a file at the front, but Derek made no move to retrieve it. His assistant manager sat in his favorite spot by the window.

"I spoke with both the D.A. and Eric," Derek said. Eric Henshaw, the Port Oso's Chief of Police and Derek's good friend. "It's an ongoing investigation and they're not ready to make any arrests. Eric said a couple of his detectives searched the house—based on some confidential information; then they all went downtown for a talk. Zack and Sheila both. They don't have enough to arrest Mills. Not yet … but Eric says he's their man."

"Gawd, I can't believe it," Perry said. "W-why would he do something like that?"

"That…" Derek made a feint toward the swagger stick, but drew his hand back, "they didn't know."

"They'll need a motive to make their case," I said. Seems like I'd read that somewhere.

"Why're they talking with Sheila?" Perry asked.

"Is she involved, too?" This from Liz.

"Of course not." Perry's head snapped around and he shot daggers at Liz. I could tell he was having trouble not adding, "stupid," or something like that.

"They must think she knows something about it," I said. I was remembering my first dinner with her and what she had said about Zack, although she'd never brought it up again. Nor had I.

"She's his alibi, Eric says." Derek wasn't pacing today, but he was rocking his chair back and forth behind his desk. He looked over at his assistant manager, who had been maintaining a sullen silence. "What do you think we should do, Layton? We can't have them back in the plant now."

"Fire his ass," said Layton. Perry and I both started shaking our heads.

"He's not charged with anything ... yet," I said.

"That's right, boss," said Perry.

"How about her?" Liz.

"So, what do I do with *him*?" Derek asked, looking at me.

"Suspend him, pending the outcome of the investigation."

"Do I have to pay him?"

"Well, if he's not the one who did it, yes. Or if he's not convicted of something." Out of the corner of my eye, I could see Layton glaring at me. "But you can make it without pay for now," I added.

"How about his wife?" Liz asked again. "She has a confidential position in HR—just down the hall. How can you trust her after this?"

Perry's face grew redder as Liz spoke. He was shifting in his chair and his jaw was working. I was afraid he was going to jump up and shout at Liz. Instead, he stayed in his seat and spoke calmly.

"She ... she's worked for me over a y-year now, and she's done an outstanding job. Always reliable ... Always ... She's smart and I trust her. She doesn't go running to the union with everything that goes on up here."

"That doesn't mean a thing," Liz said, sitting erect in her chair, her knees to one side and her briefcase and purse next to her feet. She shook her head, her lips in a tight line. "This has *got* to be a family thing. I don't see how she couldn't *know* what happened."

I grimaced at her. Sometimes she was a real pain in the ass. Strictly by the rules, don't trust anybody, question everything. And I was feeling bad for Sheila.

"We don't have any proof that Sheila—or Zack for that matter—did anything," I said. "You can't just put 'em off work without something…" I shook my head, "some evidence."

"I don't think either of 'em should be back in the plant," Layton said. He was slouched down in the chair and still skewering me with the evil eye.

"I don't know," Derek said. "Maybe we need to give this a day or two."

"At least bring Sheila in and talk with her," I said. "You won't get Zack to say a thing, not if he has a lawyer. But you should do some sort of … I don't know, due diligence or something with her before you tell her she can't work, especially if you're not paying her."

"She's not going to tell you anything," Liz said. "Not if it was her husband who plugged the guy."

"It was a shotgun," Perry said.

"What?" Knocking over her briefcase, Liz turned to stare at him.

"He blasted him with a shotgun," Perry said. "I mean whoever did it."

Liz tossed her eyes and turned back to Derek. "She's not in the union and you don't have to pay her while she's off. You can do whatever you want with her while you wait to see what the cops do. This is an employment-at-will state." She had me there. And she was trying to show Derek how tough she was.

"We have policies on the treatment of non-union people," I said, struggling to remember one that would apply. "You don't want to treat 'em any worse than if they had a union." Nobody said anything, all eyes on me. I shrugged. "That's to keep 'em from getting a union."

"I'm sure Dan can *make sure* none of the policies apply in this case." Liz smirked at me as she said it. "Anyway, the policies aren't binding, and we can change them." She leaned back in her chair. "Or *interpret* them, as Dan knows."

"Dan's right," Perry said. "We should at least give her the chance to tell her side. And if she has to stay out, I want to keep paying her."

"Ah, shit!" said Layton. "Why would we pay someone we think—?"

"Wait," said Derek, holding up his hand. "We don't know the truth here … I agree with Perry. He should talk with Mrs. Mills and get her side before we do anything." He looked at Liz, and one eyebrow went up. "That okay with Houston, Miss Johnson?" The tone was patronizing. I was pretty sure he didn't care if it was okay with Houston HR or not.

"It's okay with me," Liz said. "But I want to hear what she says before you agree to let her work during the strike. Or you pay her."

Derek gave a small start, then leaned forward and picked up his swagger stick off the file. I wondered if he felt he needed it for protection.

"You'll talk to her, Perry?" he said, hitting the palm of his other hand with the end of the stick.

Layton stood and turned toward the window with his back to us.

"I will, I will," Perry said. He nodded vigorously, a pleased smile on his face.

"And let us know what she says. By the end of the week."

But Perry didn't talk to her. Nothing more happened with the criminal investigation—that we heard of—before the strike started. Sheila called in sick with the flu, then nervous exhaustion, and Perry

59

gave her sick leave. New Year's passed; contract negotiations hit high gear over the following weekend and during a three-day extension of the old contract, and then hit a wall on January 8th.

At the stroke of midnight, pickets went up outside all three gates of the plant. The hourly workers didn't walk off their jobs—not in a petroleum refinery where things can blow up if you aren't careful, or people can get roasted alive. The union gave us an orderly shutdown of the units, and supervisors and engineers took over the ones the company still wanted to operate.

From the security bunker, Perry and I watched the picketers pace, back and forth, full of enthusiasm and bravado, illuminated by bright spotlights and clearly displayed in black and white on the bank of monitors we had installed. A small crowd had gathered at the main gate. The strikers and their supporters milled about, but it was peaceful, and only ten or so picketers were left after an hour or two.

Tomorrow would be a long, first day. More union replacements—company supervisors and engineers eager to fatten their bank accounts by working a strike—would be arriving, along with caterers and additional security forces. With an uneasy feeling, I coasted past the pickets at two-thirty in the morning, on my way to the Drifting Sands Motel to catch a short night's sleep.

It proved to be a very short night.

Part II

Chapter Eight—A Riot

THE THROBBING OF THE PHONE less than two feet from my head plucked me out of a dark, foreboding dream in which Dana played a central role. I fumbled for the lamp and managed to turn it on and at the same time stop it from flying off the nightstand. As I picked up the receiver, I looked over and saw the clock. Five-twenty.

"Dan, this is Derek Frazier," came the clipped response to my mumbled hello. "You need to meet me at the Port Oso town hall in fifteen minutes."

"What?"

"There's a disturbance out at the plant. The main gate. Hundreds of people. The mayor and chief of police want us downtown. With the union."

"My God! Why on earth—?"

"It started when the caterers showed up. Chief says he doesn't have enough men to stop it, and the sheriff refuses to get involved. Not his area."

"Why don't they call the DPS?" The Texas Department of Public Safety for the highway patrol.

"They called and so did I. It'll take hours, even days. Look, we don't have time to talk. Be there in fifteen minutes." The phone went click and all I heard was a dial tone.

Dressing and on the way to the station, I puzzled over what was going on. Why would the catering company cause such a ruckus? The plant always used an outside caterer during strikes and there had never been a problem before. And hundreds of people? Probably an exaggeration. As soon as I left the Sands, I turned on the local all-night radio station, but all I got was "Moon River."

Except for the police station, the town hall was dark. There were only two police cars parked out front, but in the lot across the street, there must have been a dozen civilian cars and a couple of pickup trucks.

The station, ablaze with lights, was empty except for the desk sergeant and a shabbily dressed man asleep on a wooden bench across from him. The sergeant directed me to the second floor, up the elevators, second room on the left.

It was an interior conference room of middling size. In the center was a scratched-up black conference table with inelegant chairs pulled out at odd angles. Above the table hung a wavering pall of white haze suspended from a trio of bright fluorescent lights. The room stank of acrid tobacco smoke and late-night sweat and seemed to growl with low, discordant voices.

It was full of people—all standing in disparate clumps, away from the table, and talking among themselves. The clump by the door held my only affinities: Derek, Perry, and Layton Van Horn. Hurrying to join them, I took stock of the other clumps.

On the far side of the table were several men in suits, one of whom I recognized from news photos as the mayor. Nearer to us were three uniformed police officers, one with enough gold braid and silver on his jacket to peg him as the chief. Stiff and erect, close to Derek's age, he was taller and stouter than the others and looked the part, with silver-gray hair and rosy cheeks. A thin white scar ran from his left ear to his chin.

At the far end of the table, the union chairman Frank Landry, his sidekick Pete Reneau, and two other men in street clothes, their backs to us, were drawing coffee into Styrofoam cups from a silver urn. Forming an isthmus between the union's and the mayor's clump was Tony Joplin, holding out a stubby cigar in one hand and facing the mayor. Joplin had the physique and bearing of Napoleon, but with a mod hairstyle for the thick brush he had left around his tonsure. The mayor wasn't much taller than Joplin, but he was paler, more rumpled, and better fed. He was jabbing a finger at Joplin, and Joplin was jabbing back with the cigar.

I dropped my briefcase between the table leg and a chair and shoved it out of the way. A scuffed-up Samsonite box, it accompanied me everywhere in my lawyer role, and it carried everything I needed for survival in legal combat, including my Dictaphone, breath mints, and a candy bar.

"What happened?" I said, trying to keep my voice below the general muttering in the room.

"Fuckers started a riot." Layton's response was loud enough to turn heads at the coffee urn. He was the only one in our group not in a suit and tie.

"They attacked the caterer's trucks when they tried to come inside last night," Derek said, then looked at his watch. "This morning." He kept his voice low and motioned for Layton to do the same.

"R-rocks, bottles, and ... and tire irons," Perry said.

"We need to get this worked out," Derek said. He motioned with his head toward the door, and we followed him out into the hallway.

"We've got to get the gate cleared," he said when we were outside, "and before the shift comes in at seven."

"They were shooting at the trucks," Layton said. "Autry in security told me."

"W-wasn't bullets." Perry bobbed his white marble head at me. "All security saw was slingshots. Nuthin more'n BB's or pellets that hit a car."

"Those can *hurt* people," Layton hissed at Perry, but he was looking at me. "Put out an eye or kill somebody, if one of those things hits 'em right."

"Doesn't matter what it is," Derek said. He was starting to pace in small circles. He looked naked without his swagger stick. "We've got to stop it."

"What started it?" I asked.

"The caterers got there not long after we left," said Perry. "They got separated ... comin' over from Houston. Convoy ha ... had to stop and regroup along the road, o-over Gator Bayou ... So they could all come in together."

"Convoy?" I asked. "How many trucks were there?"

"Twenty-three," said Layton. "They had all their equipment ... and all the food. They brought enough for the next month."

"Some were refrigerator trucks," Derek said.

"Took 'em almost an hour to get ready to come in, security said." Perry paused to hitch up his pants and tuck in the front of his shirt. "The bus drivers refused to cross the picket line, so they—"

"Bus drivers?" I said.

"The caterers had two busloads of workers they hired in Houston," Derek said. "To run their operation. And they brought over some outside security we hired."

"They had to put the workers in the trailers—"

"Trailers?"

Ignoring my interruption, Perry continued, "And while they were doin' it, a crowd st-started gatherin' and—"

"They must've been tracking the trucks all the way from I-10," Layton said. "Used CB radios to spread the word over here."

"They put the workers inside the trailers?" I said.

"Yeah," said Perry, "security called me about an hour ago. There was well over a hundred people out there, and when the convoy came through the gate, or started comin' through, they tried to move 'em fast, but there were so many people, they blocked the trucks. Kept movin' in front of 'em. They hit the truck cabs and ... and the trailers, with everything they could find. Rocks, bricks, and tire irons at first, then slingshots, maybe even pellet guns."

"And there were people inside the semitrailers?" I said. "What

65

if one of 'em had caught on fire?" Not an unlikely occurrence in a situation like this, I was thinking.

"They could've gotten out," Layton said.

"In the middle of a pissed-off mob of people?" I said and had another thought. "What if someone had opened the back doors and attacked them?"

"They had the doors padlocked," Perry said. "They couldn't—"

"That wasn't real smart," Derek said. There was silence. Derek stroked the back of his head and looked at the floor.

"They had to, boss," Perry said after a moment. "People were yellin' that those ... those were strikebreakers in ... in there. Security told me they were sca-scared someone would jerk the doors open and drag the caterers out. There were even women."

I didn't know if he meant women in the crowd yelling and throwing things or inside the trailers. I suspected both.

One of the men in business suits came out of the conference room door and beckoned to us. "Gentlemen, can you come in now? The mayor's finished talking with the union, and they're going to calm their folks down."

We started in, Derek first and me last.

"Chief Henshaw thought it'd be helpful for us all to watch a news video and see what actually happened," the man said as we filed past him.

Once we were inside, no one shook hands or uttered a greeting or even acknowledged the other contingent's existence—except for Derek and the chief of police, who nodded to each other—and no one sat in the chairs pulled out from the table. At the union's end was a green ceramic ashtray in which a cigarette still smoldered, next to the upright dead stub of Tony Joplin's cigar. My throat was already burning, and my eyes were watering from the haze of smoke. I was glad now that I hadn't had time to put in my contact lenses.

"I think this was all just a misunderstanding," said the mayor, moving up to the far side of the conference table. On the wall behind him, I could see an aerial photograph of the town. Black and white. On one side of the photo was the refinery's tank farm, its white tanks like huge flat marshmallows.

"They're strikebreakers," Frank Landry said. "You can't expect people to stand by while someone takes their jobs. The bread off their table."

"They were food workers and a few private security guards," said Derek. "We always bring them in at the start of a strike."

"I've been here twenty years and it's never been like that." Frank chopped at the air with his big hand, and there were mutters of concurrence from his side.

The mayor gave both Frank and Derek a sour look, then addressed Derek. "Well, it would've helped if you'd told the union what this late-night convoy was *all about* before it got here."

"We don't have to negotiate..." Layton started.

"No, no," Derek said, motioning at Layton with his hand. "You're right, Mayor Lee. We should've given the union a heads up."

A uniformed officer with the bars of a lieutenant cleared his throat. "We have the video running," he said.

We all turned to the TV in the corner next to the table with the coffee urn. The picture went in and out of focus on faces in a crowd, then the camera swung around to show an eighteen-wheeler slowly moving forward into a mass of people, men and women in plain work shirts, jackets, and jeans, indistinguishable except for the longer hair on some, and a few women in housedresses. One man in a red-plaid hunting jacket and tan cap, his back to the camera, was wielding the short end of an L-shaped object against the door and side-view mirror of a semi cab. A tire iron. There was no sound on the video.

"Let me show you what we've been dealing with," said the lieutenant. He pointed to the screen.

Everyone watched in silence as the man in the hunter's jacket leaped onto the running board of the truck and brought the tire iron down on the windshield in a roundhouse motion. The glass shattered and bulged in on one side. He brought the iron down again, and the windshield ballooned inward. Then the man fell away and almost went under the wheels of the slow-moving tractor before two others in the crowd leaped forward and pulled him clear.

"Gawd damn, they almost got him," said Pete Reneau.

"Lucky they were going slow," Layton said. I saw him smiling grimly at Reneau, and I was sure I heard a twinge of regret in Layton's voice.

The camera pulled back and panned over the crowd. Most were only milling about, but a dozen or so of the bravest were edging backward along the road in front of the trucks, waving their arms and shouting at the drivers in pantomime on the silent screen, or darting back and forth and pounding on the hoods or sides of the trucks as the big rigs slipped past and through the open gate. An object arced over the crowd where it was thinnest and hit the side of a trailer. Then another hit the cab. And another. When one object bounced off the truck's hood and skidded through the gate, the camera zoomed in on it. A brick.

The camera veered up and back to show the next truck. Running alongside the trailer was a man waving a baseball bat. He swung the bat, hitting the trailer, then swung it again and again as if he were aiming for the leftfield fence. On the passenger side of the truck, a spider web of shattering glass spread out across the side window. No one was there with a tire iron, and I hadn't seen a brick. A dark figure inside the truck dropped down below the dash.

"Was anybody hurt?" I asked.

"Two people in the hospital," Perry said. "I hear they'll live."

"Union people were hurt, too," said Reneau.

"Or family members," Landry said.

"Probably hitting each other," Layton Van Horn said.

"Okay, folks," said the mayor as the film continued to run. "The chief here doesn't have the men to handle this. Mr. Landry has his committee out there now—right, Frank?" Landry nodded, his lips drawn in a tight line and his eyes narrowed. "They're settling things down and sending everybody home," the mayor finished and looked around.

"Well," said Frank, "we have to keep our pickets out there ... and some observers. We don't trust the company not to use strikebreakers. We don't know who all's in there working now."

"We only use our own employees to run the plant," Derek said.

"Lot of strange faces in town," Reneau said. He had been edging around the table and along our side, toward Derek.

"We have trained people from Houston and from all over our system." Standing his ground, Derek fixed Reneau with an unblinking glare.

"Mayor." It was the police chief, Eric Henshaw. He stood beside a uniformed officer talking on a telephone near the TV, on which the silent videotape was still running. "Patrol just called in; most of the crowd's gone. Only about twenty or thirty left and the trucks are almost all inside."

"Fine," said the mayor. He looked at Landry and his crew, then over at Derek and us. "I'd like you gentlemen to talk over your differences and work 'em out. What you do with your contract and stuff is your own damn business, but we can't have a riot on the streets of this town. I don't want this kind of thing to happen again."

Everyone nodded and mumbled their assent.

We were outside in the hall when the chief of police caught up with us and pulled Derek aside. Layton and Perry continued on to the elevators, but I lingered behind in case Derek required a legal assist. When I heard the chief say, "Mills," I edged in closer, staying on the periphery of the conversation but not part of it.

"We booked both of 'em last night," the chief was saying. "Detectives have been working on her for the last week." He dropped his voice, but I could still hear. "That Ranger—he's a lot smarter'n you'd think ... sicced us on her right off the bat. She finally confessed last evening."

"Confessed?" Derek said, his first reaction to what the chief had been saying. I was as shocked as I suspected he was, but I didn't say anything, just moved closer to hear better.

"Confessed. One of those, 'I admit it, he did it.' But she was in on it all along ... up to her pretty little neck."

"What's she charged with?" I asked. The chief gave me a look that told me I wasn't welcome in this conversation.

"Murdering Earl Graham."

"You mean Sheila? She's charged with murder?" I didn't believe it.

"Yeah, the wife. She was right there when Mills pulled the trigger. She's the one that set it up." He turned back to Derek. "Just wanted to let you know since it'll be in all the papers. Probably on the radio soon as somebody comes over to check the bookings from last night. We're not making a big deal out of it, but I can't speak for the D.A. Bail hearing's later this morning."

"Thank you for telling me, Eric," Derek said, nodding, grim-faced. "And I appreciate what your men did last night."

"Sorry we couldn't clear 'em out of there, but..." The chief shrugged his gold epaulets and patted Derek's arm, the only time I'd ever seen anyone do that.

"You did what you could," Derek said. The two started off slowly down the corridor.

"Call me if you need any help," the chief said. "But you have to remember, Derek, I got a union, too, and a lot of my guys have relatives out in your plants. They'll stop the violence, but they won't help you break a strike." He shook his head. "No sir. Don't let 'em catch you with strikebreakers in there. They do, all bets are off."

"I understand," said Derek. "I promise you, they're all our people except for the caterers and a few private security guards. All our own people on the gates." They turned to go toward the elevators, and I trailed along slightly behind Derek. Everyone else had already left.

"Make sure they..." the chief was saying, but I was only halfway listening now. I was thinking about Sheila and puzzling over why she had been charged in Earl Graham's murder. I wanted to stay for the bail hearing, but I couldn't. I had to get to work on a restraining order against the union.

I looked at my watch. It was only six-thirty. Enough time for breakfast and I could still make it to Jim-Bob Lloyd's office by nine. We'd already agreed to meet, part of the usual strike routine, but now we'd have to prepare the papers for the TRO—mainly fill in the blanks on drafts we'd already done, but also scramble around to collect affidavits from managers and witnesses. And then find a friendly state court judge to issue the restraining order, all by the end of the day. We'd expected problems, but not a riot. With the violence on video, the TRO should be easy. So I thought.

Chapter Nine—Nothing's Easy

THE TRO WAS ANYTHING BUT easy. Judges in Texas are elected and there were a lot of union voters in Jefferson County. The duty judge was Sam Houston Brewer, formerly a plaintiff's lawyer who wasn't known for his friendship to big corporations, however much money they pumped into the local economy, and into his campaigns. Of course, we always supported his opponent, and it didn't help that our CFO, a resident of Connecticut, had referred to the Texas Gulf Coast on an open mike as the smelly armpit of the nation, or something like that. Even though his company's refineries and chemical plants contributed to the atmosphere of the place in more ways than one. To me, "The Golden Triangle" was a misnomer and one of the most forlorn places I'd ever seen, right up there with north Jersey or the Mekong Delta.

It took only a short visit with Jim-Bob Lloyd—a thin angular Texan with a shock of wiry blond hair and a craggy face that complemented his west Texas drawl—to plan our strategy and prepare an order that would forbid acts of violence and mass picketing and limit the number of people assembling anywhere near the plant's gates. Fortunately, the duty judge could sign a temporary restraining order without notice to the union and without a hearing. Unfortunately, the order was good for ten days only, after which we'd have a formal hearing for a temporary injunction.

Back at the plant, I rounded up all the affidavits we needed for the TRO, and I was almost out the door to head back to Beaumont when Jim-Bob called. He'd been over to the courthouse to have coffee with the judge.

"Dan, Judge Brewer won't sign the TRO unless we tell Joplin and his boys about it and let 'em have their say."

"We don't have to have a hearing," I said. "Not for a TRO."

"Oh yes we do. He's the judge."

"That's just bullshit. They get their hearing on the temporary injunction."

"I know that and you know that, but this is the free state of Jefferson, and they make their own rules here. Judge says he wants to see some proof we got a problem down there 'fore he goes signing restraining orders."

"Goddamn it, they've been showing the video on the news all morning. He can't—"

"Oh, he's gonna grant it. We just have to go through this little char-ade is all. He's on the ballot in November, you know." He paused and I considered what this meant. "Be here by three o'clock, Dan. Bring Derek and Perry along with you. Maybe a supervisor or two who got hit by something and a couple of other people who saw what happened."

"How about the video? Isn't that enough?"

"Probably not. But bring a copy of whatever film your folks made. We have to be at the judge's courtroom at five. He's got a jury trial goin' til then."

"Shit," I said. "That's cuttin' it pretty tight, to round up all the people—"

"Get here soon as you can. We just need to be in court five sharp. It'll be us—whoever you can bring, and the union. Maybe a few of the press."

I looked at my watch. It was already one o'clock, and all I'd had to eat since breakfast was doughnuts and coffee. "We'll be there," I said and wondered how we'd ever make it.

But we did. A half-dozen more doughnuts, three cups of coffee, and a Coca-Cola later, I led the parade to Jim-Bob's office, and then we followed him over to Judge Brewer's courtroom. It was five-to-five when we arrived and we didn't finish our face-off with Tony Joplin and his clients until late in the evening.

After hearing from Derek and then a supervisor with a bandage over one eye and a couple of security guards, and watching the videotape of the riot, we recessed to the judge's chambers where we spent another hour arguing about the wording of the order. The union insisted that it be "reciprocal" and prohibit any violence by the company. By the time we'd agreed to some innocuous language and had the judge's signature on something everyone could live with for the next ten days, it was nine-thirty and I was starving and strung out on sugar.

We all went our separate ways, and once I'd stopped by the restroom and finally limped down the front steps of the courthouse, everyone else had disappeared. I fastened my coat against the cold night air and looked up to see the stars. There were none, just the reflection of the streetlights off the low clouds. My car was parked down the street, in the lot across from the police station and town hall. Where we had started out that morning, several geologic ages ago.

I was crossing the street to go past the town hall when I saw three women come out of the police station. Moving away from the steps, they stopped and turned toward each other under the floodlights illuminating a row of police cars parked in front of the station. When they stopped, I angled out of the crosswalk and into the shadows at the corner of the building, where I could watch them as they stood talking. It was Sheila and a stooped older woman who was thin like her and another woman who dwarfed them both. I guessed that the thin woman, who put her arm around Sheila in something that wasn't quite a hug, was her mother. The super-sized woman was Mary Magdalena Albright, a freshly minted female partner in Tony Joplin's law firm. She handed Sheila something, a small envelope it looked like, and pointed down the row of cars in my direction. I slid deeper into the shadows. I didn't want to interrupt their conversation, and I didn't especially want to talk to Sheila, or Ms. Albright—not with all that had been going on. But I wasn't about to hurry past them and across the street like I was scared of them. I waited, trying to decide what to do. I was curious, and anyway it looked like I was trapped.

The trio broke up. The other two women started across the street, toward the parking lot where I was headed, while Sheila turned and started off in my direction. She was wearing a light jacket, zipped up against the cool air, and faded blue jeans.

I sauntered out of the shadows, as if I were just now coming around the corner, while she walked slowly down the row of police cars toward a few civilian vehicles parked at my end of the street. She was looking at the cars, and not toward me. But I wasn't going out of my way to avoid saying hello. She stopped in front of a two-tone Oldsmobile Cutlass and, staring at it, shook a key out of the manila envelope Mary Albright had given her.

"Hi, Sheila," I said.

"Oh!" She jumped back a step, her hand with the key pressed to her chest. She stared blankly at me a moment, then said, "It's you, Dan."

"You get your car back?" I nodded at the Cutlass.

"Yeah." Her eyes shifted to the car. She sighed. "I guess you know what happened. I just got out." She paused. "On bail."

"Hmm." I nodded. "That's good." I tapped the side of my leg with my briefcase. What do you say to someone just released from jail under a bail bond? Congratulations? A patrol car coasted to a stop in front of the station, and we both turned to watch as a uniformed cop jumped out of the driver's side, leaving the door open, and ran inside the station.

"Zack still in there?" I gestured toward the building with my free hand. The cells for short-term prisoners were on the second floor in the back.

"Yeah," she turned toward me, and her eyes seemed to focus on the knot in my tie. "My mother posted bail for me," she said. "We don't have the money for Zack's." Her eyes came up to mine, a look of defiance in her face. Without her makeup, no eyeliner, no lipstick, she didn't seem as youthful—or sexy—as she had sitting at her desk outside Perry's office. Deep lines furrowed her brow; dark crescent-like moons underscored her eyes. But under the bright station lights, the eyes were still a pale blue, like a distant piece of the sky I'd seen between dispersing storm clouds at sunset.

"The union's gonna help him, but it'll take a few days," she said.

I shrugged. "Good for them." I started to move past her, to cross the street. Time to end this conversation. "I'll be seeing you, I guess."

"Dan." She placed her hand on my arm, not grabbing it, but gently stopping me from going. "Don't believe what they say. Okay, Dan?"

Turning, I met her gaze and tried to stare through those blue eyes into her soul or heart or mind or whatever it was you could see there. Probably nothing more than you could see in a glass mirror. But I didn't say anything.

"It's all a terrible mistake," she said. "Those two detectives," she was shaking her head, "when they questioned me, they kept telling me these things ... I didn't know what to say to them. They kept accusing Zack, us ... saying that Zack was gonna die for killing Billy." Her hand tightened on my upper arm. "I was so upset ... you don't know what it was like ... how they do. They kept after me for hours." She kept shaking her head and now she was shaking my arm.

"You don't know how it is, Dan. They tell you things ... They promised if we'd just confess, they could keep him off death row. But if we didn't..." Her voice broke. She was shaking my arm like it was Derek's swagger stick now.

"Whoa, whoa," I said. "Don't rip me apart here." I placed my hand over hers to try to settle her down.

"You've got to believe me, Dan. They said if I told them about Zack..." A sound that could've been a sob came from deep in her chest. "About Zack killing Billy, they could help us. But it wasn't like they say. He was only trying to protect me. I couldn't hurt Billy. Not for anything."

Her eyes brimmed with tears and glistened in the light. Her hand continued moving back and forth under mine, although she'd stopped shaking my arm. I reached over and grabbed her shoulder.

"Just calm down, Sheila. I don't need to be hearing this." Even though my curiosity was piqued, and I was feeling sorry for her. "Is Mary Albright gonna handle your case?"

"No. The union's got Mr. Joplin to represent Zack, so she said I'd be better off to get a lawyer who's not with the same firm."

That's interesting, I thought. They see a conflict in defending both. To Sheila, I said, "Makes sense. Do you have someone in mind?"

"No ... Could you help me?"

I stifled an incredulous laugh that ended up sounding more like I was choking. "I'm the company's lawyer. I can't—"

"No, no," she said, once more tightening her grip on my arm. "Would you get me the names of someone, some lawyers ... who could help me?"

"Well, I don't know. We aren't—"

"Please, Dan. Don't leave me to..." She shook her head and tightened her grip some more. I couldn't resist the pleading look of furrowed brow and teary eyes—and the death grip on my arm—even if I had doubts about giving her the name of a competent lawyer who could potentially become my adversary.

"Okay." If my smile was a bit strained, my good intentions weren't. "I'll get you the names of a couple criminal lawyers you can call."

"Thanks, Dan." She snaked her arms around my waist and gave me a hug before I could consider backing away. "You don't know how much this means to me ... I won't forget it." I tentatively returned the hug with one arm.

"I'm not sure you should be talking to me," I said and, shrugging out of her embrace, backed up a couple of steps.

"I don't know anybody better I want to talk to." She gave me a whisper of a smile and her eyes searched mine. Or maybe it was the other way around. "You believe me, Dan, don't you? I wasn't involved—not in the way they say. You do believe me?"

"Sure," I said, but I was wondering what it was I was supposed to believe. "How do I get in touch with you?" I didn't have her phone number and I wasn't so sure I wanted to call her at home.

"I'll call you. The Sands, right?" Now she gave me a real smile.

It was only after I was across the street and unlocking my car that the thought occurred to me: surely Mary Albright or Joplin had recommended a lawyer to her when they told her they had a conflict. It puzzled me, but I pushed it aside. No time to worry about *that* with everything else I had going on.

Chapter Ten—The Shadow

A COUPLE OF DAYS LATER, Sheila tracked me down in Perry's office, where I was spending most of my time—when I wasn't in Jim-Bob Lloyd's conference room preparing for the next round in our battle with the union. Sheila's replacement from Houston HR gave a discreet knock on Perry's doorjamb and poked her head inside just far enough to catch my eye.

"Mr. Esperson," she said, her voice professionally neutral, "Sheila Mills is on the phone for you." Both Perry and Hank, Perry behind his desk and Hank on the other side of the conference table, gave me quizzical looks, Perry staring over his reading glasses. I shrugged at Perry.

"Thanks, Andrea," I said, "I'll take it across the hall." Where I'd set up shop in an office left vacant by a manager out working in the plant during the strike.

Andrea was young, probably not much older than my daughter. I had found out from talking with her that she was far too ambitious to spend her life as a secretary. Perry said she volunteered for strike duty because her boyfriend in Houston engineering had come over to work as an operator on a unit. I suspected she was Liz Johnson's secret eyes and ears to keep tabs on what was going on in this place.

As soon as I picked up the phone, Sheila apologized for calling me at the plant. She had tried the Sands and when I didn't answer there—

"That's okay," I said. "Do you still need to find a lawyer?"

Jim-Bob had given me the names of two former prosecutors he said were aggressive and competent. When I told him who needed a criminal lawyer, he shook his head and gave me a knowing, one-eyebrow-raised look.

"Yes," said Sheila. "My preliminary hearing's next week."

"All right. Let me get my notepad. I've got a couple—"

"Why don't we meet for lunch?" she said. Her voice had an eagerness that made me uneasy. "Do you have time, Dan?"

I looked at my watch. It was after eleven.

"No, not really." I was torn. Maybe I could make time. Then I thought about the entanglements and conflicts Sheila presented. I cleared my throat and spoke slowly. "It's probably not the right time now ... since you may have to file a claim against the company." And since it wouldn't look too good if someone saw us together. In fact, I had my doubts about talking to her at all, and here I was, helping her find a lawyer I might have to face in a couple of months.

"Oh, Dan," she said, "I can't imagine suing anybody. I'm sure this'll all work out. Anyway, I just wanted a chance to see you again." A siren song if I'd ever heard one. And I had heard a few, even if they were far, far in the past.

As tempting as it was to see her, whatever that meant, I resisted. But I did hesitate a moment, and I looked at my watch again. I couldn't just leave my meeting with Perry and Hank. What would I tell them? We were busy preparing for our own hearing in court next week.

"Maybe some other time," I said, and without giving her an opening to answer, I added, "Let me get those names for you."

After I retrieved the names and finished with Sheila, I rejoined Perry in his office. Hank had left on an errand to the main gate.

"What was that all about?" Perry asked as I settled into my chair at the conference table, a fresh cup of coffee and two fresh doughnuts on a paper plate in front of me. Stacks of food were all over the place now—much of it assured to expand your waistline and clog your arteries, though we paid little attention to that, at the time.

"I gave Sheila the name of some lawyers. For her hearing next week." Another basic rule: never lie to your client. I bit into a strawberry cake doughnut. "Ran into her outside the police station ... when she got out on bail. It was right after we had our little ordeal on the TRO."

"She called me, too," Perry said. He swung his chair back and forth, but he looked steadily at me. "She wanted to come back to work."

"Huh?" I stared at him, my doughnut suspended in midair. "You told her she was relieved of duty, didn't you? ... Until she's cleared?"

"Oh, yeah. I told her." But Perry looked sheepish, and he swung his chair a little faster, his eyes not meeting mine. "Maybe I wasn't as clear as I should've been." He flapped his hands out to his sides. "She understands it now, though. I made sure of that." The hands came back to the chair arms and he stopped his fidgeting. He gave me a wistful look. "They need the money, you know."

"Yeah, I know." I finished the last of the doughnut. I was thinking that Perry was a soft touch where Sheila was concerned, probably more than I was. I just hoped he was tougher—and more direct—with the union. If he wasn't, Liz Johnson would ram a firecracker up his ass and light it. And she'd know if he wasn't tough, with Andrea there to watch him.

"Why the fuck do we have to go back to court, Esperson?" Layton Van Horn barged through the door like a tank. "We already had one hearing in front of that fucking judge. Now you're telling us we have another one?" He jerked out a chair across the table from me and plunked his square form into it. "What more does he need? You're tying up several of my best people."

"Should be only a couple of days," I said. I was sure he'd been there when I told Derek how the TRO worked. "Maybe a half-day to get 'em ready."

Layton eyed me coldly with his Rottweiler stare, then pulled an ashtray closer in front of him and extracted a pack of cigarettes from his shirt pocket. The admin building was about the only place in the plant where you could smoke, and Layton was one of the few who did. But he never smoked in Derek's office or in his own, next to it.

"So why do you need 'em?" He lit a cigarette.

"We *need* live witnesses who've been injured or had their cars hit. Our outside counsel *needs* to talk to them the day before, and they'll *need* to be available"

"Why can't Perry here," he jabbed the cigarette toward Perry, rocking gently in his chair, "and the security guards show him some of the damn videos we've spent a fortune on."

"We *need* witnesses who can identify the people in the crowds. It has more impact if it's someone with stitches—"

"We've done this once already."

"Like I said, we have to go do it again. The TRO expires—"

"What a fucked-up mess."

He crushed out the half-smoked cigarette in the ashtray. It wasn't worth explaining to him that the hearing on the TRO had been both bizarre and unnecessary and nothing but a CYA for the judge to keep the union vote. That would only make him madder.

"We're going to file for contempt against some of the goons," I said, hoping to mollify him. My stomach was beginning to churn and the discomfort spread all the way up to my chest. "The ones we can identify on tape. If we can get that heard—"

"If we identify them, we'll fire their asses," said Layton.

"We'll have to reinstate 'em at the end of the strike," Perry said. He had stopped rocking in his chair.

"Not this time, we won't," said Layton. "And there's no goddamn contract, so we won't arbitrate the fucking discharges either."

"That'll extend the strike," Perry said. The chair was going again, and he swiveled it back and forth.

"Let 'em stay out the whole damn year. We make more money

when they're *not* in here than with 'em. Teach the bastards to stop suckin' eggs."

"We fire anybody, we need to make sure we have the evidence," I said. One of these days I was going to have a heart attack dealing with this shit. "*And* we need to make sure we have witnesses who'll testify."

"That's right," Perry said. "When it's all over, everyone here still lives together; they work together, pray together, and play together. Most of 'em just want to forget it." I noticed he wasn't stuttering.

Layton glared at him, then at me. He lit another cigarette and slumped down in the chair. Perry eyed him warily, then jumped up and went to a gray file cabinet in the corner, to one side of the window that provided me with a view of the plant's silver and gray piping and white steam.

"We've been collecting evidence," he said, opening a drawer, "so we can prove what they been doin'." As Perry pulled out three manila envelopes, Layton blew a stream of smoke out his nostrils and darted his small dark eyes back and forth between us.

"Dan told us how to secure the stuff and do a chain of custody," Perry said. He shook one of the envelopes, dumping out three "X's" of crossed nails bent over each other. "Russian stars. We picked these up at the terminal gate."

"I know," said Layton. "We're gonna try filling the tires with polystyrene foam." He waved a hand at my coffee cup. "Like Styrofoam."

Perry replaced the nails and opened another, larger envelope. From it, he extracted a slingshot.

"One of 'em dropped a wrist rocket at the main gate," he said, placing the metal support over his wrist. He pulled back the rubber surgical tubing and released it with a snap. "They're shooting those porcelain balls we use for packing catalyst—"

"Where are they getting those?" Layton asked.

"Hell, they're all over the place. Probably been stocking up on 'em for months." He stopped at the sour look Layton gave him, then shrugged. "It's better'n if they were using ball bearings."

I figured it was better for me to stay out of this. Layton didn't seem too impressed with our efforts. Perry shook out another envelope and held up a white ceramic ball about twice the size of a marble. "These only shatter the windshield and don't go on through—"

"Still could hurt somebody." Another streamer of smoke.

"We've got a ton of videotape, and we're going over it to identify who's been firing these babies at shift change." Perry slipped the wrist rocket and the porcelain balls back into their respective envelopes. "Once we have a fix on the perpetrators—"

"Hey, guess what we got." Waving a sheaf of papers in front of him, Hank Greenberg bounded in through the door to Andrea's (formerly Sheila's) little office. I knew what "we got" as soon as I saw the long pages he held out.

"A new lawsuit," he said, handing the papers to me. To Layton, he added, "Just picked it up outside the main gate. Deputy wouldn't cross the picket line."

"Why didn't they send him away?" Layton asked. "We don't have to go rushing out just to get sued."

"We've already been sued," I said, reading quickly over the caption and the first few paragraphs. "And there's lots of ways we can be served." I looked over at Perry. "But they still have to get personal service on Perry and Derek and whoever this John Doe turns out to be."

"Me!" said Perry.

"They're suing you and Mr. Frazier," Hank said, going over to Perry's desk. Perry stood motionless by the file cabinet, the evidence envelopes suspended over the open drawer.

"Frank Landry and the union local are plaintiffs," I said, studying the caption. "Landry claims you've been spying on him— him and some others in the union, trying to intimidate 'em and invading their privacy. I think there's also a few labor law violations alleged in here." I flipped through the pages. "They'll have to take those to the NLRB."

"Spying on the union?" Layton said. He was staring at Perry. Perry dropped the envelopes into the drawer and slid into his chair, but he didn't respond to Layton.

"This is crazy," I said, continuing to skim the paragraphs. "They're alleging that you and other employees and agents of the company were watching their houses and following their cars." I stopped at a paragraph on the third page. "What's this about Gene Jarvis?" The paragraph alleged that one John Doe had followed and taken pictures of Frank Landry while he was riding in Gene Jarvis' car.

"Oh, shit," said Perry. Both Layton and I were staring at him now. "You tell 'em, Hank." Perry was studying the backs of his hands on top of the desk.

Hank cleared his throat and edged toward the file cabinet. Leaning his elbow on top of it, he shifted from one foot to the other.

"We had one of our security guards watching Jarvis. He—"

"You remember," Perry said, looking up at Layton, "we ... we were g-going to try to get some p-pictures of Jarvis—"

"Yeah, yeah, I remember," said Layton.

"You ... you okayed us using plant security," Perry said. "Remember?" He shifted his eyes to me. "Rather than ... than an outside investigator, you ... you know, a detective, we ... we decided we'd use our own security. It ... it was a lot cheaper."

I resisted the urge to groan out loud. That wasn't what I had recommended. I stole a glance at Layton and found him giving Perry a tight-lipped "shut-the-fuck-up" look. Perry clamped his mouth shut.

"So, what exactly did this John Doe you got to watch Jarvis do," I asked, waggling the suit papers toward Perry, "that brought all *this* about?"

"His name's Pierre Lamont," Hank said. "And he didn't get any pictures."

Perry didn't say anything, just looked like he wanted to be elsewhere.

"I need to talk to this guy," I said. "Not only did he *not* get any fucking pictures of Jarvis, it says here they got pictures of him."

Pierre Lamont was nowhere to be found. From what Perry and Hank finally admitted to me—once Layton left for the john or some other urgent business—plant security had assigned this untrained security guard, Pierre Lamont, to tail Gene Jarvis and get some video if he caught Jarvis working or lifting or doing anything that violated his doctor's restrictions. So that the plant could fire him. Mr. Lamont wasn't supposed to be anywhere near Frank Landry or anyone else with the union local. The assignment had lasted only a day. The mission had been discovered, the security guard's cover blown, and he returned empty-handed.

No one seemed to know what exactly had happened, and Pierre Lamont had gone home for a family emergency back in New Iberia, Louisiana. Not only was the lawsuit a complication in the middle of a strike, I was also concerned that Mr. Lamont would become an issue in our hearing on the temporary injunction. And possibly turn this into an unfair labor practice strike—for which the company would pay dearly.

Chapter Eleven—Preliminaries

SINCE THE DAY SHE LEFT, I hadn't heard from Dana. But then I hadn't been home much, not after the strike started. No one answered the phone there, and when I called her office, I got a mumbled conversation through someone's hand over the receiver and then her secretary came on the line. Dana had quit. Last Friday, she said. Not even given two-weeks' notice, just packed up and left. Said she was leaving the law and going to be a violinist. Full time. Professional.

I about dropped the phone. There went the house in Aspen was my first thought. We could never afford it on my salary. My second was to wonder what the hell was going on. I asked her secretary where Dana was. The secretary said she didn't know, but I knew she wouldn't tell me if she did. Dana always said she had a damn good secretary.

The hearing for our temporary injunction took a long day of evidence, up to seven o'clock on a cold January night, and then a half-day of bickering the following morning. I didn't have to worry about the union's spying claim, though. Judge Brewer refused to hear it. All that happened before the strike started, and anyway the union had a suit filed in federal court. I hadn't heard the last of Pierre Lamont.

The good judge also refused to cite the union and three of its most fervent supporters for contempt. He was dissolving the TRO, and "all that stuff" was in the past. He was sure everybody would comply with his temporary injunction. No more violence and no more mass picketing. Right.

By the time Joplin stopped objecting and we had verbiage that suited everybody, it was well past lunch when his honor signed the injunction. This done, Jim-Bob Lloyd disappeared and Derek, Layton, and Perry returned to the plant. Hank Greenberg and I, having a few hours respite, trudged upstairs to the second floor of the courthouse—to see what was going on in the preliminary hearing for Zack and Sheila Mills.

We slipped inside the courtroom not long after the hearing started. A police officer was testifying about his search of the area behind the StarLite Drive-in Theater where a jogger on his early morning run had discovered Earl Graham's body. Other than the victim and his car, all the officer found was some faint tire tracks and a single shotgun shell casing. From a sixteen gauge.

Pausing to listen to the officer's soft Cajun brogue, I looked around. This was an old courthouse and the courtroom had the same fine old polished wood and polished brass I had seen in other old Texas courthouses. In this one, the wood was blond oak: blond tables and benches, railings and wainscoting, and a high podium for his honor. Dark oil portraits of judges all the way back to the Civil War—or more likely, to the end of Reconstruction—hung along the side walls. Above the judge's podium, in what looked like a pewter inset, was the great seal of Texas: his honor's ultimate imprimatur of authority.

Hank and I slid onto a bench seat against the back wall. Straining to see past heads and shoulders—Sheila's mother and others I took for family members and supporters, along with Pete Reneau and J.C. Ledbetter from the union—I managed to get a good view of the defendants and their lawyers. Sheila sat slightly sideways to me on the far left of the defense table. Next to her was a husky lawyer with brown hair down over his ears: Edgar Day, one of the lawyers I had suggested. He appeared to be busily taking notes while Sheila, dressed in a navy-blue jacket, her straw-blond hair pulled back under a blue headband, sat stiff and straight beside him. Zack was at the other end of the table, and beside him, Tony Joplin, which explained Joplin's sudden eagerness to finish up his bickering in front of Judge Brewer. The two lawyers sat side-by-side, their clients on the outside of them and away from each other.

On the other side of the courtroom, at the very front and just behind the prosecution table, were three rows of heads and shoulders of African-Americans. Men and women, young and old, and even a couple of teenagers. At the near end of the front row sat Earl Graham's brother, George, next to an elderly woman who was so small and stooped her gray head barely showed above the back of the bench. George Graham was staring at the defendants' table as the officer told of examining Earl Graham's pockets and not finding a wallet or any identification. George's face was rigid except for his jaw, which was working like he was grinding nuts with his teeth. His fist, clenched in a hard knot, rested on the railing in front of him.

The next witness was a ruddy, round-faced deputy sheriff with a swagger to match his puffed-out chest and military haircut. He testified about finding a sixteen-gauge shotgun in the Mills' house. The house, he said, was still pretty much in disarray, even though the family had moved in weeks ago: furniture in odd spots, no pictures on the walls, boxes all over the place. The shotgun was stuck way back in a utility closet behind a bunch of half-empty boxes, along with several other lethal weapons. The sixteen-gauge was on its way to Austin, as was the shell casing from the murder site.

When the prosecutor, an assistant D.A. named Hastings McHugh, produced photographs of the gun and the shell casing for the deputy to identify, Edgar Day made as if to rise. Joplin's hand on his shoulder stopped him. No use fighting this battle now, I thought. Joplin wants to see if the forensic tests are inconclusive, while holding in reserve his motion to suppress the evidence. This was only the preliminary hearing and he would want the prosecution to lay out their case for him.

89

After the deputy stepped down—first twisting his body to smirk at the reporters in the jury box—McHugh called a Port Oso police detective to the stand, prompting a flurry of whispered conversations at the defense table. Detective James Robinson reminded me of the salesman from whom I bought my last Buick. Long dark sideburns and pompadour, sharp nose and chin, a well-brushed suede sport coat, light tan.

Once past the preliminaries, Detective Robinson testified that he and his partner had interviewed both Zack and Sheila Mills, and while Zack refused to talk without his lawyer, Sheila had been most cooperative and talked freely. In the end, he said, she had confessed that her husband murdered Earl Graham.

Both Eddie Day and Tony Joplin were on their feet.

"Your honor," said Day, "we object to this and—"

"Whatever Mrs. Mills said to Detective Robinson isn't admissible against her husband," Joplin sang out, overriding Day's voice. "One spouse cannot testify against another in this state—not in any way, shape, or form—so long as the two remain bound in their holy marital union."

Sheila's head was down. I couldn't tell whether her face was in her hands or what, but she wasn't looking at Zack. He, on the other hand, was glaring at her, past the two lawyers standing between them. I could see his profile etched against the judge's podium.

"Hold on, counselors," said the judge, raising his hand. Judge Carter was a small, wizened man who had wilted away his years on the criminal bench, worn down by all the sadness he'd seen and heard, or so I thought. His thin hair was swept back from a high forehead, both skin and hair so pinkish-white it was hard to tell where the skin ended and the hair began. Wire-rimmed glasses hid his eyes and flashed back and forth between the lawyers arrayed in front of him. In his black robes, he gave me the impression of an emaciated vulture perched on the stump of a giant tree. Despite that, he wasn't known as a hanging judge.

"Your honor, we haven't even heard what the detective has to say." Hastings McHugh. His tone was pleading, almost whining. A tall, big-boned man with the lugubrious mien and three-piece, blue pinstripe suit of an undertaker, he was known around the courthouse as the D.A.'s murder guy.

"This is only a preliminary hearing," the judge said, motioning with his hand to silence the overlapping voices. "Counsel can file a motion to exclude—"

"Your honor, it would be highly prejudicial to my client to air this so-called confession," Joplin said, "now or at any other time." All I could see of him past the spectators was his rounded shoulders and his hair, stylishly long on the back and sides and graying around a well-tanned bald spot.

"The press is here," he was saying as I contemplated his well-coifed hair and wondered if he had it done at a beauty salon. "The marital bond of silence will be torn asunder before the entire world." He rapped the table hard enough that it resounded in the back of the courtroom. "My client has the right to maintain that sacred privilege ... essential to the unity and peace between husband and wife. There is no greater privilege ... no greater privilege before the law, not even between lawyer and client."

Eddie Day jumped in as Joplin took a breath and I was thinking, what a pile of bullshit. This time Joplin didn't try to override Day.

"This ... this confession," Day said with earnest disdain, "if that's what the prosecution's trying to call it—was *no* confession by my client of any guilt whatsoever. *And* it was obtained under *dur-ess* and false pretenses." He glanced at Joplin and I could tell he was hurrying to get his point made before Joplin or McHugh or the judge interrupted him. "Mrs. Mills was distraught. She was upset. She had been badgered and bullied for hours, and through it all, she was lied to—"

"Oh, come on," McHugh said. Up to this point, he had let the defense lawyers have their say. "Let's not cast aspersions on our law enforcement—"

"Gentlemen, gentlemen," said Judge Carter. "Why don't we try to keep this civil? Only one of you at a time." He smiled benignly at McHugh, then at the defense table. "I'm inclined to let Mr. McHugh tell us how this is admissible against Mrs. Mills, and if it is, let the detective tell us what she said to him ... them. There's no jury here. I'm just trying to determine if there's enough evidence to bind these defendants over for trial."

"Your honor, Mrs. Mills admitted to participating in the murder of Earl Stanley Graham," McHugh said. "What she said to the detectives therefore falls within an exception to the hearsay rule."

"You have a signed confession?" the judge asked.

"No, your honor," McHugh said. "She refused to sign anything, but we have the detective ... and his partner, to testify to what she said." McHugh turned to look at the three reporters who had staked out a spot in the jury box. "And we have a tape recording—in her own words."

The defense table erupted. "I object," shouted Edgar Day. Not only the lawyers, but also Zack was on his feet—until Joplin quickly placed a hand on his shoulder and pressed him back into the chair. Sheila's head had jerked up, and she half rose from her seat, too, but she didn't stand.

Day was visibly bouncing up and down on his feet. "If there's any recording, it was made through stealth and deception, and..." He stopped. I could see Sheila tugging at this sleeve.

"May I have a moment, your honor?" Without waiting for the judge, Day bent over to listen to her.

His gavel raised, the judge had been glaring at Zack and Joplin. "Mr. Joplin, you're busting to say something. If you got your client under control now, go ahead and say it."

Joplin was shaking his head. But I got a glimpse of what looked like a smug, satisfied smile when he glanced over at the reporters before addressing the judge.

"Judge Carter, this just goes to show the problems with this alleged confession by my client's wife, who, by the way, is also his co-defendant. This tape cannot come into evidence in any proceeding against Zack Mills, and the DA's office has no business airing it in public and trying to use it against him—not now, not ever. It's simply not admissible for any purpose. Not against him, it isn't. And it's highly prejudicial."

Still in the witness box, Detective Robinson had been watching all of this in silence. For the first time, I saw some slight furrows of concern on his brow.

"Your honor." McHugh now. "All we're offering this tape for at this time is to corroborate the detective's testimony in order—"

"Judge Carter, this is an absolute travesty." Edgar Day had finished whispering with Sheila. "This young woman had no idea a tape recording was being made, and if it was, it was against her express request that she not be recorded. Moreover, this is the first anyone's ever told us about a recording."

"I just did..." McHugh started.

"For God's sake, this is a preliminary hearing," Judge Carter said, his glasses flashing toward Day. Then to McHugh, "Do you have this tape recording?"

"Yes, your honor. Right here." McHugh held up a white cassette.

"Well, I..." the judge motioned toward Joplin and Day for them to keep quiet. "I want to hear it."

Tony Joplin stretched forward over the table, his arm extended, like he was going to grab for the cassette. "But your honor—"

Whap, whap. The judge brought his gavel down to stop the objection. "I said I want to hear the tape ... We'll do it in my chambers, *in camera*, before we have any more testimony from Detective Robinson or put that tape into the record—if we do." He motioned the gavel toward Joplin, to stop him from speaking. "You'll get your say, when the time comes, Mr. Joplin. You, too, Mr. Day ... How long's that tape?" he asked, turning his head toward McHugh.

"Only fifteen, maybe twenty minutes at most."

"Court's recessed until," he tilted his head to look at the clock on the wall behind me, "three-thirty. That should give us enough time. Counsel," his glasses shifted back to the defense table, "you'll join me and Mr. McHugh back in my chambers, won't you?" A command masked as a question. Both Joplin and Day nodded their assent.

"Miss Doré," he said to his clerk, down below the podium, "rustle me up a tape recorder that'll play that thing." He pointed to the tape that McHugh was obligingly holding out to her.

The judge and lawyers left, along with many of those in the gallery, forming separate phalanxes, white and black, out the rear doors. Zack and Sheila remained at the defense table, talking in low voices, Zack moving a hand in a rubbing motion on the polished surface and Sheila giving brief shakes of her head. A sheriff's deputy stood close by, keeping an eye on Zack. After watching them a moment, I left with Hank to go downstairs to the coffee bar in the basement. I hadn't eaten since my breakfast of Danishes and doughnuts that morning.

By three-thirty, the defendants and their partisans and adversaries and the onlookers and court staff and reporters were all back in place. But there was no judge and no lawyers or prosecutor. Sheila and Zack sat well apart at the ends of the long defense table. In the jury box, there were three more reporters and, out in the hallway, a television crew in tow of an evening-news-pretty young woman wielding a microphone. My affable nod and friendly smile drew no request for an interview. Or any other response.

Finally, at four o'clock, Joplin, Day, and McHugh reappeared through the side door for jurors, and the bailiff ordered everyone to their feet. Judge Carter swept past him and ascended his throne. Settling his robes about him, he began perusing a yellow legal pad, mouthing words to himself, and stopping to mark out something and scribble something else. At the defense table, the lawyers whispered with their clients. Clothes rustled in the gallery—along with a few coughs and whispers and the other indefinable sounds that seem to fill any threatened gaps of silence in a crowd.

I was watching Sheila. As Day pulled back from speaking close to her ear, she dropped her face into her hands.

"You ready," said the judge, his glasses angled toward the court reporter, who sat with her fingers poised above the keys of her machine. She nodded.

"This is one of the strangest hearings I've ever had," Judge Carter said, his glasses toward the news reporters in the jury box, then shifting over to the defendants and their lawyers. He took a breath. "I'm reserving ruling on this confession of Mrs. Mills," he paused, "or whatever it is ... until we can have a complete airing of the circumstances under which it was obtained." He looked down at the legal pad and back up at the defense table. "But I'm binding Sheila Ann Mills over for trial in the meantime." He pursed his lips, and the glasses flashed to the prosecutor side. "That's based on the D.A.'s representation he'll submit the case to a grand jury. Right away ... Bail is set at twenty-five thousand dollars."

The judge waited as Edgar Day stood and voiced an objection—mainly on the bond, nothing more about the tape or the grand jury, although the last seemed a bit cockeyed to me. Maybe Day hoped for better luck there.

"That's the same bond she's under now," the judge said to Day. "Your argument's already in the record, and I'm not reducing it."

Day slumped back into his seat and turned to whisper something to Sheila, who was sitting straight and erect in her chair once more. The judge looked back down at his legal pad.

"As to Mr. Zackery Taylor Mills," he said, "I find insufficient evidence admissible at law to bind him over for trial. Neither his wife's testimony nor any statement she may have made may be used against him in this state. Moreover, absent some proof that the shotgun shell they found at the site came from a gun over which he had control, or some possible control, there's no evidence before me that would justify trying Mr. Mills for the murder of Earl Graham." His head came up from the pad. "Accordingly, Mr. Mills is released from his bond."

Joplin slapped Mills on the back; Zack turned toward him and the two shook hands. Neither looked over at Sheila, whose head was bowed almost to the table. What began as a low muttering on the far side of the gallery rose to a cacophony of protests and a few sobs. The defense side in front of me was filled with more subdued whispering, but I saw J.C. Ledbetter put his hand on Pete Reneau's shoulder and give it a shake.

The judge rapped repeatedly with his gavel, and the noise level dropped. "Okay, let's settle down in here." The gavel descended again, and a bailiff advanced past the judge's podium to stand in front of George Graham and the rows of Billy Graham's family and friends, who remained visibly agitated even as they lowered their voices.

"I'm not finished," the judge said. He leveled his glasses at Joplin and Zack, who had been making their own share of the noise. The sound level diminished to something near to silence.

"Mr. Mills, I want to remind you that while you're free to go, the charges against you have not been dismissed, and Mr. McHugh may … correction, he *will* continue his investigation, and he may submit all of his evidence, including the forensic results on a number of items found in the search of your residence, to a grand jury." The judge stopped but continued to focus the glare of his lenses on Zack. "I wouldn't plan on taking any vacations outside the county any time soon." He looked down at the court reporter. "We're off the record now, okay?" Then back up at Zack and Joplin. "And I'll tell you this, Mr. Mills, you leave to go anywhere without Mr. McHugh's *written* permission and I'll personally take that as an admission of your guilt. You got that?"

To my surprise, Joplin didn't object, even though I had my doubts that the judge could make his threat stick. But he was the judge. Zack must have responded with something, but it was inaudible to those of us in the back of the courtroom.

"Okay," said Judge Carter, "Sheila Ann Mills shall remain free under the existing bond." He looked down at the court reporter again. "That's back on the record." Then over at McHugh. "Provided the D.A. has no objection."

"Not for the present, your honor." McHugh popped up and down.

"I want to talk with counsel at the bench about when this case might go to trial. Court's adjourned."

"What was that all about?" asked Hank as we stood to leave. He grabbed my elbow. "How could he let Zack walk out of here ... and make Sheila go to trial? That's what he did, isn't it? Everyone knows Zack pulled the trigger."

The reporters had broken for the exit ahead of everyone else, leaving the lawyers and their clients huddled together at the counsel table. I figured Sheila was trying to figure out what had just happened, as well. McHugh's assistant was busy packing a briefcase, while McHugh was already at the judge's podium, looking over at the defense table and waiting for Day and Joplin to join him. Eager to get outside and meet the press.

"I'm not sure what happened when they went back there," I told Hank. I stopped to watch the Graham contingent on the other side of the room. They were milling about, not toward the rear doors, but in the same area where they had been seated. Most were conversing among themselves, some heatedly, and a few were gesturing toward Sheila and Zack. I saw Tony Joplin glance back at the gallery and then slide over to a bailiff who was standing at the side door usually reserved for jurors.

"Ah," I said, nudging Hank, "they're slipping out the back door." I pointed toward the jurors' door. Joplin was motioning for Sheila and Zack to go out that way. Day went to the podium, and after a brief conference with McHugh and the judge, he followed the defendants out. Joplin gave the judge a wave and then he, too, left. The bailiff closed the door behind them.

Bench conference postponed, I thought. Smart move. Avoid any contact with the media and postpone any discussion of a trial date.

"Is he going to get away with this?" Hank asked. Without waiting for an answer, he added, "Why's the D.A. going to the grand jury now?"

"Good question." I was watching McHugh pack his stuff while trying to ward off George Graham, who was talking to him in a low voice, but waving his arms. "My guess, he's being extra careful—and it gives the judge some cover. You heard Jim-Bob Lloyd: it's the free state of Jefferson."

We were out the door now. Somehow McHugh had managed to shake off George Graham, and he squeezed past us to make contact with the plasticized blonde with the microphone. The bright lights of the cameras came on, and I pulled Hank out of the line of fire.

"You don't want to end up on the national news," I said. "Not about this, not if they see it in New York."

But I paused outside the cone of lights long enough to hear McHugh say, "Our investigation is continuing. He can't hide behind some claim of privilege."

"If she can't testify against him, will he just go free?" Hank asked in a whisper. When I shrugged, still listening to McHugh, Hank added, "What if she divorces him?"

I hadn't thought of that.

Chapter Twelve—The Indictment

THE DISTRICT ATTORNEY MOVED quickly to indict Sheila as an accessory to the murder of Earl Stanley Graham. Zack was named as the shooter, but he wasn't indicted for the crime.

Sitting in Derek Frazier's office, I read through the indictment and tried to visualize how the murder had happened. Even with the paucity of detail Hastings McHugh had included, it seemed clear that it had taken place where the victim and his car was found, behind the StarLite Drive-in Theater, and that Sheila was present, along with Zack, in her car, the two-tone Oldsmobile Cutlass the police had seized and then returned to her the night I saw her outside the jail. The indictment stated that Sheila had willfully assisted Zack in the murder, allowing him to hide in the trunk of her car and leading Billy Graham to the murder site. When Graham got out of his car, Zack shot him. She hadn't tried to stop it; she hadn't reported it to the police. She had lured Billy Graham to his death.

This couldn't be true, I told myself, shaking my head as I skimmed the boilerplate paragraphs on the last page. Not the Sheila I knew. There had to be an explanation. But the indictment said that Sheila had confessed all of this to the two Port Oso police detectives.

I looked up to find Layton glaring at me from his spot by the window. I shifted my eyes to Derek behind his desk. He was watching me and tapping his palm with the swagger stick, slowly, rhythmically, like he was hammering nails.

"Everyone read this?" I asked, holding up the indictment and looking over at Perry on my left. I was wishing I had a soda or something to get the taste of bile out of my throat. I must have downed too many cake doughnuts in Perry's office.

"I haven't," said Hank from the other side of Perry.

"We all have," said Layton. I passed the papers over to Perry, who handed them to Hank.

"The D.A. called me as soon as it was signed," Derek said. "Zack Mills shot Mr. Graham and Sheila Mills helped him. It's all in the confession they got from her ... on tape."

"He tell you anything that's not in the indictment?" I asked.

"No," Derek said. "I talked to the chief, too. That's all they feel free to tell us—except they're still going after Zack Mills."

"There'll be a motion to suppress the confession—and the tape recording—and to quash that indictment," I said, waving my hand in Hank's direction. "Or something like that ... before she ever goes to trial."

"I want to fire them both," Derek said. He brought the swagger stick down on his desk with a loud thwack. "I know enough from what's in that," he pointed the stick at me and, not finding me holding the indictment, swung the end over to Hank. "I have enough there to know those two killed one of my supervisors, and I want them off my payroll. Now!" Whack went the stick again.

Layton was silent, for once keeping his thoughts on firing employees to himself.

"I don't know, boss," Perry said. "She might just be innocent. What if Zack forced her to go with him?"

That thought had occurred to me, as well, but I wasn't about to speculate, not in front of Layton. And why would Zack want to kill Billy Graham, anyway? Then I remembered; she had told me at our first dinner that Zack had called Graham some names out in the plant. They must have gotten into an argument. But why? And why hadn't she told me more about it?

"If she was forced into it," Hank said, "why didn't she come forward?" Hank was becoming a little bolder in these discussions. "Say something to someone about it?"

"Maybe she was afraid to," said Perry.

I was trying to remember the dinner at Caprice's. She hadn't seemed especially upset, but then when we were out in the parking lot, she'd sounded like she was afraid of something. But I didn't think it was Zack. Yet, right after Zack's interview with the Ranger, I'd seen Zack grab her wrist, and the two of them seemed to be arguing. Derek's voice cut into my thoughts.

"George Graham caught me after mass on Sunday." The swagger stick was still. "Out by my car ... He was almost crying. He asked me not to let these people get away with ... with what they did to his brother."

Layton was slouched down in his chair, studying his fingernails. I figured there had already been some discourse between him and Derek about this.

"I promised we'd do what we could." Derek paused, elbows on his desk, the swagger stick in both hands out in front of him, thumbs on the underside pointing toward each other. "I've been trying to reach out to the black community, and this may be a way to do it."

I knew he was tolerant on race issues, not a bigot by any means, but I couldn't believe he'd gone liberal on us. I didn't need to worry, though. Derek gave a slight smile.

"George told me he'd try to help us end the strike. He might even get some of his folks to cross the picket line."

Perry was shaking his head—vigorously. "Derek, that'll ... that'll tear this place plumb apart. It ... it might give the union a fit, but it'd cause more trouble than it's worth ... That's only a fraction of the hourly people he ... he can speak for and the hard-liners'll go after 'em so hard..." He was still shaking his head. "No one's gonna come back for long."

He was right. I had visions of another riot, this one a race riot. Maybe even cross burnings—or worse.

"I don't care," Derek said. "When it comes to right and wrong, we can't be timid." I winced at the loud whack of the swagger stick on the desktop.

Layton had stood and was staring out the window, his back to us. I followed his gaze. It was a cold, gray day. A misting icy rain had fallen through the night, and when I came in the gate at six-thirty that morning, no pickets greeted me, only two "On Strike" signs wedged between bricks on either side of the entrance. Icicles hung along the bottoms of the signs, at one down-tilted corner almost to the wet asphalt. Bright lights illuminated the entrance like spotlights on a stage, ushering me inside past the union's picket shack, an old shipping container with no windows. High above the gate, cameras like twin tubular eyes rotated back and forth. The plywood door to the picket shack was pulled tight, and from a pipe on the roof rose a thin streamer of gray smoke.

I sighed and returned to Derek and the present. "Nobody's been convicted of anything," I said. "Not yet. If we're challenged on a discharge—Zack or Sheila—we have no proof. Not until there's some evidence we can use in an arbitration."

"She's an at-will employee," Layton said, turning away from the window. "And the union won't fight us on him." His tone was milder than usual.

"I ... I wouldn't bet on it," said Perry. "Zack's in tight with Pete Reneau and his gang on the west side, and they never let any discipline go ... go by without filing a grievance. They think that's their God-given mission."

"We have the burden of proof," I was shaking my head now, "if we have to arbitrate. They both pled *not* guilty, and the DA's not even pursuing a case against Zack—not yet at least."

"Innocent until proven guilty," Hank said, chiming in.

"She said they did it." Derek had stood, and he was pacing behind his desk, the swagger stick going all the time. "What more do you need?"

"A conviction," I said.

"There's a taped confession," Derek said, stopping and staring at me. I was surprised it wasn't Layton making these arguments, but Layton was back in his chair, busy examining his manicure.

"Can we get a copy?" I asked.

"No-o-o," said Derek, and stopped. We all waited for him to finish. "I asked the D.A. ... and the chief."

"They wouldn't let you have a copy," I said. I wasn't surprised. "And we aren't likely to get the *only* two people who heard this confession to come testify in any arbitration hearing. Certainly not with a criminal case pending."

Derek didn't respond. I suspected he had asked the D.A. and the police chief about the two detectives testifying, as well. He'd been in refineries long enough to know how these things worked.

"We don't know what happened out there," I said, "or why ... or how. Why don't we wait until after the trial?"

"That Zack Mills may never be tried," Derek said. He was pacing over to the window, the swagger stick in his hands behind him. "Or Sheila Mills, if what you tell me is true." He turned toward me and nodded. "You know ... what they'll try to do with her confession."

"We can cross that bridge when we get to it, boss." Perry finally gave me some help. "Neither of 'em is being paid while they're off."

"You know, Derek," said Layton, looking up at his superior, who was still standing beside him at the window. "The lawyer's right."

I about fell out of my chair.

"We don't know what happened." Layton shrugged and extended his hands out in front of him. "Maybe Zack Mills had some justification for what he did—defending his wife or something, protecting her from a bullying supervisor who was trying to take advantage of her ... It happens, you know."

Narrowing my eyes, I stared at Layton Van Horn. What the hell was he up to? This sounded like a lynching defense. Protect the pure white woman from a rapacious black man.

"Maybe they were having an affair and Zack caught them." Hank's voice came from the other side of Perry.

All of us strained to peer at him. I'm sure disbelief was written all over my face. Glancing around, I saw disgust in Layton's and impatience in Derek's. Perry's face stayed toward Hank and I couldn't see it.

"You have some reason to think that?" Derek said, moving away from the window. He snapped his head around to Layton before Hank could answer. "Or you. That killing someone like that could ever be justified?"

Hank's "no" was overridden by Layton's response. "There's some circumstances where a man's justified in defending himself and his kin, especially his wife."

I had never seen Derek glare at Layton, but he did now. The silence hung like a shroud between them. I certainly wasn't going to inject my thoughts into this one. Derek seemed to be handling it quite well.

"I don't know what happened among those people," Layton said, breaking the silence.

Derek had stopped beside his desk. He was still staring at Layton, or maybe out the window past Layton. I couldn't tell.

"I don't care what the circumstances were," Derek said. "A man—one of our supervisors—was shot dead ... he was shot multiple times ... and we *know* who did it." Leaning against his desk, he pivoted to look at Perry. "I want those two discharged and I want it done today—effective back when we relieved them of duty."

"What about Houston, boss?" Perry asked.

He'll need the concurrence of Human Resources in Houston, I thought.

"I'll take care of them. Miss Johnson won't buck me on this one." Slapping his hand with his baton, he stared at me now. "Counselor, your job's to make this stick."

"Yes, sir," I said. No use raising any more doubts. I shifted to advocate mode, ready to don my game face and make life miserable for the other side. Though sometimes it was a shared misery. I felt a twinge of guilt over Sheila. And I almost felt bad for Layton Van Horn, slouched down in his chair and looking like a beaten puppy.

Part III

Chapter Thirteen—The Shadow Knows

THE STRIKE WAS INTO ITS second month and we were in court again. After a long day of testimony, the judge denied our motion for contempt against the union and three of its members, including J.C. Ledbetter, despite our video of the three leading an assault on the main gate every morning for the previous week: hurling rocks and bottles and shooting wrist rockets at cars and pickups at shift change.

His honor had doubts about the identification. There hadn't been any serious injuries, not since the first week under the old TRO, and it had been dissolved. Only broken windows, dents, and punctured tires. And we couldn't show that the union had sponsored any of the violence.

In return, the union claimed that supervisors had harassed the strikers and that the company was spying on the union's leadership, watching them even as they slept. There had been mysterious happenings at their homes: broken windows, dead cats in their driveways, and disabled cars, bass boats, and trucks. Had to be the company goons, Frank Landry said on the witness stand.

Wearily staring at both sides, Judge Brewer said he had heard enough. This was a private dispute and he wasn't going to referee it. He didn't want to see any of us back in his court again.

So, the strike went on, and the company fired J.C. Ledbetter for shooting a wrist rocket and breaking Layton Van Horn's windshield with a ball bearing—and being dumb enough to do it on camera.

Two others who launched porcelain balls at indeterminate targets, we promised to suspend for thirty days once the strike was over. After that exchange, things settled down, although I had to rescue Andrea's engineer boyfriend from drowning in the Sands swimming pool. Crossing the courtyard just before midnight, I spied two dark figures holding a man upside down by both legs and dunking him headfirst in the water. When I ran toward them, they fled, dropping their victim into the murky pool. I had to jump in and fish him out as he flailed about. He couldn't swim.

There was plenty to keep me busy—charges from the NLRB and OSHA, as well as the stupid spying lawsuit I was trying to make go away. All that didn't stop my nagging worries about Dana. It seemed that more and more I needed a midnight beer or scotch to help me sleep and then some Maalox to settle my stomach.

The one time I went home to replenish my wardrobe and pay the bills, I found most of Dana's clothes gone from the closet and a brief note that she had rented her own apartment. She already had her own bank account and savings, so she had the economic freedom to do whatever she wanted, even without her day job. I wondered if she had gone to Mexico. In a weak moment, I called a member of her string quartet—in what proved to be a fruitless search—and learned that her violin teacher or whatever he was, Tim Oakes, the guy I saw kissing her at the Christmas party, had absconded with the group's small kitty of accumulated earnings and fled south across the border, abandoning his cancer-riddled wife and small son.

Dana ended her note to me, saying: "Heard about the strike. Hope you are doing okay. Miss you. Dana." She'd never been much for writing letters.

On my return to the plant, I finally interviewed Pierre Lamont, the security whiz kid assigned to spy on our slacker-in-chief, Gene Jarvis. Mr. Lamont was all of twenty-eight, a criminal justice program graduate from some junior college in Louisiana, and so polite and unassuming that I actually liked the guy, despite the trouble he'd caused us.

We sat catty-cornered to each other at the table in Perry's office—Perry was out roaming the plant on Derek's instruction to see for himself what was going on out there. Good practice for when the hourly workers came back.

Hank Greenberg sat in on the interview. I thought the experience might prove educational, help him avoid crap like this in his future career. He was going places, while I was staying here, going round and round, like a squirrel on an exercise wheel.

Pierre said I could call him Pierre or Pete. He answered to both. A south Louisiana Creole with neatly trimmed black hair and moustache, Pierre or Pete was too small and thin, to my mind, to be a security guard, although the pressed Khaki uniform he wore and the .45 he carried probably made up for that. He said he hadn't been armed and he was dressed in civvies when he went out on his special assignment.

"Okay," I said, "you ended up spying on our union chairman, as well as Jarvis. Can you tell me how that happened?"

"Yes, *sir*," Pierre said. He gave me a nervous smile and shrugged, which he often did in answering my questions. "I knowed this lady that lives down the block from Jarvis. I didn't want to park in the street, you know, so I asked her if I could park in her driveway, and she let me park there."

His voice was quiet, mellow, with a Cajun lisp. "There" became "dare" and "the" became "da" and "this" became "dis," and "that" became "dat."

"Did you have a telescopic lens or something?" I asked.

"Yeah ... yes sir, and I had a pair of binoculars." He took a swallow of Coke from a can on the table. "I got there on a Sat'day—back before Christmas, 'cause I figured he might of been doin' something 'round his house, you know ... His was about five down, and there wasn't no trees or bushes or nuthin like that between me and it ... Only a big bush right beside the car and there was an openin' I could see through."

"He couldn't see you?"

"That's why I picked the spot. I knew he couldn't. My friend, the lady in the house, checked it out. Walked down the street with her dog. A little poodle thing." He held his hand down low to the floor, and I grimaced at him. He shrugged. "From where he lived, he couldn't tell nobody was in my car."

"But somebody saw you." Not a question.

Pierre shrugged again and gave his nervous smile. "Guy in the house next door. Guess he's that Landry fellow that filed the lawsuit."

"Ah, shit," I said. "You parked next door to the union chairman?"

"That's what it looks like," Hank said from the other end of the table. "Rumor in the plant had it that Landry thought it was the police after his son. For smo—"

"Hold on," I said and held up my hand. "Let him tell it." I didn't want Hank to influence the witness, not at this stage. I needed the straight story. "So, Landry saw you and confronted you there, thinking you were watching his house?"

Another smile and shrug. "Well, not right away. I was using the bi-nocs a lot, and I guess he must've seen 'em." Pierre's dark eyebrows went up. "I reckon he figured out I was watching Mr. Jarvis down the street, 'cause along about noon, he come out of his house and walked down to Jarvis' and went inside. He's a big guy, you know, sorta like Frankenstein when he walks." Pierre moved his upper body back and forth and grinned at me. I didn't grin back. "Anyways, the two of 'em, they come out and got in Jarvis' car—I'd seen him in it the day before—and they backed out in the street. So, I backed out too—and started followin' 'em."

"Why did you follow them?"

"Mr. Comeau told me to stick with him all day for a few days. Like butter on toast, he said."

I stared at Hank. He gave me a sheepish look and shrugged. It was becoming contagious.

"Then what?" I said to Pierre.

"They was driving mighty slow, and I ended up right behind 'em at the stop sign—end of the street. When I stopped, the big guy—Landry I guess it was—got out and came over to my car." Pierre stopped now for another swallow of Coke.

"Your side, right? What did he say? Your window was down?" I was getting impatient.

A shrug and a smile. "He told me he didn't mind me followin' 'em, just not to be so obvious about it ... It was embarrassin'."

I rolled my eyes and looked at Hank again. He was studying the legal pad in front of him on the table.

"So, this is where you gave up the chase?" I hoped.

"No, sir." There it was again. "I kept followin' 'em."

I sighed and slowly shook my head. I didn't want to ask why. "Go on."

"They went over to that Eckerd's on The Groves' highway and stopped in the lot, and that other guy went inside."

"Landry?"

"Yeah. He went inside for a few minutes, then he came back out."

"Where were you?"

"On the other side of the lot."

I stifled a groan. "Did you keep following them?"

"Well," Pierre's head seemed to shrink down into his shoulders, like a turtle, "he came over and started takin' pictures."

"You're kidding," I said.

"He must've bought one of those little automatic jobbies in the drug store. I saw him unwrappin' somethin' when he came out."

"How many pictures did he take?"

"A few. My car. The license tag in back. Then a couple of me."

I was shaking my head, staring first at him, then at Hank. Why

111

hadn't Pierre just left? Why hadn't they told me about this when it happened?

"So, is this when you stopped following them and came back?" I asked Pierre.

"Well-l-l ... no. They went back to Jarvis' house and stopped out front, and I stopped down the street a ways." Upending the Coke can, he finished it and gave a strangled cough. Waiting on him, I stretched my back and shoulders. We needed to finish *this*. I had a meeting with Joplin in less than an hour.

Gently setting the empty can on the table, Pierre resumed telling his tale. However bad it was, he didn't shy away from looking me in the eye.

"They got out and went inside, but another car pulled up right behind me. I'd seen it in the parking lot at the drug store, but I didn't pay no attention to it then." Pierre shook his head. "This fellow got out of the passenger side—there was a woman driving—and he came up and tapped on my window, so I rolled it down."

"This wasn't anyone you knew?"

"Well, yes and no. But it wasn't Landry or Jarvis."

All I could do was shake my head and look over at Hank again.

"He asked what I was doin' there ... And I told him."

"What exactly did you tell him? Whoever it was."

"Oh, it was that guy they arrested for killin' one of your supervisors."

"What! Zack Mills?" I shifted forward, closer to him.

"That's him. He wanted to know if I was there watchin' him and his wife."

"Oh, shit! Why were they out there at Landry's place?"

"Like I said, they must've been at the drug store and maybe Landry said somethin' to 'em." Pierre shrugged, raising his hands out to his sides. But not smiling. "Later heard they had a new house down the street ... Anyway, I told him I was watchin' Jarvis, to see if he did any work 'round his house. He asked who I worked for, as if he didn't know, and I told him. Then he asked if I was recordin' the conversation."

"Why'd he ask that?"

Pierre reached up to his shirt pocket and pulled out a ballpoint pen. "I was clickin' my pen." He held it up and began clicking the cartridge in and out, in a steady rhythmic motion. "I was nervous," Pierre said and gave me his nervous smile. "That's all. I think he recognized me from before."

"Before what?" Hank said, leaning forward on the table.

"You see, in thinking about it, I saw him and his wife back in the fall. I wasn't full time then and I had temp jobs doin' night security and I saw 'em both at a 7-Eleven off the highway goin' into Port Arthur. He let her out at the store, then drove the car over to this car wash, a self-serve one, down on the other side of the lot."

"Fine," I said, "but this doesn't have anything to do with *our* problem." Then I had another thought. "Did you know him back then, before the strike?"

"No, but I'd recognize her anywhere. Seen her up here in the office." He waved his hand toward the door.

"Sheila?"

"Yes, sir. And she walked right pass me, goin' into the store. Didn't say anything, just had her head down. Seemed odd they were goin' to wash their car that late at night."

"Okay ... was that all you said, or he said, when you were watching Jarvis?"

"He told me I'd better stay away from him and Sheila and mind my own business. Then he left and they drove off, the two of 'em, and I came back here to give my report."

I guess this little wrinkle should've caught my attention and made me ask more questions, but I didn't. I had a lot on my plate and it just didn't register. Until later. And I had half an hour to make it to Joplin's office—and convince him to drop his damn lawsuit.

Chapter Fourteen—What Joplin Says

WHEN I EXPLAINED TO JOPLIN that it was nothing but a little mix-up on our part, he scoffed at me and told me he wanted a million in damages and an injunction against the company spying on any of its employees or the union for the rest of eternity. I ground my teeth together to keep from telling him to go fuck a tree.

We were meeting in a humongous conference room on the fourth floor of the Joplin Building, a glass and steel monolith that was the tallest inhabited structure between Houston and New Orleans. Paid for by the likes of Texaco, Gulf, Mobil, Fina, Goodyear, and a number of other corporate contributors to Joplin's ever-increasing wealth. The building was only the first of several marvels that always struck me when I was forced to visit Joplin's office.

The Joplin firm itself occupied the middle three floors of the building. The rest he leased to the doctors, radiologists, and other retainers who assisted him in his personal injury enterprise—founded upon the suffering of maimed and diseased workers who yielded up to the Joplin firm thirty to forty percent of what recompense Joplin could wring out of the employers and contractors for their employees' cancerous lungs and brains and polluted blood or busted and missing limbs. Or from the millions he won for their widows and orphans.

Once inside the gleaming structure, the first thing I noticed—and the second thing that amazed me—was a female staff that could've graced the pages of the slickest glamour magazine in any airport newsstand. Almost all were younger than thirty; thin, shapely, and outfitted straight out of Vogue, skirts shorter and necklines lower than I'd ever seen in any corporate office or any other law firm I'd ever visited. And poised as any model or third-generation Southern debutante. A few even had olive skin, and one a rich ebony color, which was a bit daring for a major law firm in this part of the country. But none were lawyers.

Sitting in the waiting room and walking down the long hall to the conference room, I checked out each and every one as they went past me or I went past them. I wondered if they could type.

Then there was Mary Albright. Order of the Coif at Duke followed by a Federal clerkship. Antoine Joplin's partner after only three years of practice, the only female partner. She was adept at hammering defense lawyers against the hard anvil of redneck, Cajun, and black jurors who shared a common bias against big corporations and Yankee executives, bankers, and lawyers in Brooks Brothers suits—and an abiding prejudice against people who flew in private jets, rode in limousines, stayed in penthouse suites, and toasted any victory, however ephemeral, with Dom Perignon champagne. Of course, I knew, and Antoine Joplin knew, that he, Joplin, fit that same bill—off stage.

Sitting across the table from Tony Joplin and Mary Albright, I presented reasoned arguments as to why their spying claims weren't worth a shit. No injury, no statutes violated. Not even an actionable invasion of privacy.

"The case is in federal court, Danny boy," said Joplin.

"My judge," added Mary Albright. "Judge Gadsden." For whom she had clerked.

Mary lit another cigarette and politely blew smoke toward the glassed-in corner of the room, away from my side of the table. She wore a solid blue dress, a rich hue to go with the honey blonde hair, which I suspected was all-natural but didn't care to check out, and the heavy gold chain that circled her neck just below her third chin. Fifty pounds lighter and she'd be really attractive, sexy even, I was thinking as I insisted on the fairness of the federal courts.

Behind her on the long wall next to the door was the third thing that amazed me about Joplin's offices: a huge painting—a colorful collage that covered half the wall. Joplin had told me it was by a Port Arthur native, a man who had become a famous artist, something I found hard to believe. I never could remember the name—something German with "berg" at the end. But the painting, with its lurid colors and patterns, always drew me into it, and I'd spent a lot of hours studying that painting while I listened to bullshit from Tony or Mary or one of their cohorts.

"So, you're gonna have a lot of problems," Tony was saying, "pleading stupidity in front of Judge Gadsden. A fortune five hundred corporation. With all the resources you have … In Beaumont, Texas."

"There's no injury here, Tony." But I knew he was right. "It was just a mistake … a little mistake by an inexperienced—"

"Ha!" said Mary. "You admit you were negligent in hiring your agent?"

"Well, this sure as heck ain't going anywhere," I said and picked up the complaint and my legal pad and pulled my briefcase out from under the table.

"We'll want some depositions," Tony said. "Derek Frazier. Maybe your CEO." He was grinning at me, like a wolf salivating over a meal.

"Don't be silly," I said, plopping my briefcase down hard on his shiny blond conference table and hoping I scratched it. "We'll give you Perry and the security guard any time you want." I opened the briefcase and tossed in the complaint and legal pad. "I'm over here full time now, it seems."

"Then you'll be happy to hear Sheila Mills can come back to work," Mary said, taking a last draw on her cigarette and snuffing it out in a silver ashtray.

I snapped the briefcase shut and stared at her. "I don't think so.

You don't expect..." Something in her look brought me up short. My face must have shown some disquiet, because Mary smirked up at me as she took the ashtray and dumped it into a plastic-lined trashcan by her leg.

"Judge threw out that confession ... so-called confession." A stream of smoke came downward from her nostrils. "He's going to dismiss the case."

Standing the briefcase upright, I leaned on it and stared down at her and her huge blue-silk bosom draped over her pale arms on the edge of the table.

"When did this happen?" I asked.

"Judge called Edgar Day this morning," said Joplin. I turned toward him. He was leaning back in his chair and grinning at me. "Guess you folks'll have to take her back ... Zack, too."

"Zack? He's still under investigation," I said. But I was thinking about Sheila.

"There's no evidence against him." Joplin waved an index finger over the table like he was tapping out a beat. "He'll be ready and rarin' to go—once the strike is over."

"Sheila told me she's looking forward to seeing you again ... Dan," Mary Albright said. She favored me with a sly smile.

I picked up my overcoat from the chair next to the one I'd been sitting in.

"Is the D.A. going to appeal?" I asked.

"I wouldn't think so," Mary said. "Those two Port Oso detectives stepped on their dicks when they questioned her and he knows it. Didn't even advise her of her rights."

I shook my head. "If what's in the indictment is true ... and Zack did what it says, there ain't *no way* either of 'em is coming back into the plant." I started out. I needed to get out of there and digest what they had told me.

"Come on, Dan," Mary Albright said. "You wouldn't do Sheila like that, would you?"

I avoided looking at her as I headed around the conference table to the door. "It's not my decision," I said, and left. But I was wondering: if Edgar Day is Sheila's lawyer, how does Mary Albright know so much about *what* Sheila's saying about anything—much less about me?

Chapter Fifteen—When Circe Beckons

IT TOOK A FEW DAYS FOR THE news to hit the local papers, and then it didn't even make the front page. The judge's order said that Sheila's confession was inadmissible because it had been obtained through oppression, deception, and false promises—after hours of interrogation and without her being read her Miranda rights. With no confession, there was insufficient evidence to continue the criminal prosecution of Sheila Mills, and the indictment was quashed. Case dismissed. But it could be refiled.

The state crime lab had completed forensic tests on the shotgun found in Zack and Sheila's new house and the spent shell found at the murder site. The results would not be made public. Assistant D.A. McHugh was quoted as saying that the investigation continued, and he called on anyone with information on the crime to come forward. Sheila's lawyer, Edgar Day, declined to comment, but Joplin managed to get quoted at length. He just hoped that Sheila and Zack Mills "could now put this terrible, terrible ordeal behind them." In a separate article, the local NAACP offered a ten-thousand-dollar reward for the arrest and conviction of the killers of Earl Stanley Graham.

Derek Frazier knew damn well who killed Billy Graham, and he remained hotly adamant. Not even the Supreme Court of Texas could make him reinstate those two murderers and it was my business to make sure they never set foot in the plant again.

Two days after the news report, Sheila called. I had just returned to the Sands from a solo dinner in Beaumont.

I was thinking about her when I came over the bridge into Port Arthur and saw the myriad explosion-proof lights of the several refineries, a wide field of dull yellow pinpricks punctuated here and there by garishly billowing flares, all of it spread out like a vast medieval tapestry across the mudflats and marshlands toward the Gulf of Mexico. Steam and mist had coalesced in a massive cloud above this preternatural canvas and reflected a pulsing red glow back down on the flat landscape, making the scene a surrealistic vision of Dante's hell. I wondered how Sheila and her husband and the other workers endured in this place.

The phone rang as I was taking off my shirt and tie. I answered, hoping it was Dana.

"Dan, can I see you again?" Sheila said. Still recovering from my surprise, I didn't answer right away. "Guess you saw the judge threw out that ... that case against me," she added in my silence.

"Yeah," I said, sitting down on the bed and looking at the clock. I was wondering if she wanted to see me tonight. Thinking that might not be such a bad thing. Or maybe it was.

"D.A.'s still going after you," I said. "You and Zack."

"Mr. Day thinks he'll drop it. So does Mary Albright." A pause. "Eventually." Another pause. "I really would like to see you."

"Jeez, Sheila. I don't know if that's such a good idea." The voice of reason taking over. "The union's filed a grievance for Zack, and you may—"

"I want to tell you my side ... It's not what they said. The cops. That damn D.A." Her words tumbled over each other; her voice had an urgency that tugged at me. "What *you* think is more important. I don't care about the job. I just care about what you think ... about me. You've always been ... so nice. I don't want you to think I'm a bad person or something. I'm not. I don't want you," there was a catch in her voice, "to hate me."

120

There was a long silence, and I waited, torn on how to respond to this plea.

"Dan?"

"I'm here."

"Will you meet me? Any time you want. Any place."

"Where's Zack?"

"He's in New Orleans. He has a construction job over there."

"I thought the judge told him not to leave the county."

"Hah! Mr. Joplin took care of that. Told the judge Zack couldn't get work here. He needed to support his family ... Promised he'd make sure he came back."

I sighed. Despite my better judgment, I wanted to see her. But that could get complicated, especially now, in the treacherous depths of a strike.

"Why can't you tell me on the phone." My better judgment winning.

"That's not the same. Please ... Dan?" A catch in her voice.

"Okay." I ditched my better judgment. "But it can't be anywhere around here. I'm going home Saturday ... overnight. Why don't you meet me Sunday afternoon, say three?"

"Can we make it later? In the evening?"

"Later's fine, but not around here. Let's meet at the new Pizza Hut on I-10, the one at the cut-off to Winnie. Can you do that?"

"Yes ... Seven okay?"

"Seven's okay with me." There was nothing in Houston to control my schedule. "I can start back over a little later."

"You may not recognize me. I've dyed my hair."

"Dyed your hair?" I thought about her straw-yellow hair, how it fell on either side of her face and on her neck.

"Actually, brown's more my color anyway. I didn't want people to recognize me, you know, from the pictures."

"But you have those blue eyes."

"You can have blue eyes with brown hair. It's longer, too. I think you'll like it."

"I'm sure I will." And I was sure.

"I'll wear my trench coat—and the red scarf you said you liked."

"I'd know you anywhere."

AT HOME, I found a thick envelope on the kitchen table. Inside it was a short note from Dana and a thick sheaf of legal documents. Nothing on where she was or what she was doing.

The legal papers were a contract to sell our house in Aspen. Disclosures and disclaimers and the like. And a two-page document releasing any claim I might have to her law firm profit sharing and benefit plans. I started to tear it all up, then stopped to reread the note from Dana, searching for some hidden message between the lines and beneath the neatly inscribed words on the page.

There wasn't any hostility there, or any affection. Not even "I miss you." Just a matter-of-fact request for me to sign. She needed the money. I sat looking at the note, no more than six lines, a long time. Remembering: dinners, vacations, diapers; the sharing of worries, joy, and pain; the daughter who, I feared, despised us both for the alien creatures we had become.

Last May, the three of us had gone to Cancun, a growing but not over-crowded beach resort on the Yucatan Peninsula. To swim and snorkel and decompress, Dana and I from work and Susan from school. Susan stayed on the beach or in the cantinas, and met a new guy we all liked, while Dana and I spent most of our time at the poolside bar, drinking margaritas and quarrelling. Petty things, but it was really over what we'd done with our lives as we sped toward the half-century mark.

Neither of us was the same person the other had started out with the long years before. We didn't move in the same orbits; we didn't even talk the same language half the time. We didn't know each other and we weren't sure we wanted to find out who the other was. The counseling hadn't started until the fall and it lasted only two sessions. It ended before the Christmas party, and Tim Oakes.

I signed the papers and replaced them in the envelope and left the envelope on the kitchen table. I didn't leave a note.

Chapter Sixteen—A Little Pizza Never Hurts

WHEN I REACHED THE RESTAURANT—a little late because of the traffic—Sheila was already there. A blue norther had swept the air clean, or as clean as it ever gets next to the freeway, and you could see a few stars through the lights of the parking lot and the bright glow from the Texaco station next door.

As I turned into the almost empty lot, I spied Sheila's two-tone Cutlass and pulled in beside it. She came over to greet me from where she was walking, hands in her trench coat pockets, near an area of newly planted grass covered by straw. We hugged tightly. More like, she hugged me and I responded in kind. For quite a long time.

Inside, coats off, pizza ordered, and a pitcher of beer and filled mugs between us on the table, she began to tell me her side of the story. We were off by ourselves, in a corner. The restaurant was suitably darkened, the dinner crowd thin because it was a Sunday and the place was new. It hadn't yet become a teenage hangout.

Sheila was wearing trim dark slacks and a white V-neck sweater that was smooth and silky to the touch, cashmere or a good quality imitation, and her red silk scarf. After I helped her out of her coat, she removed the scarf from her hair and tied it around her neck, the loose knot to one side of her throat.

Taking the trench coat, I admired her once again: hair, face, and body. Despite three kids, she was still slim, but rounded in the right places. Unlike Dana who had grown thicker and fuller as we aged.

And unlike me, who had matched Dana in pounds and wrinkles all along our extended journey together.

Sheila repeated much of what I'd already read and heard. She had been bullied and tricked and confused when she gave the taped confession. It was true that Zack shot Billy Graham, but it wasn't like they said in the indictment.

"Zack made me go out there with him, Dan. He said he was just going to talk to him." Sheila was leaning over the table and speaking in a low whisper. I was hunched forward, too, my elbows resting on the tabletop, my face not far from hers. Separated only by the two beer mugs.

"Talk to him? What about?" I had other questions, but they could wait.

"It started at the plant, but Zack couldn't really say anything to him there." She shrugged. "You know how it is. Billy was a supervisor. You know what would happen if he argued with a supervisor."

"I understand. But what were they arguing about?"

"Billy was coming on to me."

I stared at her. Into her pale blue eyes. "He was doing what?"

"He wanted me to go to bed with him." She looked down at the table and moved her fingers through a wet ring left by her beer mug. "He left a box of candy and some flowers on the back seat of my car ... Zack found them. At work."

I was trying to visualize that. She parked behind the admin building, and the car had to be left unlocked there. It could've happened like she said.

"Sheila," I said, "I don't understand why he ... Billy, I mean, would do that." I was thinking, there must have been something that made him believe she was interested. But I could see why he did it. It was right in front of me.

"I'd always been friendly with him, you know, when I worked as a truck driver." She looked up at me. "He was my supervisor. I couldn't exactly blow him off if he got fresh with me."

I didn't say anything, just looked at her, her face, her mouth, her eyes, trying to see what lay behind them. She gave me a sad little smile.

"I still joked around with him some when he came up to the office. But I didn't mean for him to take it seriously ... You believe me, don't you, Dan?"

"Why did you go with him ... or why did you and Zack go out to that old drive-in and him follow you or you follow him or whatever it was? And why was Zack in the trunk of your car?"

"It was a trick, Zack said. He wanted to teach him a lesson ... I know this sounds crazy." She shook her head, and her hair, now light brown, splayed out around her face and neck. She pulled it aside. "Zack said if I led Billy out there and he jumped out of the trunk, it'd scare hell out of Billy, and he'd leave me alone. He'd be too embarrassed to retaliate—otherwise he could've made life miserable for Zack, and maybe even for me ... even if I was up in the office."

I was beginning to understand. "So, by following you out there like you two were going to have a little ... a little tryst or something, he would be compromised ... and Zack and you would tell everybody about it, if he didn't leave you alone." Her eyes on mine, she was nodding rhythmically to this, with one long finger moving in the wet rings on the table, then up the side of the beer mug.

"But what proof would you have?" I asked, shaking my head. "Didn't you consider that they might ... get into a fight? Did you know about the shotgun?"

"No! No!" With her head tilted down, her hair swung back and forth in front of her face. Then her eyes came back up to mine. Her face reminded me of a fairy's I'd seen illustrated in some children's book I read to my daughter long ago. High cheekbones and cheeks still flushed from the cold—or maybe from baring her soul to me— a sensual mouth that when she smiled made dimples in her cheeks.

"Zack told me he'd just talk to him, that's all ... He'd have him in a trap and he couldn't deny it." Her eyes were searching mine, looking for sympathy, I guess, or understanding. "He didn't give me any choice, Dan. I had to go."

"Folks, here's your pie. Pepperoni, mushrooms, and extra cheese." A tall teenager whose face looked like it had been splattered with pizza sauce was standing over us. As we drew back and pulled the mugs aside, he swiftly dropped the metal disc in the center of the table. "I'll bring you some plates," he said.

"Extra napkins ... Okay?" I snapped and quickly brought my eyes back to Sheila, who was staring at the steaming pizza as if it were a crystal ball. She looked up and, to my surprise, gave me a shy grin, like she'd just thought of something. The grin was a little crooked on one side, showing a tiny gap in the front teeth. Her eyes seemed to sparkle in the rising steam.

We ate. I wasn't feeling hungry, not for food. Perhaps I was nervous, wondering where we were going from here.

"So, you didn't know about the shotgun," I said. The first bite scorched my mouth and I'd taken a long draw on the beer. "How'd he get the shotgun into the car without you seeing it? You didn't see it, did you?"

"He fixed up the back with some blankets. Before we left the house. He must've put it in then."

"He was in the trunk the whole time?"

"Right. If you leave the key in the lock, you can open it from the inside."

I was thinking: has she just confessed a murder to me? Do I have to go to the police with this? Nah, of course not. What she says is no good against Zack, and she's telling me she had no role in it. Well, not up to this point. She lacked any *mens rea*—criminal intent. Up to the point Zack shot Graham. The way she'd told it to me. But then she became an accessory after the fact, helping him conceal the crime. Maybe I had already heard too much.

"Sheila," I said, leaning forward and shaking my head, "you

cannot tell me what happened after that. You'd probably be admitting a crime, and I'd have to tell the DA"

"But you're a lawyer." Eyes pleading, face brimful with innocence.

"That's the problem. I'm a lawyer, but I'm not *your* lawyer. I can't give you legal advice, and I don't think I can keep anything you tell me confidential."

"But, Dan." Her hands were on the table, beside her plate, and she reached across and grabbed my wrist. She looked stricken, almost panicky. "I trusted you ... I trust you. You're not going to tell anyone what I said, are—"

"No." I sighed. "Not unless you confess a crime ... to me, I'm not." Pulling my wrist free of her grasp, I took her outstretched hand in both of mine. Her long fingers curled around my fingers. "I don't think..." I paused a moment. "I'm not in a position to say whether anything you did violated any criminal law. Not from what you've told me." I squeezed her hand and tried to divine who she was from her face, from her eyes, still a disconcerting blue. "But I don't want to hear any more ... It could cause problems—for both of us ... Okay?"

"Okay." Her fingers tightened around my hand, her face relaxed, and a weak smile replaced the frown. In silence, we sat like that for I don't know how long, our eyes drawing us together. I began to feel an overwhelming hunger to kiss her mouth, her bare neck above the scarf, to hold her—to make love to her—and I quickly pulled my hands away and picked up a piece of pizza. It was cold.

A thought struck me, and I put the pizza down on the plate. Sheila was cutting a corner of hers with a knife and fork, the way she'd been eating it.

"Sheila, is that why you wanted to see me? Just to tell me ... this?"

Leaving the knife and fork over the pizza, she looked up. "Yes. I wanted you to know..." Our eyes stayed locked. Then her utensils sank onto the plate. "To tell the truth, Dan, I'm lonely. I needed to talk to you—you're so gentle and caring and ... and understanding."

Those weren't words I was used to hearing. That wasn't how I defined myself, even though I was a pretty good listener, most of the time. Even when my ears were disconnected from my brain.

"And Zack barely talks to me now," Sheila was saying, her face contorted in a grimace. "When he's home ... Dan, what are you thinking?"

I smiled at her. My distraction, or the electric current coursing through my body, must have been obvious. "Where are your children?" I asked.

She sighed, and rubbing her forehead with her hand, she pushed her hair to one side. "My parents have been looking after them ever since ... ever since this thing started and they searched our new house."

"Would you like to go see a movie?" An irrational, animal force had seized me.

Her face brightened. "Oh, yeah." She nodded. "That'd be really nice ... In Beaumont?"

"Why don't we go back to my place—in Houston?" I kept my eyes on hers, wanting to see her reaction. Her eyes narrowed slightly, but there was a spark of interest. "We ... I have one of those new Betamax video machines," I said. "Wave of the future."

She leaned back and cocked her head, a smile playing along her lips. "Isn't your wife there?"

"No." I shrugged and reached for my coat on the seat beside me. There was only one thing I wanted now. "I'll tell you about that."

"Can I leave my car here ... you know, til tomorrow?"

"Why not?" I pushed my chair back and stood. She did, too, smiling broadly, expectantly, at me as I reached across to help her with her coat.

Chapter Seventeen—All or None

THE NEXT MORNING, IT WAS after ten o'clock by the time I reached the plant. There were already a half-dozen pink message slips waiting for me. The one that got my attention was a call from Roy Rogers, the Texas Ranger—marked urgent, with a number in Waco.

Perry and Hank asked no questions about where I'd been all morning. With the Jarvis/Landry lawsuit and a couple of NLRB charges, along with our efforts to put together a contempt case for strike violence and a few matters I had going on back in Houston, I came and went as I pleased. Good cover to do what I wanted.

Tossing my overcoat across a spare chair in my temporary office, I grabbed the phone and, without going behind the desk, dialed the Ranger's number. The one window in the office looked out over the former plant manager's house and the dead lawn and struggling oleanders around it. In the ship channel beyond the house, a long oil tanker was sliding past—going out to the Gulf of Mexico, on its way to some exotic destination. Or maybe to Newark. It was a cloudless blue-sky morning, crisp and clean, if you could ignore the refinery odors seeping through the interstices of the old building. Odors infused there day-by-day over the last seven decades.

There was an answer on the fifth ring. "Yo. Who's this callin'?" An out-of-breath tenor.

"Dan Esperson. Mr. Rogers? You called me."

"Oh yeah, Dan." A deep breath and exhalation. "I need to see you. Got somethin' that might help you with that Mills matter."

Mills matter now, not Graham. I shifted the phone to the other ear. "What's that?" I said, not sure I wanted to know.

"You fired 'em, didn't you?"

"Ye-ah. The company discharged them both, but—"

"Ol' McHugh may not be able to prosecute, but we sure as hell want to make life difficult for those two ... hard as possible. Maybe even get the woman so she'll talk—for real."

I was staring out the window, trying to think. After last night, this was the last thing I wanted to hear ... or to discuss with the Ranger, or anybody else. But I should've known something would come along to mess up my little idyll.

"I don't understand," I said. "I thought the case against her was dismissed."

"You know as well as I do it can be refiled ... Look, I'm over that way Thursday. How about you and me havin' dinner?" I was silent, so he went on. "Say that little Mexican place we went to last time. That'd do just fine."

Curious, puzzled, I agreed to meet him. The only answer to my question about what exactly he had for me was that he still needed to run some traps. He'd show me Thursday, if it all worked out.

Sheila and I managed to get together a couple more times that week—before Thursday. Not at the Sands or any other place in the Golden Triangle. She knew a little out-of-the-way motel down the interstate toward Lake Charles, so we went there. It was a time like no other I could remember—well, not for years. The nights revived me, and the days left me sinking hourly into weary exhaustion.

Thursday after lunch, I was almost asleep in my office, when Perry startled me awake. "Dan, Landry wants to talk about the strike discipline ... after the bargaining session. I need you there. He's bringing his lawyer."

"All right," I said. I looked at my watch. The Ranger. "I've got to meet somebody at seven. Will we be through by then?"

He gave me a funny look, like maybe he expected I was meeting a woman or something. Or maybe I was just feeling guilty.

"Prob'ly. Mediator called this meeting, so we have to go through the motions, keep him happy. I don't reckon it'll take more'n hour or two."

"I can cancel my dinner," I said. "It's the Ranger—you know, the one who—"

"Oh, yeah. Why you talking to him?"

"He called me." I stretched to get a kink out of my neck. "Wouldn't say what he wanted—real mysterious like. Care to join us?"

"Not tonight. Promised the bride I'd take her out. It's been a while."

THE COMPANY and union were holding their negotiations at a local motel owned by someone's friend, Johnny Holiday, who had mounted a large green-and-white Holiday Inn sign out by the highway. Each side had a command center in a "room with two queens" down the wings from the conference room. Now that the strike had settled in for the long haul, actual bargaining took place only at irregular intervals—and occasionally at odd hours and late into the night.

Propped up against the headboard of a queen bed, my eyes shut, I waited with Perry's new secretary/assistant and an HR clerk for Perry's summons once the Federal mediator gave up for the day. Shortly before five, I was dozing and Andrea reading a magazine when the call finally came.

As most of the negotiating teams exited, I slipped into the conference room and went to join Perry and Hank Greenberg on the side of the table away from the door. Facing them were Frank Landry, Pete Reneau, and a union committeeman who introduced himself as Harold Kaufman. Harold was older, a grandfatherly sort, pleasant and deferential to everyone. I wondered why he was on the committee. Probably because he did what he was told.

We waited while Landry called Joplin's office to find out where he was. Leaving my briefcase by the chair and my legal pad and pen on the table, I wandered down to the far end of the room to retrieve a soft drink from a tray in which a few remaining cans floated in tepid water.

Like the motel, the conference room wasn't fancy: two long tables with spindly legs, pushed together and covered with three overlapping white tablecloths, hard straight chairs, frayed gray carpet, and sliding glass doors facing the swimming pool. Drawn partially across the doors was a gauzy curtain on which I spied a long brown roach track in a crease near the refreshment table. Above it all, the bright fluorescent lights permeated a floating haze of cigarette smoke. Full ashtrays, empty drink cans, and half-empty glasses of water littered the white tablecloths—among a few brown coffee stains and round cigarette burns. Cellophane candy wrappers were scattered on the table and on the floor around one empty seat.

Joplin and Mary Albright swept in as I meandered back to my spot.

"Let's get started," Joplin said. "I don't have all day." Like we were the ones who were late.

Joplin dropped a bulging briefcase on the floor without opening it, while his subaltern produced a pad and pen from a thin attaché case that seemed dainty next to her. The table creaked and shook as she levered her body into a chair and placed the case and her purse under the table.

"You aren't going to resolve this thing until you deal with the discipline," Joplin said to Perry, seated at my elbow. Joplin's face was red like he'd been out in the sun too long, but his nose was even redder. I wondered if he'd had a few nips of scotch before he got here. It was after five.

"Everybody's mad as hell about J.C. and the others," Landry said. "I couldn't sell 'em on any kind of contract so long as you refuse to talk about the discipline."

"It's not a negotiable item," Perry said, leaning forward and looking down at a typed page. "My management says you can stay out til hell freezes over if you expect us to reinstate somebody who was taking shots at our people coming to work." Perry didn't stutter or hesitate when he was scripted.

"Oh, for Christ's sake," said Reneau, "it was nothing but a damn wrist rocket. All they did was break a car window or two."

"Somebody could've been hurt," I said. I needed to show that I wasn't irrelevant. At least let them know I was here.

"They weren't." Mary Albright doing her part. "Those porcelain balls only make a loud noise and break up. They don't go on through."

"How do you know *that*?" I said, rolling my eyes.

"We watched the video you gave us. Did our own little test."

"Bet you got lots of slingshots and ammo you can use for that," Perry said. He turned his head toward Landry. "But it wasn't a porcelain ball J.C. Ledbetter was using. It was a ball bearing and he picked the wrong target."

"I warn you," Landry shifted his bulk so he could wag his big index finger closer to Perry. "We all come back together, or we ain't coming back."

"It's your choice." Perry kept his elbows on the table, not backing away from the finger.

We went on like that for almost an hour. In a side conversation at the coffee urn, I suggested to Perry that we agree to arbitrate the discipline. Perry said he couldn't do that. Derek wanted to stand on his rights, and Layton Van Horn was mad as hell about the ball bearing whizzing past his face. No contract during the strike so no arbitration. Simple as that. It was clear that the discussion was going nowhere when Joplin changed the subject.

"Well, you're gonna have to reinstate Zack Mills," he said.

"I ... I don't think so," Perry answered, after hesitating a moment.

"There was a contract then..." Joplin started.

"He was discharged after the strike began and the contract ended," I said.

"No, you made it effective before the strike." Mary Albright.

I started to answer, then stopped. That was right. Zack and Sheila had been relieved of duty before the strike and their discharges made effective retroactively to then.

"The decision to discharge him was made after the contract expired," I said. "You didn't file your grievance until—"

"You'll have to arbitrate that," Mary said, "and the arbitrator will want to hear the whole thing. You won't win on some technical nicety."

"Derek w-won't re ... reinstate either of 'em," Perry said. "It *don't* matter what an arbitrator does."

"I think it does," said Joplin. "He's not above the law." He paused. "You are going to reinstate *Sheila* Mills, aren't you?"

"She ain't our concern," said Reneau, frowning at Joplin.

"Not anymore," Landry said. The grandfatherly union rep, Kaufman, seemed to be studying the wall behind me. I was wondering what was going on here with Joplin and his clients.

"You don't have any basis to keep either of 'em out." Joplin.

"We represent Sheila, too," Mary Albright said, shaking her head at Landry. "She waived any conflict and it's best for both of them to have the same lawyers."

Ah, I thought. Now I see.

"Zack's the union's concern. That Sheila ain't." Landry leaned on the table to look sideways at Mary, then shifted to stare at me. The coffee in my cup on the table almost sloshed over the sides. Shaking his finger to emphasize almost every syllable, Landry added, "You're gonna have to arbitrate Zack's discharge—no matter what you do with the wife."

"And you don't have any evidence, not that you can use," Joplin said. Now he was trying to placate his client. "You don't have a criminal conviction. You don't have witnesses. You don't have jack shit."

It was like tennis except the other side hits multiple balls at you at once. I was trying to think how we were going to win an arbitration with the union over Zack. And worrying about Sheila. What all this meant for her. And for me.

"How about Sheila," I said. "She's a witness and she's not in the union ... And the detectives, the ones who interviewed her? They're witnesses."

"She's not going to testify in any *kind* of proceeding, period." Joplin grinned at me. "And you'll never get those detectives down here. I'm damn sure of that. Not after the royal cluster-fuck they got themselves into."

My mind was racing. Anything Sheila said in an arbitration could be used against her in the criminal case. No defense of coerced or wrongly obtained confession. And Joplin would argue that she couldn't be compelled to incriminate her husband, even in a private arbitration hearing. That would produce a transcript, or at least a half-dozen witnesses who could testify about what she said when she was under oath.

"We'll subpoena the detectives," I said. "The arbitrator can issue subpoenas." I hoped he could, and would.

"Derek's got friends with the city," Perry said. "The chief of police was with Patton—"

"You'll see." Joplin was on his feet now and Mary Albright was struggling to rise with both hands on the table. Leaning back in their chairs, the union reps were enjoying the show.

"You want to make this difficult," Joplin said, seizing his briefcase and hitting the table with it. "That's fine with me. We'll fight you the whole damn way. But you better go talk to Derek before you go digging your hole any deeper." He turned to stare at me. "In fact, maybe you better go talk with those jokers in New York—about Mills *and* the strike discipline."

"Look, Tony," I said, using my best voice of reason. "Zack Mills killed a supervisor. You can't really expect us to reinstate him. Think about the reaction in the plant."

"That's *your* problem," said Landry. He and his fellow committeemen had slid back from the table. The other two were watching him, waiting on him to stand, but he kept talking. "You don't know what happened out there—or why it happened. You can't do anything to him without something from a court of law."

"You don't have a leg to stand on," said Mary Albright, now on her feet. "You have to follow the labor agreement ... and the laws of the land. Innocent until proven guilty." She was puffing a bit from the exertion of rising. "Beyond a reasonable doubt. You can't take the man's livelihood from him without just cause. That's what the contract says."

"Killing a supervisor's gotta be just cause to fire him," I said.

"Burden's on the company to prove he did it," Mary said, with such emphasis she knocked her chair over.

Kaufman stood and hurried behind her to pick it up. Landry and Reneau were up as well.

"You don't have any evidence," Joplin said, looking over his shoulder. He was on his way to the door, Landry, Reneau, and Kaufman following in his wake. Mary was still trying to shove her legal pad back into the attaché case with one hand and retrieve her purse off the floor with the other.

"What if she divorces him?" Hank said. "And agrees to testify."

Joplin stopped and turned, almost causing Landry to plow over him. Mary Albright was quicker, though, on the reply.

"Ha! It'll never happen." She shook her head, the blond curls bouncing around her face. "That woman will stick with her husband until your proverbial hell freezes over." She smirked at Hank, then at me. "You just watch."

I thought I caught the hint of a wink in my direction.

"You can't treat Zack any different than her," said Joplin, and resumed his march to the exit. With Mary as the caboose, they disappeared out the door.

"Is he right?" Perry asked after they had gone and Hank closed the door. He was looking at me. "Is there nothing we can do? You know, Dan, to keep Zack out of here." I noticed he didn't mention Sheila.

"I need to think about it. Do some research." I was on my feet now and looking at my watch. "You need to talk to Derek. Make sure Houston will back us up."

I was thinking about the Texas Ranger, and hoping he could help. And puzzling over the way Mary Albright looked at me just before she left.

Chapter Eighteen—Roy Rogers, Again

THE RANGER WAS WAITING FOR me in the foyer at Mi Casita Bonita. We shook hands and followed a pretty *señorita* in a frilly red skirt and scooped-neck white blouse to a table, this time well away from the restrooms. At my request.

The restaurant was mostly empty, the red carpeting clean of the broken tortilla chips we had crunched through the last time. The union workers and their families couldn't afford to dine out, while the company supervisors and engineers were eating catered food every day inside the refineries: grilled T-bone steaks and shrimp and ten different kinds of vegetables and desserts. Or they were staying home during the few non-sleeping hours before their next twelve-hour shift.

I ordered a margarita, the Ranger an iced tea. Something in his lingering look at the margarita told me he was in AA. His lingering look at the *señorita* told me that something else was missing in his life.

"Dan," he said after our drinks had appeared, "you know about the problems we've been having with our case against the Mills couple?"

I nodded and jabbed the straw at the lime in the bottom of the margarita. "It's been in all the papers," I said and took a long pull on the straw.

"Damn case has both me and the D.A. buffaloed. We know they did it, but we can't get to first base on gettin' 'em convicted." He was drinking his tea but still eyeing my margarita. "Now that her damn confession's been thrown out, we're left with practically nuthin."

"How about the shotgun and shell the cops found? You given up on that?" The drink was improving my mood already—and making me more daring.

"Well, hell ... that's not enough. We have a match, but it ain't that good. The shell was damaged, probably run over. And the damn tire tracks could belong to several hundred vehicles in Jefferson County. There and all over southeast Texas."

"No footprints?"

"All kinds, just can't tell whose."

"So, what have *I* got to do with all this?" The margarita was almost gone and I was ready for another. I waved to the waiter.

"The chief called me. He and your boss have been talking."

Eyeing him, I gave a brief nod over my empty glass. Chief, Port Oso police. Boss, Derek.

"The chief says you'll have to arbitrate the husband's discharge ... with the union, I take it ... but your plant manager's tellin' *him* the lawyers are concerned they don't have any evidence."

"Ye-ah. That'd be me, I guess."

My drink arrived, along with a second waiter bearing plates with still-sizzling steak *tampiqueña* and the usual sides of Spanish rice, *frijoles*, and *pico de gallo*. And warm tortillas. Figuring the margarita was no match for the peppers, I ordered a beer.

Prayerfully, the Ranger sniffed the rising steam from his plate. "Had to twist the DA's arm a bit," he said, addressing the steak as much as me, "but I've got the solution to your problem."

My mouth full of steak and peppers, I swallowed and stared at him. "What's my *problem*?" The *jalapeños* were making me long for my beer.

"Proving your case."

The beer appeared and I grabbed it before the waiter could pour it into the chilled mug he brought. Dropping the lime slice into my water glass, I took a swig from the bottle. The Ranger was working his jaw on a piece of steak.

"Proving my case?" I said, swiping my mouth with the back of my hand. I upended the Tecate bottle over the frosted mug.

He was looking at me now with a big smile on his face. Reaching inside his coat, he pulled out a folded-over manila envelope. Tonight, he wore a blue plaid shirt and bolo tie with his usual camelhair coat and blue jeans. The white hat he'd left on a peg in a row of empty pegs near the entrance.

Keeping his eyes on me, he laid the envelope on the table. "This is her confession—the one she gave those two dumb-ass detectives." He pushed the envelope toward me, carefully avoiding the wet spots left by the drinks.

I looked at the envelope, but I didn't reach for it. "What is it? A tape recording?"

"Yep."

"Why are you giving me this?"

"So, you can prove your case."

"How can it be admissible?" I stared at him. "It was thrown out by the court. How can I authenticate the damn thing, anyway?"

"You're a lawyer, I'm sure you can figure out a way." Now he was grinning at me. His teeth were white and even. Too even. Have to be false, I thought and took another bite of the steak. How was I going to handle this? The tape was probably useless and I didn't know if I wanted it anyway. For a number of reasons.

"Will the detectives testify?" I asked.

"Not likely." What Joplin had already told me.

"We can try to make them testify, I guess." I cocked my head and sighed and gave him a look out of the corner of my eye. "Will you testify?"

He shook his head. "Probably can't—but I don't have any problem with your saying where you got the tape."

"How does this help the DA? We're just trying to keep them ... Zack at least, out of the plant."

"Play this at the hearing, it'll be the first time the man's ever heard it." Stopping the relay of food to mouth, he shook his fork at me. "You see, it's like a chess game. Keep moving the pawns, keep the pressure on and see if one of 'em will break. Panic or run. Sooner or later, one of 'em's gonna tell somebody what happened out there so the D.A. can use it." He dropped the fork and shrugged. "Or lead us to somethin' ... If we can't keep the two of 'em in jail, we can at least keep 'em lookin' over their shoulders."

"Sheila says she was forced to go out there with him."

The Ranger drew back slightly and frowned at me, his eyes narrow under his bushy white eyebrows. "Who told you that?"

I tried to remember if I'd heard it from anyone other than Sheila. I wasn't about to tell Roy the Ranger I'd been talking to her. Much less have him guess I'd been sharing a bed with her.

"Isn't that what her lawyers are claiming?" I mustered a look of pure innocence. "I don't know what happened, but I do know Sheila—from work ... and I can't believe she'd *willingly* participate in a murder." I threw my hands out to show my incredulity at the very idea. "She's not the type."

The Ranger leaned back in his chair and scratched a fold in his neck above his bolo tie, his eyes narrowed to suspicious slits and his mouth pulled down at the edges. His steak was gone, but I'd eaten only about half of mine. No longer hungry, I was relying on the remnants of my margarita for fortitude.

"You need to listen to that tape, Mr. Esperson. See what you think after that."

"What if Graham was trying to force his attentions on her?" It was one of those things that when it's out of your mouth, it doesn't sound like you intended.

"You mean like the innocent little white girl," he said, grinning at me now, "bein' taken advantage of by a mean ol' buck nigger, and the white man, the poor ol' husband, steps up to protect her. That what you mean?" He leaned farther back, so that the shadows fell across his face. His eyes receded into dark holes.

"Not exactly," I said, grimacing at him. "What I *mean* is that Graham could've been trying to get something going with her, using his position as a supervisor, and she thought her husband was just gonna talk to him ... She didn't know he was gonna shoot the man."

Bending forward, the Ranger rested his chin on the back of his hand, his one elbow on the table. He stared at me.

"You been talkin' to her about this? ... You two have something goin' on?"

I felt a flush of anger, or maybe it was embarrassment, rise from my gut all the way up to my receding hairline. I gritted my teeth before I answered, but I kept my eyes on his.

"I'm just trying to look at all the angles," I said. I pushed my plate away and grabbed my margarita glass. The beer was long gone. "The EEOC's issued some new regulations—sexual harassment, they call it." I waved my hand at his skeptical smirk. "That's something you're gonna hear more about—it means a supervisor can't use his position to get sexual favors from a woman who works for him."

"She didn't work for him."

"She used to ... and he was still a supervisor."

"Hm-m-m. So, you think that could've happened?"

"Could be—she could've been pressured by Billy Graham and she told her husband. Then he—"

"I think somebody's been feedin' you a line." He leaned over the table and shook a big index finger at me. "Let me tell you a little somethin' about women ... Any time they don't like what a man's doin', that's what they'll yell—sex-u-al her-ass-ment. That what you call it?"

"Harassment."

"Sexual hair-ass-ment." He shook his head, his finger hanging in the air between us. "I'm tellin' you there's a deep vein of *art*ifice in the female of the species that don't exist in us men." The finger wagged again. "They have a deviousness they use to convert their physical weakness into a shield—and a weapon ... Oh, you think I'm a country bumpus, but I've taken a course or two in psychology ... and I've known a lot of women over the years."

"No," I said. "I don't—"

"Made a study of it ... criminals, witnesses, victims ... read books on it. Over the eons, females have used their wits and wiles to turn aside the male's sexual assaults—or play them against one another."

I eyed him with some distaste, thinking this ol' boy's quite a barroom philosopher ... and full of bullshit. "So, what are you sayin'? That all women are deceitful and made that way as a necessary defense against men." This had started out as a discussion about Sheila, but now I was thinking of Dana. She's not like that. She couldn't be.

"You got it."

"That's quite a theory, or whatever it is," I said, shaking my head. "But, you know, I don't think it's a male or female thing. Men are just as deceitful. They use fraud and deception as tools ... for money and power ... and sex."

Yeah," said the Ranger, "but the male doesn't need this deception to get what he wants. Only the weaker, subservient ones—"

"Shit!" I said. "Half the male population in this damn country must be weak and subservient then."

"Maybe so. But they're not as good at it as women. For women, keeping secrets, secrets from men, is second nature."

"For a Texas Ranger, you seem to know a helluva lot about human nature and psychology." Not to mention bullshit.

"Like I said, I've read a lot, and I've studied a lot of people in my job."

"I just can't accept what you're saying. Every human being is different." I downed the rest of my margarita, not using the straw.

"But you have to agree," he said, jutting out his chin, "deception's a way for all of us to deal with life's challenges."

"Maybe self-deception and—"

"Women are good at it. The deception." He grinned at me and set both elbows heavily on the table and his chin on the backs of his folded hands. "Somethin' else I've learned," he said, his forehead deeply wrinkled. "Each person has three faces. One they show the world—by what they do, action and inaction—and that's what the world sees, maybe not the same as they intended. The second is what they say out loud and what the world hears. The third face is the unseen, unheard core of their being that their deeds and speech only partly reveal. Some's conscious; some's unconscious—"

"Sounds like Freud," I said.

"Freud got it only half right—all that stuff about id and ego." He cleared his throat and shifted back in his chair, letting his jacket fall away from his big gut. Tonight, he wasn't wearing his six-shooter.

His face was red now, and he continued venting with what I decided was *his* personal rage at the hand life had dealt him. Or perhaps it was because of what he'd seen in his job as a Texas Ranger.

"Let me tell you about the core. The male and female are different. Deep in each male—those with the usual chemistry and equipment," his finger was wagging again, "is an aggressive, sexual animal that seeks the pleasure of copulation. The male, stripped to this sexual id, if you want to call it that, would..." He paused and took a deep breath. "You see what I'm sayin'?"

He came forward over the table again and I stared at him, my lips clamped shut at his sophomoric logic. So he went on.

"At the female's core is her defenses against this male animal—her reactions over the ages ... to use the male to procreate and protect her offspring. So, you see, she has to use deceit and manipulation. You see?"

"What about love, companionship, and all that?" I couldn't keep quiet any longer. "Mutual support, affection ... that's all real—"

"Another story ... I'll tell you about it sometime. But at the woman's core is the wiles that preserve her and obtain the favored seed for her womb. All she has is deception and her favors to obtain her ends. That's what gave rise to Eve ... you know, the apple in the Garden of Eden, and equipped her for survival ... and the survival of the human race." He hit the table with the palm of his hand. "Why would you think that where a woman *works* is any different from anyplace else?"

"You've thought this all through? Thought about it a lot?"

"An awful lot—I've studied it and I've lived it."

"It *is* possible, isn't it, that you've got it all wrong? That's there's no core, male or female, just individual people. And that Sheila Mills was just as much a victim as Billy Graham?"

"Just listen to the damn tape." He shoved the manila envelope across the table, and I barely managed to catch it before it slid off the edge. "There's only this copy and the original, so don't lose it."

"Okay," I said. "I'll see what I can do." But I was thinking this guy could spout more B.S. than a brace of lawyers. He gave substance to a vocabulary word I'd found only mildly interesting in high school English: "misogynist," and this was the most misogynistic bastard I'd ever met. My margarita was gone, my steak was cold, and I was ready to get the hell away from him and his warped philosophy.

Chapter Nineteen—The Tape

INSTEAD OF GOING BACK TO THE Sands, I drove to the plant. At the main gate, two picketers stood next to a barrel with a fire in it. One had his sign, "Local 88 - On Strike," propped on his shoulder as he rubbed his hands together above the low flames. The other man's sign rested upside down at his feet.

Watching the two as I went by ... and them warily eyeing me back, I felt a certain sadness. Not pity exactly, but a feeling that whatever their ideals and wants and reasons, all this was a terrible waste, their sacrifice and their families' suffering. All for naught—knowing what I knew. But how else could they make their case? Rise up against us, the corporate monolith and its minions, with raised fists?

Behind them shone the dull lights on the refinery units and high above the units the effulgent flame of the hydrocracker flare pulsing like the fiery breath of some mythical dragon burning through the mist.

The gate was open. Exhibiting a bored expression, the gate guard waved me through and quickly retreated into the warmth of the enclosed gatehouse.

My temporary office had a Dictaphone that played standard-size cassettes. Settling into the swivel chair behind the desk, I removed the tape from the envelope and stared at the label on one side: "Interview with Sheila Mills" and the date. After a long moment filled with dread and doubt, I snapped the cassette into the

Dictaphone, pushed the play button, and leaned back in the chair with my feet on the desk. I left the office lights off and I sat in shadows cast by the hall lights outside the frosted glass in the door.

There was a minute or so of silence, only the whirring of the machine. Waiting, I stared out the window into the night. A series of streetlights shimmered near the dark Victorian house across the road. Beyond it, through the swaying fronds of the palms, I could see the superstructure lights of an oil tanker gliding up the channel. The wheels of commerce grinding on.

The first voice I heard was that of detective James Robinson, saying his name and his partner's, Sid Baggerly, and giving the date and the case—murder of Earl Stanley Graham—and then asking the interview subject for her name and address. Then came Sheila's voice.

For ten minutes, maybe less, the questions were fairly innocuous—the two detectives trying to put her at ease and, I suspected, set her up to contradict herself—things like, what was she doing the night of the murder, where was Zack, and why did she stay out of work the next day. Then the questions became increasingly aggressive, until finally Robinson's voice, smooth and pleasant, gave me a sinking feeling.

"Mrs. Mills, we both know you were having an affair with Earl—"

"That's a damn lie! I was not!"

"You can't hide something like that—not for long you can't ... The Ranger dug it up out at the plant and passed it on to us."

"And we matched the casing out there at the drive-in with the shotgun we found in your closet, Mrs. Mills." Baggerly. A low raspy voice. A heavy smoker, I decided.

"Graham told his brother the two of you had something goin' on. He called you his pretty little white girl." Robinson.

"You're lying, damn you! Billy'd never say a thing like that."

"Ah, it's Billy, is it? Billy wouldn't say that." Robinson.

There was silence on the tape and I leaned forward to make sure it was still playing.

"If you want to save your husband, you have to tell us what happened." Robinson. He spoke slowly, deliberately, with long pauses. "Right now, it looks like cold-blooded murder ... and in a robbery ... That's death for sure ... Only way you can save Zack is if you tell us the truth."

Silence, then a cough and a low noise that could have been crying.

"He's gonna die for sure ... your children won't have a father. You don't want that, do you, Mrs. Mills?" Below the sound of the raspy voice asking the question, came faint sobs, followed by a series of choking coughs.

"You can help save him." Robinson's low soothing voice. "If you tell us the truth, we may be able to keep him off death row. But we can't help you, or Zack, if you don't level with us ... This goes any further—you keep trying to hide what happened—Zack's a dead man."

"Turn ... that thing ... off." Sheila's wavering voice was punctuated by hoarse sobs. "I won't talk with it on." I could see her pointing at the tape recorder, her head down, or maybe she was looking up at Robinson with wet eyes, pale blue eyes, wild like a cornered animal. Pleading.

"If we turn it off, will you tell us?"

"Yes! Jesus, yes! Just turn it off."

There was a click on the tape. Then a second click and the sound came back on. This time it was Sheila talking in a voice laden with tears.

"... and he knew I'd been having an affair." A sob. "But he didn't know who it was with."

My stomach rolled over. The steak and *jalapeños* and margaritas were vying with each other to rise into my throat. I didn't know how long the detective's tape recorder was off, but from the way it started back up, I couldn't believe Sheila knew they'd turned it on again.

"Then while we were working on the house this summer, I told him."

"You told him it was Graham?"

There was a sob and silence, then a faint, "yes." She went on, without any interruption, telling about how Zack wouldn't touch her, how angry he was, especially because it was a black man. But they had kids and a new house, so she was going to stay with him even if they didn't have feelings for each other.

"We had too much to lose!" came out in a jagged sob.

I was in agony at the pain in her voice. How could someone as lovely as her, the intelligence I knew she had—how could she get herself into such a mess?

"When did you decide to kill him?" Robinson asked, not as gently as before.

"We'd just signed the final papers on the house. We were going to move in in a few weeks."

It was all downhill from there, my heart falling into the pit of my stomach. What finally set it off—Billy left a box of candy and some flowers in her car with a note. She had moved up to the admin building. And Zack found them.

"He was taking my car home." A sob. "The note." Silence. "Oh, God! His ... his car was in the shop." She was sobbing hard, and one of them brought her some water. There was a long silence until Sheila started talking again, sniffling but not crying.

Zack said they had to clear the air between them before they moved into their new house. So, they went looking for Billy at Lamar U, where he was in night school. When they found his car, she drove around the block and Zack got out of her Olds and climbed into the trunk, but he left a key in the lock so that he could open it from inside. That's when she first saw the shotgun, when Zack got into the trunk.

She parked in front of Billy's car, and when Billy came out of class, he came over to talk to her. After she thanked him for the flowers and candy, she told him to follow her. He did, out to the old StarLite Drive-In Theater—with Zack telling her where to go from the trunk. They'd been out there before and they knew the place.

There were more questions, but I was thinking back to one the detectives hadn't asked. Why had she and Zack been out there before? But I had to concentrate on listening; Sheila's voice had gotten lower. I dropped my feet off the desk and turned up the volume on the tape player and leaned closer to it. Her voice was quiet, almost lethargic. No crying at all now.

"Where was Graham?" Robinson continued to ask most of the questions.

"He came up behind me and pulled on by…" I listened intently as Robinson established where the cars were, what Graham was doing, and what Sheila could see in the dark. I heard her take a deep breath and let it out in a long sigh.

"When he reached my car, I rolled down the window. That's when I heard the trunk latch."

Baggerly interrupted to ask if Billy said anything to her, and Sheila said "no," Billy just looked back when the trunk lid came up, then started running. And Zack shot him. Another noise like a sigh, this one turning into coughing.

"Have some water." Baggerly.

There was a long silence until Robinson asked how far Billy had gone when Zack fired the shotgun, and after a moment, added, "To the corner of the room, right?"

I could see Sheila nodding and pointing. He didn't fall, she said, just kept running, maybe stumbled, but kept on running. She didn't know how far he'd gone when he finally fell. There weren't any lights.

Robinson interrupted and said the man was shot six times.

There was a deep breath, almost a shiver I thought, and Sheila said in a rush, "Zack went over to Billy ... lying on the ground and fired two more shots." She saw Zack bend over the body then hunt around and pick up the shotgun shells. When he got back in the car, he said he took Billy's wallet to make it look like a robbery.

"Could you see if Graham was dead," Robinson asked, then without waiting for an answer, added, "Did you ever considered trying to help him?"

There was a long silence. I could hear Sheila crying again, not sobs, but low agonizing moans, subsiding into hiccupping sniffles. Somewhere away from the microphone, Robinson and Baggerly were whispering. I hadn't heard them get up, but I heard chairs scraping on the floor as they sat back down.

The questioning continued. Sheila drove when they left the drive-in, going back to the highway and to the 7-Eleven on Merryman Avenue. They stopped there and Zack bought a couple of Cokes and got some change; he wanted to wash the car, make sure it was clean. There was a car wash next door.

A little light bulb went on in my mind. Pierre Lamont, the shadow, said he'd seen Zack and Sheila at a car wash, next to a 7-Eleven. The night of the murder? It had to be.

After they washed the car, they drove to their old house, and on the way, Zack threw Billy's wallet and the spent shotgun shells into the canal.

"You went home and you went to bed?" Baggerly said in his raspy voice. "You and your husband. In the same bed? ... Did you have sex?"

"I don't have to tell you that!" Sheila was yelling at him. "It's none of your goddamn business."

"We know you two went dancing the following Friday, Mrs. Mills." Robinson again. "And Saturday, you went shooting with some friends out on your hunting lease. Isn't that right?"

There was a long silence, and I checked the tape player to

make sure it was still on. Then Sheila asked, "What are you going to do with us?"

"Right now, Mrs. Mills, we're going to type up your statement. Just like you told it." Baggerly.

"Then you can read it and sign it." Robinson.

"I'm not signing anything. Not 'til I talk to a lawyer. You told me you'd help us ... You'd keep Zack from ... from the electric chair ... or whatever they do. Promise that in writing and—"

"We can't promise you anything." Robinson, his voice not so gentle now. "But maybe if he comes clean, who knows?"

After a moment, Sheila asked, "What happens now?"

"Well, you're under arrest and I'm going to read you your rights, just like in the movies." Robinson, in an unpleasant, sarcastic tone.

There was a click and silence. I let the tape run almost to the end and flipped it over to the other side, but there wasn't anything more. I wondered if the two detectives had meant for it to run as long as it did. My memory of the preliminary hearing was that Sheila didn't know the tape existed, at least not the part *after* she told them to turn the recorder off—not until the D.A. sprung it on the defense. What they said at the end meant they probably hadn't advised her of her rights before she talked—and confessed to a crime. And I knew from the hearing and the newspapers that she'd never signed any confession.

I took the tape out of the Dictaphone and replaced it in the manila envelope. Standing and opening my briefcase on the desk, I tossed the envelope inside, on top of a pleadings file from the Jarvis case. I started to reach for my coat on the chair but paused to press on my stomach, trying to make it stop hurting. Thinking, what am I going to do with this? What am I going to do about Sheila? The hot peppers and margaritas burned in my gullet, ready to erupt. I needed something to drink. No more alcohol, but maybe a soft drink from the machines at the Drifting Sands Motel. And some Tums or something.

153

When I got back to the Sands, I found a folded-over sheet of paper ripped from a steno pad taped to my door. I dropped my briefcase on the concrete walk and, holding my cold soft drink can in one hand, pulled the note off the door and read it under the yellow bug light. It was from Sheila, telling me not to call her at home. Zack was coming in for a few days before he left on another construction job, this one in Baytown. She'd call me. Next week.

Chapter Twenty—Fly Away

FIRST THING THE NEXT MORNING, I tracked down the Ranger. He was visiting with the Port Oso police chief, his and Derek Frazier's good friend.

"Okay," I said once I had him on the line and my door closed. "I listened to the tape and I can see why the D.A. can't use anything Sheila Mills said."

"You're the lawyer." The Ranger wheezed on the other end, like he was short of breath.

"I don't know if I can use any of it either—if the union wants to arbitrate Zack's discharge. That's civil, not criminal, and the marital privilege doesn't apply ... shouldn't apply." I had done some quick research before I went back to the motel last night. The plant had its own law library, all of the Texas statutes and reports and even a set of ALR's with cases and commentaries on legal issues.

"I don't know if I can get the arbitrator even to listen to it," I said.

I waited, but he only wheezed into the phone. Placing my feet up on the desk, I leaned back in the chair and stared out the window at the tops of the palms swaying above the roof of the old Victorian house. Stared at the gray sky. It was a gray, dismal day.

"Why wouldn't he?" Another wheeze.

"It's out of thin air. How do I authenticate it? ... You're there with the chief. Will he make sure the detectives come testify?"

"Nope. Already talked to him. Those boys are in deep shit for fucking up the confession. They're not taking any more chances."

155

"Did they advise her of her rights? Before they started in on her?"

"Dunno. That's sure her on the tape, though."

"How will the arbitrator know that? She's not going to testify ... How about you? Will you testify?" I watched a seagull alight on the chimney of the old house and tuck its wings in close and scrunch down against the cold.

"I'd have to be subpoenaed," said the Ranger, "and the lawyers would fight it ... Matter of principle in private civil matters." A wheeze. "Could you get a subpoena?"

"I don't know ... Probably not." A second seagull joined the first.

"Then I can't testify."

"How about something to certify the tape's a true copy? Will you give me an affidavit, you and the chief?"

"Hold on a minute. He's across the hall." There was a clunk and silence except for the sounds of footsteps and a door.

Across the road, the seagulls were facing into a brisk wind from the northwest—gray wings, white bodies, black heads, the faded red brick of the chimney against a gray sky. As I waited and watched the gulls, I realized that I was tired of it all: my job, the people I worked with, my wife, probably soon to be my ex-wife. I was nothing more than a hired gun, doing the client's bidding and getting paid for it. I couldn't define the origin of my discontent, at times almost despair. Maybe it started with Dana, then Sheila, and now the tape. Or maybe because I was trapped in a morbid and mundane job, not fulfilling any higher purpose. The victories I'd won were not for any noble or enduring cause. Only to advance the aims of a giant, heartless corporation that cared only for profit. Yet most of my legal allies and adversaries were my mirror image. All of us pawns in the same game. Except maybe Tony Joplin, for whom the clients were his pawns.

One of the gulls stretched out gray wings and the wind lifted it from the chimney, then it peeled off to the north in an effortless glide. I was growing tired of waiting. Why hadn't I told him to call me back? A container ship coasted up the channel, past the vacant manager's house and out of sight.

I was sick of all my Hamlet-like agonizing and uncomfortable with my role in this mess: the Graham murder, the arbitration over Zack Mills' discharge, the strike. The union and its leaders weren't the cause of my discontent. They were just a counterpoint to the company and its executives, with whom they shared the same drives for power and authority.

Maybe I should quit and fly away like that seagull. Do like Dana and go pursue my own dreams. Hang out a shingle somewhere in a small town. Maybe write a book.

Was there anybody I cared about, other than my daughter Susan and sometimes Dana? Before Tim Oakes. But I still cared about her. Loved her? What the hell was I going to do about her? Us? And Sheila. What was I going to do about her?

Despite my dilemma, the days and weeks seemed to creep past in endless monotony. Then some idiot would open the wrong valve and blow up a unit. Or life's banalities were shattered by sudden jolts of macabre tragedy: a dump truck backs over a man and crushes his head; a worker feeds nitrogen instead of fresh air into a storage tank his buddies are cleaning; a welder falls into an acid tank and all they find are the steel toes in his boots. The tragedies were real, and terrible, and depressingly regular in occurrence, even if the gods of disaster chose to vary their methods—from fire to asphyxiation, from lightening to drowning, from scalding steam to all-dissolving acid. There were as many different ways to die or get maimed in this business as the mind could conjure.

"Daniel." The Ranger's voice brought me out of my bleak reverie. "The chief'll give you a letter to certify the tape's authentic. It'll say he gave it to me, and who's on it, and when it was made. I'll add a note that I passed it on to you."

"Not an affidavit?"

"No."

"You need to say the tape's complete and hasn't been altered or anything like that. And your part has to be certified by a notary. That you are *who* you say you are."

"We'll see what we can do." Wheeze. "What are you gonna do about the woman?"

"The woman?" I knew whom he meant, but I wasn't going to concede anything on her. Not to him.

"Sheila Mills. Y'all *will* keep her out of the plant, won't you?"

"That's up to Derek ... I don't think she can make a claim, but I don't know. There's the sexual harassment angle I told you about."

There was silence, and I watched the lone remaining gull rise from the chimney and flap off into the wind, its underside white against the gray sky. The silence on the line ended in a long sigh. "You haven't gone sweet on her, have you?"

"What do you mean?" I felt my face flush.

"I think you know ... Let me tell you about it, son. She's more like the snake than the Eve character. I knew it the first time I talked to her."

He was pissing me off. "So why didn't you arrest her ... them ... back then?"

"I had most of it figured out from day one. Who shot him, anyway, and why. We just didn't know how it all played out and who was involved ... And we needed more evidence."

"How'd you know it was Zack?"

"Earl Graham's brother knew a little about the affair. That Jones woman, the one they call, 'Too Tall,' confirmed it. Sheila did some talking to her at one time or another. Couple of others overheard Zack haranguing Graham over behind one of the maintenance sheds. And Zack told Ledbetter about the stuff he'd found in Sheila's car."

"Wasn't that enough?"

"D.A. didn't think so. Robinson and his partner were playing Sheila along, thought they'd get something more out of her without

158

an arrest. We knew those two weren't goin' anywhere." Wheeze. "We wanted to know if somebody else was in on it—one of Zack's buddies."

"Was there?"

"You heard the tape."

After I hung up, I told Perry Comeau I had to go back to Houston for a few days—but I asked him to find Pierre Lamont first. I wanted to talk to him again. I didn't mention that Mr. Lamont had seen Zack and Sheila at a car wash next to a 7-Eleven late one night—just like Sheila said on the tape. It had to be the same night Zack killed Billy Graham. If I could deliver a witness to place Zack and Sheila together and at the car wash on the night of the murder, that *might* solve my problem with offering the tape in an arbitration. And buy me some help from the Ranger and chief of police.

What Perry found was that Mr. Lamont had quit, after being chewed out by Autry, the security chief, and placed on part-time duty. Autry thought Lamont had gone back to New Iberia. That's where they sent his last check, but it was returned "addressee unknown." Perry and Autry both said they'd try to get a phone number for Lamont, and I told them to let me know if they found out where he'd gone. But that was the last anyone ever heard of the man.

Chapter Twenty-one—Choices

I HEADED OUT THE MAIN GATE and over to the Sands to pick up my clothes. What I really needed was to get the hell out of this place and think. On my route back to the motel, I pushed Sheila, and Zack, and the problems they posed for me to the back of my mind, to gestate into a solution of some kind.

The long industrial boulevard and surrounding area through which I passed must once have been prosperous. Now it held nothing more than a series of dilapidated wooden stores from World War II or before, almost all boarded up, and a modern strip mall that had recently suffered the same fate. The only open business left in the strip mall was a freshly painted pawnshop and gun store with bars on the windows. In the old wooden buildings, I made out a massage parlor, a palm reader, and a small café with matching neon signs in the two front windows. On a corner in the middle of this lonely stretch was a new 7-Eleven. A couple of cars were parked out front and one at the gas pumps. A convenient stop for someone wanting a cold six pack for the road after a long day's work. Or a couple of Cokes and change to wash the car after committing a murder. But there was no car wash next door to this stop.

I cut through an old neighborhood that in times past housed well-paid refinery workers—and still held a few stubborn retirees, along with the part-time laborers or store clerks who hadn't managed to win the prized refinery jobs. Those who had the jobs had long since fled to the suburbs, away from the towns and their re-segregating schools and dying businesses. The houses here were low-slung ranches, most with carports, only a few with garages. A spidery web of live oaks both shaded the houses and concealed the state of decay into which many had fallen. From the branches of the trees hung long gray beards of Spanish moss.

A procession of chain-linked fences and weed-filled ditches lined the streets. In the driveways that breached these barricades, there was often an old car or two—and sometimes another with flat tires in a tangle of vines on the lawn—and here and there a chopper motorcycle or a bass boat on a flimsy trailer.

Had Sheila and Zack lived in a neighborhood like this before they moved into their new house?

The long drive to Houston offered none of the variety I needed to distract me, and once I'd settled into the traffic and turned on the radio—a classical station dominated by the violins I'd come to hate—I couldn't help thinking about Dana. And Sheila. And again, what the Ranger said about women.

I had always preferred female company to any male's. And I'd enjoyed Sheila's company. And Dana's. Dana's always. But even with her, I found myself watching, and studying, other women.

An attractive woman gave me pleasure, not in a particularly lascivious way—though the impulse seized my mind occasionally—but in admiration. Of form and grace, of manner, of motion and style. Not just the components, but the gestalt of a woman: handsome, pretty, striking, unusual, engaging. Not just pleasant curves or the smooth angle of a jaw or high rounding of a cheekbone in the light. Not just the shape of her nose or the texture and tint of her hair: auburn, black, or blond, thick or curled or straight, by the ear or down her neck, on her shoulders, her back. Nor just a woman's skin, velvet to the touch and of differing hues. No, I also admired the liquid movement of a long-fingered hand—to her face, her mouth, touching my arm. Fingers pushing aside a loose strand of hair, removing an earring, checking a button at her throat or pressed in thought against her cheek; fingers smoothing out a wrinkle on a hip or in a stocking; slipping on shoes, taking off shoes, stockings. Her mouth flickering in the corners with a smile or stretching in a grimace or a challenge; her forehead furrowed in concentration. A sly, sleepy-eyed look in the shadows; a step sideways on the walk, a smile, a laugh, a sigh, a hand on my arm, a warm palm against my back or on my thigh.

Tears, though, always troubled me. I was fearful of brushing them away, despairing that I was the one who made them flow.

For the appearance of my fellow males, I gave not a whit. Perhaps to admire a muscled arm or well-shaped head. Or hair. Lots of hair, and perfect teeth. And smile. Or for the woman who was with him.

All this was shallow, I knew. It didn't speak to who the woman really was. Book and cover. The eyes, windows of the soul. Perhaps false windows, just like words. Hiding motives and desires and anxieties. Deception, deceit, subterfuge. Rouge, lipstick, fingernail polish, and eyeliner. Dyes and waxes. The flatteries of stylish clothing, furs, and expensive haircuts.

Were her actions and words true reflections of her mind? And mine, of my own mind? Not just the conscious mind, but the unconscious as well. From what in *her* life and *her* nature sprang this person's self? His self, her self, at the moment of their eyes meeting? Their lips touching? Their bodies joining?

Tired of the music, I turned off the radio. Reaching for my coat, which I'd flung across the passenger's seat, I found a pack of Juicy Fruit next to my glasses case in an inside pocket. My wrists braced on the steering wheel, I extracted a piece, peeled off the wrapper, and began viciously chewing the sugary gum in hope it would quash my heartburn and settle my stomach.

Traffic whizzed by on my left, while I stayed at a steady speed, lost in the peregrinations of my mind. I drove like that all the way back to Houston, taking my time and thinking, trying to figure things out.

I had a pretty good idea of who I was, since I had spent a lifetime in the study—forty long years, at least since my first consciousness of myself. Unless I was only engaging in self-deception, always a possibility for any of us. Yet, I'd always felt compelled to be a better person than I was, even if I never quite succeeded. But I little troubled myself, at least not for long, if I fell short. The struggle had always been to extend the same acceptance of shortcomings to others. To Dana, to Susan. To Sheila.

Could I, should I accept Sheila's shortcomings?

I couldn't. She was on the other side of some high, impassable barrier from me. She was so far removed that, as much as I admired her feminine qualities, I could never understand her. I could never accept what she had done.

As for myself, I could always manage to bury any regrets and to forget my sins—after a few remonstrances perhaps; and they—the regrets or memories of my sins—only resurfaced in odd moments now and then, prompted by a stray comment or a parallel event in the skein of life.

By the time I reached home, I was ready to bury Sheila in the past and get on with *my* life. Whatever that was.

Dana was another matter. I wasn't going to bury her and leave her behind.

Chapter Twenty-two—Dinner with Liz

TWO DAYS IN HOUSTON DIDN'T improve my mood, or my health. There was no sign of Dana. Only a note in the mail with a copy of the deed conveying away the house in Aspen.

I was spending a few hours catching up on work in my Houston office when Liz Johnson barged in. The door was shut tight, but that never stopped Liz. She caught me listening to the tape: right when Sheila was telling how Zack shot Billy Graham the first time, in the back when he was running away from the Olds.

As soon as the door swung open, I dropped my feet to the floor and reached for the off button. Liz stopped me while my hand was in mid-air.

"Wait," she said, charging toward my telephone stand, which also held my Dictaphone. "I want to hear this."

Hesitating only a second, I hit the off button. "It's confidential," I said.

"That was the Mills woman, wasn't it? You've got her confession." Liz was always quick to figure out what was going on.

"Yeah, that's right."

"Why won't you let me hear it? It's gotta be juicy." She was glaring at me, her hand poised above mine, which was still on the off button. I tried to return her glare, but I couldn't hold it.

"Okay." Why shouldn't she hear it, I thought. "I've listened to it twice already, and I was just checking this part." Not quite true.

"Well, don't just sit there; turn it on. I'm in a hurry."

I pushed play, and Liz pulled a client chair around from the front of the desk, closer to the telephone stand. As Sheila spilled her guts, I stared at the HR manager, a statuesque woman with jet-black hair and olive skin. A modern businesswoman, sophisticated, worldly, and tough. Not trusting and naïve like Dana, who always looked for the positive in everything, even when it wasn't there. Not feline and seductive like Sheila.

Liz wrinkled up her nose at something Sheila said and stretched her legs out to brace her feet against my desk, her high-heel shoes off by now. I had seen that listening stance often enough to know her habits, the little quirks. All of a sudden, it hit me that she and I were a lot alike: our cynicism, our attitudes toward the corporate world in which we lived—and toward other people. Skeptical and sarcastic, especially when we were together.

Zack was bending down to get Graham's wallet, but I was concentrating on Liz. She looked nice today. Really nice. She had more than a little Mediterranean blood, despite the name, a married name she'd kept. Her hair and complexion and angular face differed from Dana's Irish auburn and fair skin and soft lines. From Sheila's Scotch-Irish blond paleness and nymphet features.

Liz was wearing a trim business suit, navy blue, and a white silk blouse open at the throat, exposing a shiny black obsidian necklace. When she charged in, I'd noticed that her skirt was unusually short and tight for her.

Grimacing, she shook her head. Sheila was describing how Zack had stopped at the 7-Eleven, getting change to wash their car.

Her hair's longer, I thought. Fuller, a different cut. And she's wearing dangly earrings, obsidian stones to match the necklace. Blush makeup and eyeliner. Even her nails were done, with red polish. She'd changed over the years, as she advanced in the company, a change that had accelerated in the last months. Yet, she still had a way of turning up the corners of her mouth when she smiled—which she did at me while I was staring at her and assessing how she looked and deciding I actually liked her—for all the grief she'd given me.

"What do you think you're looking at?" she said. "You checking me out or something?" She threw a hand back over her shoulder, giving her hair a toss. She was still smiling.

"You look nice," I said. I reached for the Dictaphone. "Heard enough?"

"More than enough." I clicked it off. "Good thing we fired their asses," Liz said, "but that's not why I'm here." She sat up straight in the chair and placed an elbow on the edge of the desk. "I've got a problem, Dan. The prick's in town and he wants me to end the fucking strike—as if it was up to me." She kicked the side of the desk. A soft thud. The prick was Jack Dawson—her boss. "The board's pressing him to get it over with. Too much negative publicity."

"I thought you were close on the issues," I said, shifting my chair under the desk and leaning toward her. She had nice cheekbones and lovely brown eyes. And at this point, I really didn't give a shit if they got a contract and ended the strike or not.

"We're almost there," she said and held up her thumb and index finger less than an inch apart. "It's the discipline. Jughead wants to put the ones we fired back to work."

"Ouch." I leaned back in my chair. "That's a switch." We'd fired J.C. Ledbetter and two others, including one of the strikers who gave Andrea's boyfriend an upside-down swimming lesson in the Sands' pool.

Liz waved her hands in a wide arc. "Dawson was all rah-rah to do it when we discharged them ... backed us a hundred percent, he said. The slime ball."

"You free for lunch? ... We can go talk about it." I started to get up, but she waved me back down.

"Can't." She looked at her watch. "I've got a luncheon with Dawson and the coordinating committee." All the company's HR managers and their big chief. The reason she was so well-manicured, made up and dressed up. "What do I tell him, Dan? I've got to deal with it this afternoon."

"Tell him that if he backs off, Derek Frazier will ram his riding crop, or whatever that thing is, all the way up his sorry ass."

She chuckled and gave me a sideways look and a wry smile. "Seriously," she said, shaking her head.

"I *am* serious. Tell him to call Derek, get his input. That'll take care of it. Derek will never put 'em back to work ... not so long as he's there."

"Hmm. Maybe I should."

"If you need a middle ground, offer to arbitrate the Ledbetter case." What I'd suggested to Perry. "But not the other two. Those cases aren't good ones for the union and I don't think they're dues payers. The union may not push them."

"Well, maybe..." She grimaced at me. I could tell she didn't like the idea. "Guess we could talk to them about arbitrating." She shook her head and leaned down to slip on her heels.

"How about dinner?" I said as she stood up. "If you can't have lunch." I was afraid the question sounded tentative, and timid.

Liz straightened the lines out of her skirt, like she was making sure she'd be presentable to her boss, then looked at me. The turned-up mouth again, a little more on one side than the other.

"What's the matter? You lonely?" she said.

"Dana's not around." I shrugged. "And I don't like cooking for myself."

"Maybe," she said, starting out. She stopped and checked her watch again. "Got to take the prick to the airport at five. I could be back down here by seven. So-o-o, I guess..." She tapped her foot, and I found myself holding my breath. "Tony's okay?"

The cost of even the breadsticks at Tony's made me cringe, but I resisted asking if she was buying. All I said was, "Yeah, that's good."

She left and I closed the door, then turned the tape player back on. I started from the beginning, again, and leaned back in my chair, my eyes closed, trying to visualize Sheila and the two detectives. And trying get into Sheila's mind.

WE WERE halfway through dinner when Liz asked me about Dana.

"What's with you guys, anyway? I always thought you were the perfect couple."

"Appearances deceive," I said, studying my almost empty glass of wine. Dana wasn't what I wanted to talk about with Liz, still in her day-with-the-boss attire: tight skirt and silk blouse, refreshed makeup, all the accessories. In this romantic setting.

Tony's was one of the most elegant restaurants in Houston, crystal chandeliers, starched white tablecloths and napkins, and liveried waiters who acted as if they could sense power, money, and social status—and weed out the fakes like me—with a few sniffs of an upraised nose. Out front, the valet had made sure to park my old Buick far to the rear of the luxury cars facing the entrance. Mostly Mercedes, but also a couple of Rolls, and a Bentley. Ordinarily, the bottle of wine Liz ordered would have prompted me to calculate my credit card limits, but tonight I was more interested in the company than my finances.

"Appearances do deceive," Liz said, nodding. "I found that out when I was married. The jerk had gotten back with his old girlfriend and it took me two months to figure out what was up."

I smiled to show understanding and sympathy. But I was thinking of my own gullibility. "He must've been a real fool," I said. "Not appreciating what he had." I raised my eyebrows to show my appreciation of Liz.

"Hah! He found out what a royal bitch I can be when I'm crossed." Her voice had a hard edge, like she'd been told that a few times. Based on my experience, I suspected she could hold her on with any male. Or female.

"Yeah, me too," I said and grinned at her.

"Huh?" She looked perturbed, like she had taken my reaction in a way I hadn't intended.

"I can be a real bitch, too," I said, holding my grin.

Now she laughed and sat back on the bench seat across from me. We were seated French style, across from each other in a row of tables along one wall of the softly lit dining room. The dinner crowd had thinned out and the tables on either side of us were empty.

"So, why'd Dana leave?" Liz asked. That part I'd let slip to her weeks ago.

Trying to decide how to answer, I stared at the gilt-framed mirror beyond Liz's shoulder. Reflected in the mirror were the images of a few diners and empty tables with fresh white linens and place settings. On the far side of the room was a low balustrade, black, with thin black columns reaching to the ceiling to separate the diners from those waiting at the entrance.

"I think..." I hesitated a moment, "I think she was having an affair ... with this guy ... helping her with her violin." I stopped, a lump forming in my throat. Not a good subject. In the mirror, a young couple got up from the table behind me, and a tuxedoed waiter began clearing away their remaining dishes and glasses.

"She didn't seem the type," Liz said softly, toying with her empty wine glass. Our own food dishes were gone and we'd ordered dessert. Crème brûlée. Espresso for her, a medicinal brandy for me.

I nodded, but didn't answer.

"You used to talk about her a lot," she said.

"We were always comfortable with each other." I frowned at my reflection. "Well, I thought we were." The mirror provided me no new insights, so I looked down at my hands on the white tablecloth and sighed, remembering the separate paths we had taken after raising a child into junior high, the two of us together, but already diverging: my work dominating days, nights, and weekends; Dana going back to law school to escape the suburban mommy scene and then joining a big law firm. Liz was silent, waiting for me to continue, so I did.

"She changed after she went to work. Made new friends, dressed the part ... became more self-confident, things like that. Then she went off in another direction; I didn't see it coming, until it was done ... Her music. She played in a community orchestra when Susan was little—then she went back to law school and she focused on that, you know, getting the grades, passing the bar. She was always focused on whatever she was doing. But the violin was her first love." I took a deep breath. "It still is, I think."

I glanced up at Liz. She didn't say anything, just stared back with what looked like real sympathy. I drank some water and, replacing the glass on the table, kept my gaze on the water glass, searching the clear liquid for some window into my past. All I saw was a warped mirrored face reflected in the light of the candle.

"She wanted us to go to counseling." I shook my head. "Last fall. I never understood why. Maybe she was trying to tell me something." Or felt guilty, I thought, but didn't say it. "Or maybe she was trying to see if we could work things out before she left ... It ended after one session. I couldn't stand the woman, the counselor—her cloying, insipid approach to us, the stark office in a second-rate business park, the whole idea of somebody interfering in our lives—my life." I looked up, squarely into Liz's eyes. "Anyway, I saw Dana kiss the guy, we argued, she left, end of story."

I wasn't about to tell Liz that the argument had ended in my hitting Dana. That would end any chance of sympathy. Liz would brook no excuse for that. Of course, in my rational moments, neither could I.

Liz pursed her lips. "Surely, it's not what it seems," she said. "I can't believe—"

"Ah-h-h, she hasn't been back." I shook my head. "Not while I was there. As far as I know she's in Mexico with him right now."

"Do you *know* any of this?"

"I don't want to *know* anything ... I only know what I saw. But that was enough..." I threw up my hands and almost knocked over the water glass. "There was enough ... what you call *circumstantial* evidence to make me believe that something was going on. More than just a casual friendship. Based, evidently, on some mutual interest." I clenched my teeth, then willed myself to calm down, relax.

"Mutual interest? What—"

"He was her violin coach, teacher, whatever. It may still be going on for all I know," I said, closing my eyes.

"I'm sorry."

I opened my eyes and stared into Liz's, full of compassion and kindness. There was shared sadness there, as well.

"Don't be," I said. I shook off my gloom and grinned at her, holding her gaze, the reflected specks of candlelight in her dark eyes.

"Would you like to comfort me in my grief?"

"What?"

"You've never shown me your new apartment."

"Oh, for Christ's sake, Dan. Don't behave like a boorish male in rut."

My face must have dropped a few feet, but I didn't look away. Liz reached across the table and grabbed my curled-up hand, not gently, and shook it.

"Hey, I'm not going to bed with you. Not like this. I like you too much." She smiled at me, her eyes fixed on mine. "You'd just be using me to get over Dana," she said, squeezing my hand. "You still care about her, you know."

Her grip relaxed and I turned my hand over to take hers. We looked at each other a moment, then she pulled her hand out of mine, but slowly.

Dessert, espresso and brandy appeared. After the two waiters vanished, I fixed Liz with my best hangdog gaze.

"You're a very practical woman," I said. "But that doesn't help my ego."

"Screwing me isn't going to help your ego either." She gave me a wry smile as she stirred sugar into her espresso. "Or mine. You're just looking for some random sex to get over your grief."

"We've known each other for a long time." I sipped my brandy, watching her, judging her reaction.

"Never in that way, we haven't ... Look, you need to deal with this, your issues with Dana ... with your head, not with your..." She grinned at me. "You know what I mean."

"Well-l-l, yes—"

"You had the hots for Sheila Mills, didn't you? You find any solace there?" I stared at her, and she smiled back at me. "I saw you with her." The smile was still there, but the eyes were flinty.

"You *what*?" My voice went up an octave. I downed the last of my brandy with one gulp, but I kept my eyes on Liz.

"That Pizza Hut, the one on the highway near Winnie, isn't that a good place to have a ren-dez-vous with someone you don't want to be seen with?"

"You saw us?" I leaned back in my chair and slung one arm over the back of it.

"I was in the Texaco station next door. You were out in the parking lot, next to your car. Or I guess it was your car. I started to come over and then this woman in a trench coat and scarf came across the parking lot—from another car it looked like—and came up to you. You put your arm around her ... and helped her into your car. Then you left." Liz grimaced. "So, what does that seem like?"

"Seems like I was being stupid."

"So, it does."

"How'd you know it was Sheila?"

"You just admitted it." She gave a wide grin and winked at me. "I'm a good detective, aren't I?"

"Wait, you said—"

"It was a wild guess." She took a bite of the crème brûlée. "I'd seen her picture, but I couldn't tell who it was. Not really ... Look, Dan, I didn't say anything to anyone. I wouldn't do that to you." She smiled at me as she dug another hole in the dessert. "Never. You've pulled me out of too many ditches, and I do care about you ... I have to admit, I was a little jealous."

I was too interested in what she was saying tzo go after my share of the dessert. She shook the spoon at me.

"You need to be careful. You have a conflict—"

"It's over."

"And that bastard of a husband of hers might just shoot *you*, too."

I gave a choked laugh. "Oh, I don't think so." But I was beginning to have my doubts.

"That's why he killed that black supervisor, wasn't it? Sheila had been sleeping with him."

"Don't think it was quite that simple."

"It never is."

"Well, I've learned I can't trust the woman, or what she says. The Ranger, the one who figured it out, he claims you can't trust any woman, period. You're all like Eve in the Garden."

Liz's face, and body, went rigid, her eyes cold. She threw her napkin onto the table. "You believe that?" she said, her voice harsh.

"No, no." I held up my hands, then reached across to grab her hand, which was gripping the napkin into a wad. I missed and got her wrist. "I know I can trust you. You always shoot straight with me." Or I hope you do, I thought.

Her eyes stayed on mine, her lips in a tight line. The rigidity ebbed slowly from her face and body, and she slid her hand back into mine for a few seconds, then pulled it along with her napkin back into her lap.

"Anything he says about women can apply to men, too," she said. "It just gets manifested in different ways."

"No generalization's worth a damn," I said.

She smiled and shook her head. We both dug a spoon into the crème brûlée. "Don't you always add, 'even this one?'" she said after a moment. She was looking at me over the raised spoon.

"Yeah, I do ... I say a lot of things."

Continuing to look at each other, we both savored the dessert. Her eyes seemed to twinkle in the candlelight.

"Sometimes I really do think you're a nice person," she said. "You have nice eyes and you laugh a lot. Or you used to. And you're fun to talk to. If Dana ever leaves you for good, I've got dibs—but only after you've given her up."

"Can I have that in writing?"

"Hell no!"

But I knew she was only pulling me out of a ditch, trying to make me feel better about making a fool of myself.

Chapter Twenty-three—A Little Surprise

WHEN I GOT BACK TO THE GOLDEN Triangle and my lonely room at the Drifting Sands Motel, I had a message waiting for me at the desk. It was from Sheila, asking me to give her a call. I didn't. I wanted to call her, but I didn't want to see her because I knew what would happen. Like a moth to a flame.

She left another message and another. The phone rang at midnight on Friday, and I didn't answer it, even though I was awake, reading. I called the desk to see if there was a message, but the caller hadn't left one. It was a woman, the clerk said.

Settling back on the bed to read, I started worrying about whether there was a problem at the plant, so I called to make sure no one had been trying to reach me. A drowsy voice in security said everything was fine, nice and quiet. Next, I called home, and no one answered. No surprise there. Then I called Susan in L.A. and we had our first real conversation in months. But she hadn't tried to call me, and she hadn't heard from her mother since the week before. By the time I turned out the light, I was sure the caller was Sheila. Anyone else would have left her name. Even Dana.

The following Monday, Sheila finally caught up with me at the plant, in my temporary office. I made the mistake of answering my phone.

"Dan, why haven't you called me? I've called you over at the Sands at least a dozen times."

"I've been busy."

"You weren't too busy before. Don't you want to..." she hesitated, "to see me?"

"It would be best if we don't—"

"Why not? Aren't I good enough for you?"

"You know that's not it. First of all, you're married—"

"So are you."

"And I don't see a divorce in the works for either of us." I stopped, but she didn't say anything. "Secondly, we have a little conflict in that I'm the company lawyer and—"

"That didn't stop you before."

I was silent. She had me there. But I'd thought she was innocent before ... Or had I?

"I've got to go, Sheila."

"Dan, I really need to see you. Zack's gone over to Baytown on a job ... How about tonight."

"Sheila, I'm..." There was a timid knock on my door, and I stopped what I was saying. But the door didn't open right away, so it wasn't Perry or one of the managers. "Sheila, someone's here. I'll think about it."

"Call me ... okay?"

"I don't know," I said and hung up as another knock sounded, louder, and the door opened slightly, just enough for Hank Greenberg to peer in.

"Dan, you have a minute?" Hank edged inside, across the threshold. "I've got something for you to take care of."

"Yeah, no problem," I said, swinging my chair around. "I was on the phone. What you got?"

"This was in Perry's inbox this morning." He held up a set of papers. "It was sent over to the controller's office by mistake, so he just got it. He said to give it to you."

Hank laid the papers on my desk. On top was a letter from the Texas Workforce Commission, then several attachments and an envelope with a date stamp from the mailroom over a week before.

I looked at the subject. Notice of Hearing on Claim for Unemployment Benefits. Claimant Sheila Ann Mills. The hearing was set for Tuesday morning at 10:00am, in Port Oso, the Courthouse Annex.

"When did she file this?" I asked, looking up at Hank. He was waiting patiently behind a chair, leaning with his hands on the chair back.

"Probably right after the strike started. Her initial claim came in with a bunch of the union's claiming we'd locked their people out because we refused to extend the contract." He tilted the chair forward on its front legs. "One of the clerks must've handled it then. It says there," he pointed at the papers I held, "that we discharged her for cause ... so they at least got that right."

"Then she appealed, and the notice of appeal and hearing got misdirected," I said, glancing at the notice, then the date on the envelope.

"That's right," Hank said and shrugged, letting the chair drop down on all four legs. "The hearing's scheduled for tomorrow."

"Okay, I'll be there." I started to put my feet up on the desk and get comfortable to read through the notice and attachments, but Hank made no move to leave. He rocked the chair forward again. What does he want, I wondered, then realized. Of course.

"You care to go with me tomorrow?" I asked.

"Sure." His face lit up with that fresh, eager look I liked in him, even if I knew he'd lose it soon. "Perry says we have to win this one. Zack's already getting benefits and Derek's really pissed about it."

"What?" I sat up. Sheila had said he was off working. Or maybe the claim was for the time before he got the jobs. To Hank, I said, "How the hell did we miss that one?"

"The clerk didn't catch it, so no one filed an objection."

177

FOR THE hearing on Sheila's appeal, we were consigned to a sterile conference room with no windows and two dull fluorescent lights that gave the place the washed-out sepia appearance of a nineteenth-century photograph. Institutional furniture and carpet, no pictures on the walls, and no coffee or soft drinks. And certainly, no doughnuts.

The hearing officer was a jumpy little man with an anemic face and colorless lips, thin sandy hair, and glasses with rims the color of his hair. When Hank and I arrived, he was the only one there. We shook hands—he said his name was Gerald Stubbs—and Hank and I pulled out a couple of wobbly chairs along the side of the table facing the door. Mr. Stubbs was ensconced in a nest he'd made at the head of the table—piled in front of him a stack of files, notepads and pens, and a black tape recorder.

Waiting for Sheila, we chatted about the weather. A bright, sunny day in March, in contrast to the cloistered drabness of the room. Blustery, almost warm, not quite shirtsleeve weather. The azaleas were in bloom—white, fuchsia, red—in almost every yard in every little burg and subdivision in the Golden Triangle.

While we made small talk, I opened my briefcase and pulled out a legal pad, a copy of Sheila's indictment in the Graham murder, and the manila envelope the Ranger had given me. I placed all three on the table, the pad to the right, the envelope to my left, next to Hank, and the indictment in the center. With a new Cross pen, a freebie from HR, I wrote at the top of the pad, "Unemployment Comp Hearing—Sheila Mills" and the date. I looked at my watch. Ten after ten.

"The claimant is late," said Mr. Stubbs in a prissy manner I found mildly irritating. "I always allow fifteen minutes," he said, lips pursed, hands folded in front of him on the table, "then I'll hear your evidence, even without her ... Burden's still on the company, though. You have to show that the discharge was for misconduct connected with the claimant's last work." He was paraphrasing the statute.

Just as he finished, Sheila entered, tentatively at first, then stopped dead just inside the door. She was staring at me.

"Dan. Why are you here?"

"Are you the claimant?" Mr. Stubbs asked, his voice shrill.

"Why'd you file for unemployment?" I asked.

"And you, Hank?" Sheila said, like *Et tu, Brute*.

"We need to get this hearing started," Mr. Stubbs said. "I've got another one for ten-thirty. If you're Mrs. Mills, you need to have a seat close to this microphone here." He tapped on the table next to the mike, its cord snaking back to the recorder in front of him.

Sheila moved a few steps farther into the room. Despite the spring weather, she carried her trench coat draped over one arm. She had changed since I first saw her in Perry's office last summer. She was noticeably thinner, though still with a pleasing shape that was attractively displayed by tailored gray slacks and a snug pink sweater. Her office uniform. Her face had furrows and angles I'd never noticed before, and her eyes, which had once sparkled in the candlelight, now glowered at me from somber hollows. I wondered if she hadn't slept the night before. Because I hadn't called her?

"We need the money, Dan. The house..." Her voice, a low whisper, trailed off into silence. My glare must have been as harsh as my feelings toward her. Shifting the trench coat in front of her, she reached up and clutched at the top of her shirt, at her neck. She wore no jewelry.

"Okay, Mrs. Mills," said Stubbs, oblivious to the exchange, "if you'll raise your right hand..." He looked over at me. "Mr. Esperson is this your witness?" He pointed to Hank.

"No," I said. "I've got a copy of Mrs. Mills' indictment for murdering a supervisor at the plant." I pushed the indictment across the table, toward him. His eyes grew wide.

"What did she—"

"And the tape of her confession to participating in the murder." I shook the tape out of the envelope and held it up.

"Dan, how can you do this to me?" A low hard voice.

I looked up at her and tried to smile. "It's my job."

"I don't know..." Mr. Stubbs began, but he was interrupted by Sheila.

"I need to call my lawyer." She pivoted around and, clutching her coat, stumbled against the doorjamb and out the door.

"Mrs. Mills! Wait!" Stubbs called after her, his arm raised. "We have to get you sworn. I can hear the company's evidence today and maybe reschedule yours."

But she was gone. I heard her footsteps going down the hall. Running.

"She won't be back," I said.

"Well!" said Mr. Stubbs in a petulant voice. "I thought I'd seen everything, but I've never seen anything like this before." He eyed me as if I were to blame. I shrugged.

"Looks like she doesn't get any benefits," I said.

He tapped his pen on the table and stared at the door. After a long minute, during which I savored my victory, he pursed his lips again and, still tapping his pen, turned his gaze back to Hank and me.

"I'll just have to get *your* evidence." He popped out of the chair and, continuing to talk, went to the door and closed it. "It's up to the company to show misconduct or some other disqualification for her not to receive any benefits."

"What do you mean?" I said, as he resumed his seat. "Killing a supervisor's misconduct if anything is."

"Was it at work?"

"*What*?" I couldn't believe this.

"You know ... was it work-related?"

"You gotta be kiddin'. Work-related?" I was sitting up straight in my chair, my head forward, aghast. "She killed—she was involved in the cold-blooded murder of one of our supervisors. The first black supervisor in the plant."

180

"For misconduct to be disqualifying, it *has* to be *directly* connected to the claimant's last work." His narrow little jaw jutted out and he shifted some papers around in front of him, his head jerking up and down to look at the papers, then at me. "That's what the law says. Even if some act might be criminal ... if it's away from the workplace, it doesn't affect benefits growing out of her employment. Benefits that *she* earned."

I was shaking my head in disbelief. "You can't have employees going around killing their supervisor, no matter where they do it ... or whatever their motive is." I leaned over the table and shoved the indictment past his tape recorder. "If you'll read the indictment—"

"Was she convicted?"

"N-o-o ... but she confessed." I held up the tape cassette. "To the police. You must not be from around here if you don't know what happened."

Not answering this, he picked up the indictment and began reading it. I remained with my hand suspended in the air, the cassette held out in my fingers.

From beside me, Hank placed his hand on my arm and leaned closer. I dropped my hand and the tape cassette onto the table and inclined my ear toward him.

"Is he serious?" he whispered. Except to nod, I didn't reply. After a moment, Hank settled back into his chair.

Flipping to the indictment's second page, Mr. Stubbs glanced up and back down, then spoke as much to the paper as to me. "How do I know that tape is real?" His head wiggled back and forth as he read.

"You heard her voice when she came in here. You can recognize it."

"It has to be authenticated." He flipped to the last page.

"I got it from a Texas Ranger."

No need to complicate this with all the hands it had been through. Or that I was waiting on some sort of certification from the

181

Port Oso Chief of Police. Stubbs dropped the indictment onto the table and smacked his hand down on top of it.

"You won't get *him* here to testify," Stubbs said. "They never do."

I nodded toward the tape recorder. "Why don't you listen to the tape?"

He looked at his watch. "I don't have time. If you leave it with me, I might," he shook a finger at me, "and I emphasize *might*, consider it ... though without someone who was there, I think it has very little value."

"It's my only copy. I'll make a copy and mail it to you."

"I really don't have time for this." He clicked on the recorder and picked up the mike, then recited in terse, matter-of-fact sentences what had happened from Sheila's arrival, and departure, to my submission of the indictment and tape recording. What he said was accurate, as far as it went.

"The indictment appears to be a public record," he droned into the mike, "and it is admitted as evidence on the claim. Counsel for the employer admits there has been no conviction on the charges. The tape recording submitted by counsel is unauthenticated and, in any case, he has failed to provide the hearing officer with a copy at the hearing. Decision on this claim will be rendered on the record before us."

"I object..." I said, but he turned off the tape recorder before I could finish.

"If you don't like my decision, you can take it up to the appeals board in Austin."

"But that's on the record you just created."

"That's your problem." There was a knock on the door. Stubbs called, "Come in."

"Like I said, I'm sending you a copy of the tape."

The door opened and a young woman dressed in a business skirt and jacket and carrying a briefcase slipped inside, followed by an older man also in business attire. I didn't recognize either of them, but they had to be the employer reps on the next case.

"Are we early?" the woman said, looking at Stubbs, then at Hank and me.

"We're done here," said Stubbs, his chin up, staring at me instead of her.

I scowled at him, then gave the young woman and her companion a fake smile. Picking up the tape of Sheila's confession, I slid it back into the envelope and lifted my briefcase off the floor. The woman fixed me with a puzzled stare as I dropped the tape and pad into the briefcase, so I shrugged and gave her as much of a real smile as I could muster before turning to Hank.

"Come on, Hank," I said. "The man says we're done here." And I needed to find some food, anything to get the knot out of my stomach.

Part IV

Chapter Twenty-four—"Time Passes"*

IT WAS THE END OF JULY, a humidly hot and bright Monday morning. The strike was over—after six long months, the last two because of J.C. Ledbetter's discharge—and I was on the interstate back to Port Oso, this time to meet with Derek Frazier about the company's layoff plans and then to tie up a few loose ends with Joplin and the union. And to get ready for Zack Mills' arbitration hearing at the end of the week.

When I crossed the causeway over the Old and Lost Rivers, where they conjoined to form a wide pallid estuary to the east, the sun was barely above the horizon, a dull red orb in the mist. Cresting the high apex of the Trinity River Bridge, I could almost feel the exhilarating curve of the green-and-blue earth flung out before me: cypress trees and marsh grass, rice fields and lakes and bays, and beyond those, the shimmering silver water out in the Gulf of Mexico. Despite the obstacles I faced, my mood was better than it had been in a long time, and I alternately mulled over how I was going to convince an arbitrator that Zack Mills had been justifiably discharged and to convince Dana to come home.

Right before the strike ended, I found out where she was staying. Susan knew. I asked her if she knew and she told me; she gave me Dana's unlisted number and new address. I debated calling her, then decided a personal visit was best. If we could keep it polite. A big if.

---

* Virginia Woolf, *To the Lighthouse*

One Saturday morning, having escaped from the plant for the weekend, I parked outside her apartment—the place was gated, naturally—and followed her car to the local supermarket. As she was coming out with an armful of groceries, I managed to just happen to run into her.

"Can I help you with those," I said when she stopped in front of me.

She stared at me, not hostile, curious. Lightly tanned face and dark auburn hair with a few streaks of gray, combed down above one eye and pulled back behind one ear, exposing a dangling pearl earring. Earrings I had given her. Not much makeup, but painted red nails on fingers curved around one of the bags, full of vegetables and healthy foods, I was sure.

"What do you want?" she said, her voice wary, low. Not an auspicious greeting.

I smiled at her. "I can help you with those," I said and reached for a bag. "I just wanted a chance to talk to you."

She wasn't fooled by my just happening along, and I was afraid she'd say there wasn't anything left for us to talk about.

"Okay," she said and shoved a bag in my direction. "So, talk."

As she started past, I grabbed the bag and reached for the second one, but she pulled it away and kept going.

"I'm sorry," I said, going after her.

"What about?" She kept going, turning down a row of cars in the parking lot.

"About what happened to us. About everything ... I shouldn't have hit you. That was wrong."

She stopped and wheeled around to face me. She was wearing tight white jeans, perhaps a size too small for her, and a silky dark-blue blouse that she filled out nicely, far more amply than I'd realized before. Still, it was a form and a face I knew, even if I didn't understand the person that dwelt inside.

The morning was bright and hot. It had been like that for days and would be for days more, and I was beginning to perspire under the hot sun, my armpits and back growing wet.

"What are you doing here, Dan? Why are you—?"

"I want us to start over," I said.

"It's too late for that."

"It's never too late. We can start from right now ... rewind the clock or something."

She shook her head. "You told me the moving finger writes, and you can't call it back, or wash out a word of it. With all your tears ... or my tears." She turned and moved quickly toward her car, leaving me to trail several paces behind her.

"Yeah," I said after her. "It's something like that. But we can begin again, on a new page." We were at her car, a new BMW she had bought with her last bonus before she quit her job. She opened the trunk.

"Why don't you have dinner with me?" I said.

Placing her bag in the trunk, she turned and took the bag I was holding. From over it, her eyes, seemingly puzzled, searched mine. A slight smile flickered at the corner of her mouth. She nodded.

So, we had dinner. Talked about what she was doing with her music and what I was doing at my work. Banalities. And quarreled over dessert, and went our separate ways.

"What'd he do?" I asked her after a little too much wine. "Cry on your shoulder about his wife dying and not having any money?" Tim Oakes, her violin coach. "How hard it was for him with a five-year-old and her in chemo all the time?"

"You've never been in a situation like that." She was glowering at me. "How could you know how it was with him ... how he must have felt? ... His wife *was* dying."

"I don't give a damn how he felt. I only care about us. Dana, he was ten years younger than you." Then a realization. "Were you giving him money, helping him pay her doctor bills?"

She looked away, then after a moment, brought her eyes back to mine and said, "It wasn't like that. You don't understand how it was, and I don't want to talk about it."

But we were talking. Maybe I'd call her when I got back to Houston. Or maybe I wouldn't. Maybe I didn't really care. I wasn't sure.

First I needed to take care of Zack Mills and keep him fired. And that depended on an arbitrator listening to Sheila's taped confession and accepting it as proof that Zack had murdered a company supervisor. And agreeing with the company's position that the killing was workplace related and not just a crime of passion in a personal dispute over a woman—as Layton Van Horn had called it.

That the murder was work-related seemed obvious. The shriveled-up hearing officer from the TWC had denied Sheila's claim for unemployment benefits—but relying on some technicality that didn't hold water. He returned the copy of the tape I sent to him with a note that he hadn't considered "the claimant's wrongly obtained confession" in reaching his decision. I wondered if he'd even listened to it—and decided he had.

Then I started thinking about Zack and Sheila and wondering what the glue was that held those two together. Why had Sheila stuck by him through the murder and tried to protect him, even in confessing? Why had Zack stayed with *her* after her affair with Graham, if it bothered him so much? And why kill Graham? To clear the air between them? Before they moved into their new house, as Sheila put it, or she said Zack had put it to her? But there had to be more to it than that.

However beguiling Sheila looked and talked—and she certainly had beguiled me—she wasn't a sweet little angel. She was a chameleon, a phantom, and every time I saw her, she seemed to be something different.

She shared the same redneck ethos, rose from the same rawboned Scotch-Irish stock, as her husband. The offspring of rebellious exiles who had peopled the South from Virginia to Texas, bringing a tough code of self-reliance, endurance, and frontier justice—alloyed with vengeance and violence. They had cleared the trees, driven off the natives, and toiled in the red dirt and sandy soil to eke out a life in the wilderness, while bequeathing their genes and their enabling and sometimes handicapping culture to their descendants.

I'd read a lot of history, majored in it in college, studied the Civil War and the South. I knew these people, I had grown up among them, and I felt like I knew their ancestors. They were both the implements and the bondsmen—and women—of the "peculiar institution," slavery, corrupt and evil, driven to defend it by those who prospered from its continuance and condemned to suffer death, destruction, and loss of livelihood for their blind loyalty. They had endured a hundred years of consequences, backward and bitter in defeat, becoming human cogs in cotton mills and furniture factories and petroleum refineries, venting their frustrations and hatreds on black men and women who differed from them only in the color of their skin and in their greater subservience and suffering.

I had seen this. The fruits of our past. I felt it in my blood and in my bones. Through stubbornness and ignorance, this white tribe had nurtured and sustained a fractured and rotting system based on racial division even unto the present day. These white men and women, rawboned Scotch-Irish rednecks like Zack and Sheila. Like me.

MY MEETING with Derek and Layton Van Horn wasn't about Zack and Sheila or even J.C. Ledbetter, whose discharge Derek had agreed to arbitrate to end the strike. Its subject was much closer to the racial divides I had been mulling over when I reached the plant.

Perry and I had requested the meeting. Now that we had a new labor agreement, the plant was in the final stages of installing automated control systems—begun during the strike—and fewer workers would be needed. And then, with the end of the Iran hostage crisis, oil prices had plunged and New York had ordered a cut in production at the Port Oso Plant—while upgrading and expanding a nonunion refinery in Louisiana. Over the next year and a half, these changes meant a fifty-percent reduction in the Port Oso workforce. The task of drawing up plans for who got laid off, and when, had gone to Layton Van Horn.

Derek was at his desk, riding crop in hand, while Layton was in his usual spot by the window. Beyond Layton's right shoulder, the sun gleamed on the cracking towers; white steam billowed against a blue sky. For once, the flare was quiescent, and no black smoke scarred the window-framed scene.

"Layton," I said, trying to drill a hole through him with my glare, "you can't lay off every black foreman in the plant and all but one of the other blacks in white-collar jobs. You're setting us up for a class action."

"We ... we've struggled like the devil to bring ... bring these people up," Perry said. "Keep the OFCCP off our backs." The OFCCP enforced the affirmative action requirements for federal contractors—which the plant was. It had taken some convincing to get Perry to confront Layton on this, and in front of Derek. Hank Greenberg had helped persuade him with his analysis. The numbers were so stark that Perry finally agreed to come out of his CYA shell and put his neck on the line.

"That's the problem," Layton said. "The blacks we promoted weren't the most qualified." He coughed, a dry, smoker's cough. "The most qualified blacks, maybe, but they took jobs that white men should've had, based on their seniority and qualifications."

"We don't promote based on seniority," Derek said and whacked the edge of his desk with the riding crop. Perry had finally told me it was some sort of modified riding crop, not a swagger stick. I still didn't know the difference.

"The black foremen can't hold a candle to the others out there," Layton said. "They're newer, less experienced, less educated. Hell, they don't have near the hands-on training the white guys have before they get moved up."

"That's right," I said. "That's the problem. They're just now getting the education and training they never had a chance to get before. That's the purpose of affirmative action, to get 'em into the game ... give 'em a fair chance to compete."

"Well, they ain't competing at the same level," said Layton, "and that's the problem as I see it. We're not going to let good people go just so we can add color to the roster out there." He gestured over his shoulder to the window.

"Wh-what'll I do about the Feds?" Perry said. "They ... they'll be crawl ... crawling all over the place. They'll be livin' down ... down in my shop."

"Dan here will take care of 'em," Layton said. "Won't you, Dan?" He gave me a sardonic grin.

"Hasn't Reagan cut back on that kind of thing?" Derek asked. "All the government interference in our business?"

"You ... you know those damn bureaucrats," Perry said, on smoother ground now. "Presidents come and go, but they just go on and on forever."

And we went on like that for a while longer until Derek asked Layton to go back over the performance reviews for the last year and see if there wasn't at least one black supervisor who measured up. George Graham, perhaps, since he'd only been promoted to foreman at the end of the strike and he still needed a chance to prove himself.

That suggestion must have lit a fuse deep in Layton's gut. Derek had been enthusiastic about promoting George, with whom he had talked often about Billy Graham's death, and about ending the strike. But Perry had told me that Layton was hell-bent against the promotion.

Now Layton pointed at me, but he spoke to Derek. "You keep listening to that goddamn lawyer there, we might as well turn this place over to the blacks and the union. First, you agree to their demands to arbitrate cases they have no right to arbitrate, now you're telling me to keep that worthless ni ... Negro as a foreman when he's got the least time in the job."

He was shaking his finger, but not at me. At his boss.

"I'm tellin' you, Derek, we're letting the lawyers run the damn company. Keeping blacks like Graham up is the craziest goddamn thing I ever heard ... And only a fool would go to arbitration on Ledbetter." He was talking so fast he was almost panting. "Let 'em sue us. No court'll put him ... or Mills, back to work. Not in this plant."

Through all this, Derek sat stone-faced behind his desk, still as a statue, except for the riding crop beating out a slow, steady rhythm in the palm of his hand. Perry and I were hunkered down in our chairs, Perry shuffling his feet back and forth like he was ready to flee out the door. I hated that Hank Greenberg wasn't here for his continuing education.

"That fucking J.C. Ledbetter," Layton said without even a pause, "that sonovabitch knew it was me when he shot that wrist rocket ... and it wasn't one of those goddamn porcelain balls either. It was a goddamn ball bearing and it went right past my head." He waved his hand next to his head to show where the missile had gone. "It's fucking stupid to arbitrate that case. Ludicrous, insane." His arms flailed the air over his head as the last words ricocheted around the room.

Derek had continued to beat out the rhythm in his palm. His eyes, in the shadow of his brow, eyes sunk deep in a gaunt face like a statue of Lincoln, were directed at Layton. Now he spoke in a low, hard voice.

"That's enough, Layton. We've been over this before." The riding crop hit his palm with a dull thwack. "It's my decision—

Graham, the arbitrations, all of it. I'm not changing my mind." The whisper of a smile moved the creases around his mouth, and he looked at me. "Dan will win the arbitrations. I'm confident of it."

Oh, shit, I thought. Am I on the spot. I smiled back at Derek.

"I'll do my best, Mr. Frazier." But looking at his face and seeing his sharp glance at Layton, I had another thought. Layton's done it now. He's crossed Derek for the last time. And that gave me a nice warm feeling inside, even though the pain in my gut had returned during the meeting and I'd felt a small wave of nausea, sitting there in that chair, putting up with Layton's attacks.

But I had made some progress, if only a little. I had Derek's attention on Layton Van Horn's layoff plans and maybe a chance to save some of the black foremen—and avoid a big lawsuit.

Chapter Twenty-five—An Encounter

THE MORNING'S UNPLEASANT MEETING was followed by another in the afternoon, this one with the enemy. I had to admit, whatever I thought of Tony Joplin, I would've loved to work in his surroundings: ensconced in the glass smog-scraper, slinky secretaries swishing by all day, and the kaleidoscopic mural in the conference room, the one by Ralfenberg or whoever he was.

We were gathered around Joplin's long blond conference table, Perry and I facing the mural, our backs to the wall-sized windows and Joplin, Landry, and Reneau across from us. Mary Albright wasn't there. *That* I found puzzling since the two of us had agreed to talk about settling the infamous Gene Jarvis spying case. Only later did I find out where she was.

At the moment, though, we were putting the finishing touches on the strike settlement, mainly signing documents to dismiss all the claims and litigation the strike had engendered and arranging for the arbitration of J.C. Ledbetter's discharge. The impending layoffs were not on the agenda. The union was avoiding the subject, and Perry couldn't discuss anything until Layton had a plan approved by everyone lower than the throne of God. Only then would Perry tell the union the bad news. All they could negotiate over would be separation pay for laid-off workers—not how much, only when it would be paid.

Perry and Frank Landry were down to the last document when I asked a question that had been bothering me for a good while.

194

Leaning forward, my elbows on the table, I addressed Landry, who was signing his name at the bottom of a page Perry had just signed.

"Frank," I said, "one thing I want to know ... Why are you defending Zack Mills? I can understand Ledbetter, since it was during the strike and only a wrist rocket..." and Layton Van Horn, I thought. "But Zack Mills?"

Landry lifted his pen off the page and looked at me, then glanced over at Joplin, who shrugged. As Landry's lawyer, Joplin could have jumped in, or told Landry not to answer, but he didn't.

"He's a union member," Landry said, giving me a hostile glare. "Anybody discharged by the company, we take it to arbitration. That's what we've always done. That's what we're doing."

"You know he killed the supervisor ... killed him in cold blood."

"We don't know any such thing," Pete Reneau said from the other end of the table. He was leaning back in his chair, swiveling it back and forth. "He ain't been convicted of any-damn-thing. Hell, he ain't even been tried."

"And he won't be," Landry said, his eyes glued to mine. "Your girlfriend's not gonna divorce him and that's all she wrote."

It took an act of willpower not to drop my eyes from Landry's, but I didn't. I felt my face and neck flush, probably turning a bright red for all to see. I wondered what these guys knew about Sheila and me. And how they knew it.

"She's not my girlfriend," I said, "and I can't believe you'd really want the man back in the plant ... There'll be trouble."

"Why don't you give him a settlement?" Joplin said. "Save everybody a load of trouble." Landry and I were still glaring at each other, and Landry talked over his lawyer's last words in a truculent growl.

"We have a duty to represent anybody in the union who's discharged ... Zack Mills wants to come back to work and we'll stand up for his rights as long as he wants us to."

"Look," said Joplin. With some relief, I shifted my gaze away from Landry's hostile little eyes to Joplin, who was waving an index finger at me. "The union could be liable if they *don't* represent him, just like anyone else. You know *ver-ry* well he's innocent until found guilty by twelve men good and true ... And the company has the burden of proof; *you* have to prove his discharge was for *just cause* under the contract." He shook his head. "You don't have a conviction or any kind of proof against the man."

"I've got his wife's ... I've got Sheila's confession."

"You can't use it." This from Reneau. "That's what the judge said."

"Even dismissed her case," Landry added.

"This is a private matter," I said, looking first at Reneau then at Landry. "A civil case. It'll be up to the arbitrator ... what he hears."

Joplin was still shaking his head. "You can't use that tape, Esperson. I don't know how you got it. The D.A. told me he didn't give it to you, so I'm sure it was under the table. Whoever gave it to you violated some law or other."

"I got it through official sources, *and* I promise you, if you go after them, that dog won't hunt." An East Texas expression most often used against me.

Joplin changed tacks with a flip of his hand. "You can't authenticate it—even *if* you can get around the marital privilege and all the other issues."

"We'll see. The arbitrator will decide." I wasn't about to lay out my arguments to Joplin, so that he could prepare for them.

"He will, indeed," Joplin said with a smirk. I grimaced at him, then at Landry, who had gone back to signing documents. Perry had finished with his signatures while we argued. His face looked bleak.

"Frank," Perry said to Landry. "Don't ... don't make us go through this. It ... it's not worth it. Having Zack Mills back in the plant will tear the place apart."

"Just give him some cash," said Joplin.

"A couple hundred grand should do it," Reneau said, nodding.

Perry was shaking his head. "We can't do that."

"Pay off a murderer? ... Ugh," I said.

"Derek Frazier would rather drop ... drop dead first," Perry said.

"How much of the settlement would you get?" I asked Joplin. "A third? Plus expenses?"

Landry slapped his pen down on the table and pushed his chair back. "I don't need to spend my day listening to crap from a company lawyer."

"Wait," I said. "Why don't you let me play the confession? ... You've got a tape player, Tony?" I said, still looking at Landry.

Landry sneered at me. "Why do I want to hear that bitch lying through her teeth to the cops?"

"Are you going to give me a copy of the tape, Dan?" Joplin asked.

The door opened and Mary Albright sailed in, a thick case file in one hand. As she pulled out a chair, I stood and reached across the table to shake hands with her. Her hand was big and soft and her handshake not unfriendly.

"Good to see you, Dan," she said in response to my greeting. "I've gone over the drafts you sent me." She held up the file. The Jarvis case. "I think we can wrap this one up with only a few changes." She gave me a pleasant smile that creased her face and even spread to her eyes. She was being so nice that it worried me.

"Well, Dan?" said Joplin. "How about a copy of the tape?"

"I'll play it right here and now, or you can listen to it along with Zack Mills at the arbitration. I only have two copies ... mine and one for the arbitrator."

"You can make a copy for us," Joplin said. "Give it to us tomorrow."

"I don't have to give you a copy in advance. You'll get it Thursday at the hearing." I paused and watched him working the gears behind his sour frown. "Or we can listen to it now."

"I don't have the time for this," Landry said. He hefted himself out of his chair. Reneau followed him up.

Joplin looked at his watch. "Sorry, folks. I've got another meeting." A wicked grin crossed his ruddy face. "Guess we'll just have to wait and see if the arbitrator'll let you play that thing on Thursday."

"Fine by me," I said as Joplin rose to leave.

Perry and I stood and shook hands with him, then I offered my hand to Landry. Both he and Reneau ignored me, but they shook Perry's hand as if they were old friends, which I guess in a way they were.

They all left, Perry included. Mary Albright, who had been pouring herself a cup of coffee from a beaker on a hot plate at the end of the room, made her way back to the conference table. She started to sit down across from me, then stopped.

"You want some coffee, Dan?" She held out the Styrofoam cup she'd filled. "I can get another."

"No thanks. Coffeed out ... You okay with the settlement, or do we have to—?"

"No, no. Settlement's fine." Placing her coffee on the table, she smiled down at me and settled into her chair, overflowing the arms. "Just a few nits we need to fix on the agreement and proposed order." She pulled a crystal ashtray over next to the open file in front of her.

Thanks to several lengthy phone calls, Mary and I had worked out a settlement of the union's lawsuit over Perry's disastrous attempt to catch Gene Jarvis doing something for which we could fire him. No money would change hands, but the company would agree not to spy on Gene Jarvis or any other union member—away from the plant. A resolution satisfactory to Derek and Perry, although Layton was still out to fire Jarvis and still looking for a way to do it.

We went over the drafts of the settlement agreement and order and, to my surprise, managed to resolve all of her "nits" in less than half an hour. I was gathering my papers to leave when she brought me up short.

"I was just talking with a friend of yours," she said. Looking at me out of the corner of her eye, she flicked her lighter under the tip of another cigarette. Though I continued shuffling papers, I felt a sharp pulse of adrenaline course into my extremities.

She exhaled a long streamer of smoke, away from the table.

"I was meeting with Sheila Mills ... That's why I didn't make the meeting with the union." Holding the cigarette out to the side of her face, she gave me a knowing smile. "She said to tell you hello."

"She's not *my* friend," I said, lifting my briefcase off the floor and placing it on the chair beside me. I was feeling queasy, my stomach hurting again.

"She seems to think you are." Mary tapped the ashes from her cigarette into the ashtray at her elbow.

"Why was she here? Is the criminal case..." Giving her a questioning look, I paused and held up my hands.

"No." Mary took another draw on the cigarette, then held it out and stared at the burning tip a moment while I waited for her to continue. She stubbed out the glowing end in the ashtray. "Filthy habit," she said. "I need to stop." She gave a cynical laugh. "After I lose fifty pounds." The smoke rose slowly in a wreath around her face. Watching her rounded features suddenly grow disconsolate, I felt sorry for her, and almost fond of her despite myself.

She took a deep breath. "The Graham family's filed a civil suit against Sheila and Zack. Wrongful death claim, and we're going to represent them." A wry smile briefly crossed her face. "I wouldn't be surprised if you're not added as a defendant."

"Me!"

She laughed. "The company." I felt foolish, thankful she hadn't said, "Not you personally, stupid." I must be feeling guilty.

"We'll be on the same side," she said, continuing to smile at me.

I opened the briefcase, deposited my papers inside, and snapped it shut again. "Mary," I said, "I don't see how we could ever be on the same side on anything ... certainly not anything to do with Earl Graham's murder."

"They may have to sell their house." She rolled her chair back from the table as I rose to leave. "You wouldn't want that would you?"

I stopped and looked down at her, shaking my head. At the question, not at Sheila losing her house.

"That house means a lot to Sheila," Mary said, hoisting herself out of the chair.

Not answering her, I picked up my briefcase and started around the long conference table. Mary tacked along the opposite side, parallel to me. I could feel her eyes on me.

"She'll fight like hell to keep it," she said.

At the far end of the table, I stopped in front of her. "It's not my problem, Mary," I said with deliberate finality.

As I went past her, she stared at me, and shrugged, then followed me to the door. We shook hands again before I left.

After that exchange, I shouldn't have been surprised when I reached the parking lot. In the space next to my company pool car stood Sheila's two-tone Oldsmobile Cutlass.

As I approached from the opposite direction, she got out of the driver's seat and came around the rear of my car toward me. She was dressed in white pedal pushers and a fitted red shirt with the tail out, perhaps more appropriate for shopping than a visit with her lawyer. Her hair was once again a straw yellow, cut in a fashionably short shag.

"Dan, I've missed you." Her arms opened to give me a hug. "I really wanted to see you."

I managed to avoid the hug and, instead, took her right hand and gave it a squeeze in sort of a handshake. The hand was narrow, a firm hard grip, not like Mary Albright's warm soft touch.

Unlike the last time I saw her, she didn't look wan or gaunt, although she was still athletically thin. Her face was almost too perfect with makeup, eyeliner, and lipstick—a glossy pink, which drew me to her as she spoke. We came so close our noses almost touched. Pulling back, I glanced around to see if anyone was watching us. The parking lot was empty.

"Hello, Sheila." Examining her face, I couldn't repress a smile. I ended up staring into her pale blue eyes. Wondering if they were the blue of ice in an iceberg.

"Mary Albright said you were in the conference room," Sheila said, her words tumbling over each other, "so I hung around a while and waited, but you didn't come out with the others. So, I came out here and parked next to your car. I'd know a company car anywhere. And I saw Perry took the car beside yours. I was in Mary's office. I had to see you."

"You're looking great, Sheila," I said, taking another step back. "I gotta go now." I started past her, reaching for the door of my car. Her hand on my arm pulled me back, though it didn't take much on her part to make me stop.

"I need to talk to you, Dan." She held onto my arm. The briefcase dangled between us. "Can we have dinner? Tonight?" Her eyes were searching mine, her brow furrowed in a pleading look. But a smile played across her lips as I stared at her without answering. I suspected the invitation wasn't just for dinner.

"I'm meeting with Perry tonight." I sighed. My regret was real, and I didn't move to escape. I looked at my watch. "I still need to check in." Over at the Sands.

She rubbed her hand up and down the underside of my arm. "How about afterwards? I do want to see you, Dan ... Don't you want to see me?" Never had I heard the word "see" sound so seductive and loaded with meaning.

"Sheila," I said, shaking my head, "I can't ... we can't—"

"I really need to talk to you ... If you still care anything about me ... What we had." Tears welled up in her eyes; her grip tightened on my arm.

I pulled my arm free. "That's past," I said, "and you've never exactly leveled with me." I tugged my keys out of my pocket and shoved past her to reach for the car door. She grabbed my arm again, harder than before, more urgently, pulling me close to her.

"You. Don't. Understand. How. It. Was," she hissed. Her voice cracked and softened, but not her grip. "Dan, I'm going to leave Zack. I need your help."

"What?" I turned back to her. "You're leaving him? Sheila, are you ... are you telling me the truth?"

"Yes! Yes! ... But I need help, Dan ... Somebody to protect me." Her eyes dropped from mine, and she leaned against my chest so that I was staring at the top of her head. My briefcase tapped gently against my leg.

"Why not them?" I pointed with my free hand toward the Joplin building. Secretaries and clerks were starting to leave work, drifting out across the parking lot. One or two of them were staring at us as they walked.

"They can't." Sheila looked up at me. Her eyes were wet and dark eyeliner stained her cheeks. "They're lawyers for both Zack and me."

"How about your family? The police?"

"Ha!" A hollow sound from deep in her throat. "Get real. The police want to lock me up ... And my family? They say I made my own bed..." She shrugged.

More people were leaving the building now. The declining sun glinted in the silver glass along the front. I saw Joplin, briefcase in one hand and suit coat dangling over his shoulder, cross the veranda and start down the shallow steps from the temple-like entrance. Parked just below was his Porsche, in a private space. He stopped and stared in our direction.

"I don't know," I said. "What can I do?" I wanted to get out of there. At least not have Sheila so close to me, her head against my chest, her arm snaking around my waist. I found I'd placed my free hand on the small of her back.

"Can we just talk about it?" Her eyes, moist and dazzling blue in the reflected light, came up to mine. Pleading. "Please, Dan." She gave a long sigh. "Maybe you ... maybe I can help you, too?"

"How can you help me?" A tall brunette secretary, the Joplin designer type, was mincing in stiletto heels toward an older model car two spaces down from us. She grinned in my direction, or was it a chuckle? I smiled back, past Sheila's head.

"In the arbitration. I may be able to ... to tell—"

"Okay," I said, watching the woman lift a long nylon-clad leg to get into her car. "But not at the Sands." I looked around to see if Joplin was still there. The Porsche was gone.

"Do you know Pleasure Island? The county park there?" She spoke in a low voice into my shirt.

"I've been over there. Once."

I thought I remembered it. A mostly manmade island created by the Corps of Engineers in dredging a channel in Sabine Lake, a lake that was actually an estuary out to the Gulf of Mexico. To reach Pleasure Island, you had to go over a bridge from Port Arthur. The island once held an amusement park, shops, and restaurants, all burned to the ground or washed away sometime in the past. It still held a Marina and a small park, some sports fields, and trails.

"Meet me over there," she said. "Pulling her arm from around my waist, she stepped back and stared up at me. But she still gripped my arm. "Tonight. After your dinner ... But don't tell anybody about me and Zack. Not yet."

"How will I find you?"

"Go to your right when you get off the bridge." Her mouth came close to my ear, her voice almost a whisper. "I'll be in the park. By the pavilion."

"All right. But it'll have to be after ten. Maybe ten-thirty or so."

I glanced around, but no one was paying any attention to us now. Not obviously, at least. When I looked back at Sheila, she was staring solemnly at me with those pale blue eyes.

"That's fine," she said. She smiled and looked relieved, then relaxed her grip on my arm. "Fine ... I'll be in my car. I'll be waiting for you."

Chapter Twenty-six—On Pleasure Island

DINNER WITH PERRY, AND HANK, ran later than I'd expected. After the drive to Port Arthur, it was well past eleven before I reached the bridge to Pleasure Island. As I made the gentle arc over the bridge, I could see only a few solitary lights dotting the rumpled mass of the island and a few more on the smooth black waters of the lake, probably shrimp boats or night fishermen, and far to the south, a ship coming in from the Gulf. Stars filled the dark sky overhead.

The county park was exactly where Sheila said it would be, and driving around the loop through the empty picnic area, I had no problem finding her Cutlass. Parked by itself, lights off, in front of the darkened pavilion.

The heat and humidity of the day hadn't lifted and I was perspiring through the fabric of my dress shirt, even in the laboring air conditioning of the pool car. But not just from the weather.

At dinner, I'd been unable to focus on what Perry and Hank were saying—something about the layoffs and the day's meetings. My mind kept veering back to Sheila and Pleasure Island. And a singular thought that occurred to me not long after we'd parted in Joplin's parking lot. What if Zack showed up? What if this was a replay of what happened to Earl Stanley Graham? Could I be that stupid? Fall for the same trick?

I quickly rejected the thought—but I kept coming back to it and rejecting it again. Sheila wouldn't do that to me. And Zack couldn't get away with the same thing twice.

Or could he? And would she? But just in case, I'd gone light on the booze, although as little food as I ate, it still felt like too much. And I needed her testimony. That would put the final nail in Zack's coffin, both for his job and for the D.A.

I pulled into a marked space five or six down from where Sheila was parked, to the right of her car and away from its driver's side. I waited with my lights on and engine running, the air conditioner rattling away.

The only other illumination anywhere near came from two dull streetlamps at either end of the long pavilion. With crooked covers, the lamps cast slanted cones of light and wide penumbras downward at an angle on the sandy soil. No other cars were there. No one else was around. A weeknight, a Monday, and all the ballplayers and families and skateboarders were long gone. The few anglers still out this late were at the pier a good half-mile away or out in boats on the lake. Even the lovers who might come here to neck, or even abandon a used condom next to their car, had found an air-conditioned spot better than this.

Still gripping the steering wheel, I stared at Sheila's car. A figure in the front seat moved like someone looking in the rearview mirror. I could see the outline of a face and hair, short but over the ears and neck and on the forehead like Sheila's.

I turned off my lights and waited maybe another half minute, then turned off the engine and air conditioning. The driver's door of the Cutlass opened, and I rolled down my window as Sheila slipped out of her car and leaned over the top.

"Dan? Is that you?"

"Yeah." I opened my car door and quickly got out and closed it and walked toward her. She didn't move from the door of her car.

There was no need to lock my car or roll up the window. If someone wanted to search it, I didn't want him breaking things. There wasn't anything in the car anyway; my briefcase and the audiotape were safely back at the motel.

Walking behind Sheila's Cutlass, I dragged my hand along the trunk and glanced down at the lock. No key. So, Zack wasn't in there. I gave an involuntary sigh. I was glad I hadn't wasted my time buying a .38 at the gun store in the rundown shopping center near the plant.

"How are you, Sheila?" I said and felt stupid saying it.

She didn't reply. She closed the car door and reached out to me with both arms as I came up to her. So, what do you do when a pretty woman greets you like that in an out-of-the-way spot close to midnight? I hugged her. Tight against me, and she hugged me back. After a moment, she looked up at me like she expected me to kiss her. I didn't.

"Let's walk down to the beach," I said. I wanted to get away from her car and the parking lot. Somewhere more open.

"Okay, let's," she said, a hot whisper against my neck.

Reaching my hand around her waist, I guided her through a ring of light at the edge of the pavilion, into the deep shadows beneath the live oaks flung-out limbs. Fumbling and tripping across sparse patches of grass and low vines sprouting from the sandy loam under the trees, we made our way to a low wall and a walkway just above the vegetation line. Not far beyond the wall, the white sand of the beach started and stretched twenty or thirty yards out to the soughing waters of the saltwater lake. Behind us the only sound was the rise and fall of the cicadas in the live oaks. From far above, distinct from the cicadas' burr, came the muffled roar of a jet, on its descent into Houston.

Once we were on the walk, I dropped my arm from around her waist and stuffed my hands in my pockets. She briefly held onto me, then let her arms fall to her sides, the one arm brushing tentatively against my sleeve as we walked.

A half-moon, yellow in the mist over the lake, had appeared on the horizon. In its dim light, I noticed that the walk was made from some type of diamond-shaped brick, fitted together and the interstices filled with sand. In a few spots, small drifts of sand had settled over the walk.

At first we didn't speak. We strolled side-by-side toward the marshes at the edge of the island and the boardwalk that circled out over the grass. The only thing that kept me from getting soaked with sweat and sucked dry by mosquitoes was a slight breeze, cool only by comparison to the hot night, coming off the Gulf. The rising moon set a pale road across the rippling waters, almost to the horizon. As we walked, a low wall of clouds or fog eased over the moon and lifted the road up into it, until the doubly reflected light vanished. All was dark over the lake and the marsh grass in front of us. Only the lights at the pavilion and the glimmer of stars directly above limned our path to a bench near where the boardwalk began.

Taking Sheila's arm, I pulled her down to sit beside me on the bench, so that we were facing the open water. Behind the bench was a row of tall palms tilted at odd angles, their fronds rustling in the breeze. The cicadas had faded to a whisper, and I could hear waves lapping in a soft rhythm on the beach below. The air off the lake was brackish and heavy, not like the fresh salt air of the ocean beaches from my younger days.

The breeze died and I caught a whiff of perfume, sweet and full of promise. I'd waited for Sheila to speak, but she remained silent in the minutes it had taken us to walk to this spot. So now I spoke.

"You said you're leaving Zack. If you do, you could help me with my arbitration case."

She sat scrunched up beside me, bent forward, looking down at feet clad in open sandals and legs still in the white pedal pushers from the afternoon.

"You can testify against him in a civil case," I said, "an arbitration like this ... You don't have to be divorced."

I was feeling guilty at trying to use her. Maybe placing her at risk of harm from her husband. But I needed the help.

She gave a shiver. Reaching over, she took my left hand and lifted my arm around her shoulder and slid closer to me. I let my hand come to rest gently on her bare arm. She was wearing a thin tank top, not the short-sleeve cotton shirt from earlier in the day.

"I'm cold." She shivered again and pressed her right shoulder against my side.

"It's hot. How can you be cold?"

"It's the breeze." She snuggled up under my arm, then slid one hand behind me and the other across my chest and squeezed her body against mine. There was nothing under the tank top, and I could feel her soft breasts. And breathe the unsubtle aroma of the perfume on her neck.

"Maybe I'm just scared," she said. "I just want you to hold me." She reached up and pulled my hand down to her breast.

I wasn't about to kiss her, or caress her, though the temptation was overwhelming, but I held her for some time, both arms around her, and her tight against me. Then gently, I disengaged from her arms and put my hand on her face, tilting it up so that I could see her eyes. It was too dark to see their blue irises, to see anything more than the vague shape and contrast of eyebrows and eyelids and eyelashes and glistening whites, too dark to tell anything from them.

"Sheila, you said you needed my help. How can I help you?"

She was quiet for a moment, then in a soft childlike voice, she said, "Don't play that tape, Dan ... Please ... He's never heard it ... He doesn't know what all I said..."

I grabbed her by both arms, not gently this time. "Look, Sheila, you leave him, divorce him, you can testify and send him to jail. For a long damn time ... Forever." I gripped her tighter, and I felt her muscles tensing, almost rigid, but she wasn't looking at me. Her head was turned away, to one side, her eyes toward the ground—if they were open.

"Do you understand ... if he goes to jail, you're free. You're free!"

She shook her head, still not looking at me. "I'll go to jail, too."

"But you have a defense. He made you—"

"Please, Dan. Please destroy the tape." She looked up at me. I could tell she was dead serious, pleading. "Please! I don't know what he'll do to me if he ... I don't know what he'll do to *you*."

"Don't worry about me. I can take care of myself ... Sheila." I felt like shaking her, but I didn't. I made myself relax my grip on her arms. I tried to talk gently to her, reason with her. "I'm sure the police will protect you. They'll lock him up for good, if you'll only give them the evidence to do it."

She lunged forward, breaking my loose grip, and thrust her arms around me, squeezing me hard, her head against my chest. "Can we go somewhere, Dan? Can we go back to your room?"

"No," I said, not moving or returning the hug.

"I need you, Dan. I love you." Her chest and shoulders heaved with a long sob. "You mean more to me than anything else."

I held my arms out to my sides, away from her. She still clung to me, crying softly, like she did on the tape.

"Sheila, what are you going to do? You can't go on like this."

"Can't we go to your room? I don't like it out here ... Even if we just talk. No one will see us ... It's late ... Please."

She was right. No one would see us. The Sands was like a ghost town now that the strike was over and all the supervisors and out-of-town workers had gone home. But I wasn't buying what she was selling.

"No! Goddamn it!" I pried loose and pushed her away, but held onto her bare arms with my hands. "I'm not ... I'm not getting back into that. I have my own life ... Look at me, Sheila. Are you going to leave Zack or not?"

She jerked away from me and jumped up. Her arms were rigid beside her, her hands clenched in fists. I stared up at her, standing beside the bench, glaring down at me.

"Why won't you help me! For God's sake, Dan, why won't you help me?" She wasn't crying now, and her voice was shrill, shattering the lull of the night music: the sighing of the waves on the beach, the few frogs back in the park. "Don't you care about me?" she almost shouted. "What happens to me? Me!"

I stood now, as well, and took her arm. "I care," I said. "But you have to help yourself first. You have to leave Zack ... divorce him."

She shook her head, flinging the shag-cut hair back and forth. "I can't do that! I can't ... He's my husband."

I stepped back, but I held onto her arm. "Your husband? Is that what you said? Your husband?"

She looked up at me. Even in the dim light, I could see that her lips were drawn in a tight line, her face defiant. Her cheeks wet with tears.

"Yes-s-s," she hissed at me. "He's-s-s ... my ... hus-s-s-band."

I released her arm, and shook my head in disbelief. "You only came out here ... brought me all the way out here, to get me to destroy the tape—your confession to the police. Didn't you?" I thrust my face closer to hers.

The low cloudbank I'd noticed earlier was a wall of incoming fog off the Gulf, smothering the stars and covering the lake. Now it rolled over the beach and into the park, gathering around us, minuscule droplets of water cloying and clinging to our hair and skin and clothes. With the fog came an eerie gray-green light.

Sheila remained rigid in front of me, her face contorted in a way I'd never seen it before. She didn't answer, just glared at me, her body taut, her nose inches from mine. Now I was feeling chilled, but she exhibited none of her prior yearning to draw warmth from my body, or to give me any warmth from hers.

"You know, Sheila." Standing there in front of her, I experienced a blinding realization. "You've told me so many different versions of what happened with you and Zack and Billy Graham that I don't know what to believe. I don't even know if what's on that tape is true."

"It's mostly true." Her eyes, unblinking, did not leave mine.

"You've always intended to live with this ... this ... I don't know ... Zack ... what happened ... for the rest of your life ... Haven't you?"

"I didn't want anything to happen to him." She dropped her eyes and moved away from me and turned toward the sighing water.

"Billy Graham didn't force you into anything, did he? ... Did he, Sheila?"

She gave a muffled response I didn't understand.

"What?"

"No." Her voice quiet, steady.

"What did you get out of it in the end, Sheila? A promotion? ... The move up to the office ... the HR job?"

"That wasn't it."

"And Zack, what was it to him, really ... after it was over?"

She stood like a pale statue—white pants, white arms and face, white-gold hair—a white travertine statue in the gray-green mist. Staring out to a sea now completely obscured by the fog.

"You'd have done anything to help Zack, wouldn't you? ... Goddamn it, Sheila, wouldn't you!"

She was silent.

"Well?" I waited. She looked down, but still didn't answer.

"My God, Sheila ... would you still do anything for him? ... Now? Would you, Sheila?"

"Not anything."

"What *is* it you wouldn't do?"

She sighed. "I don't know." Slowly shaking her head, she glanced over at me, then back at the invisible lake. "I wouldn't have gone out there with him ... just because he wanted me to ... just to murder—"

"So why did you go?"

She didn't answer me and I was impatient. "Good God, Sheila, is what you're telling me ... you need some persuasion?" Taking a step back, I extended my hands out to her. "You need some *incentive* before you take part in a murder? ... A new house? Clear the air ... Is that it?"

"No. No." She was shaking her head, but I didn't hear any real conviction in her voice. "It wasn't that I needed persuasion. It's just ... that's the way it happened. But afterwards..." She was staring at me, her face and body telling me that I was finally hearing the truth, or something close to it. "Afterwards..." she repeated and stopped.

I could hear the water and the wind in the palms and a few desultory frogs. A jet moaned overhead as she went on.

"Zack's my husband; he's the father of my children." She shook her head, slowly back and forth, and I could see her mouth twist in a grimace of pain. "I didn't want his life to be ... Jesus God, I know," she gave what sounded like a sob, "I know what he did was wrong." She was shaking her head still. "But I didn't want anything to happen to him ... I still don't want it ... I could *never* want it."

"Shit!" I wheeled around and started to walk off, then stopped and turned back to her. "If he killed somebody else, would you protect him again?"

"Yes!" She was staring at me as she said it, one hand resting on her hip, and I knew that if I could see her eyes, they'd have a hard steely glint. Because she meant it.

"So, Sheila, no matter how many people he kills ... you're going to protect him ... as long ... as long as you two are together?"

"That's right. He's my husband ... I love him." No hesitation, not a quiver of doubt. A strong defiant affirmation of who Sheila Mills really was.

I sighed and started to leave again—and stopped again, pivoting back toward her. She stood by the bench, erect, arms limp by her sides, staring out at the water. A solitary, weathering garden statue in the low gray-green light, with the mist swirling around her.

One thing more I needed to know. "Do you have any idea ... any idea at all, of divorcing Zack?"

"No. None at all." The tone was flat, but her voice was strong and clear. She wasn't looking at me, but out at the lake.

I stalked off, leaving her there, an enigma wreathed in fog and bathed in that eerie gray-green light. Making a wide detour through the parking lot, I kept my eyes on the dark pavilion and the shadows outside the two nebulous cones of light and on the murky depths beneath the live oaks. And on Sheila's Cutlass. Especially on the Cutlass.

Nothing happened. After circling my car at a distance and carefully checking out the backseat, I got in and drove out of the lot and out of the park and off Pleasure Island. From the exit loop, I caught one last glimpse of Sheila, walking past the pavilion, Sheila ghostly vague in the mist under a cone of light. It was the last I'd ever see of her—save one final, brief encounter.

Chapter Twenty-seven—Duped

WHEN I GOT BACK TO THE SANDS—after 1:00am—I found the door to my room ajar, the lock busted from the jamb, and my briefcase gone. Along with both copies of Sheila's taped confession. So that's where Zack had been.

I felt like a complete fool.

Two police officers came, filled out a form, and left. The only thing missing was the briefcase—with the two tapes, the authentication letters, and all my notes. Only after the two officers left did I notice that my extra pair of shoes, black wingtips for the hearing, was also gone.

When the officers asked if I had any idea who might have broken into my room, I told them about Zack Mills and the arbitration hearing on Thursday. But I had no proof, not even one smidgen of evidence. They agreed, from what they could see, but they'd go by and have a talk with Zack the next day. I didn't mention that I'd been out at Pleasure Island with Zack's wife while he, or somebody, was ransacking my room.

For what remained of the night, I stayed in another room at the Sands, and slept very little. I kept going back over my rendezvous with Sheila and trying to decide what I was going to do.

There was still the copy of the tape from Sheila's unemployment case, the copy I'd sent to the TWC hearing officer and he returned to me. But I hadn't played it, and I didn't know if it was any good. Then there was the little problem of its travels, as well as its

215

provenance, that only served to compound my challenges in authenticating it. Before dozing off as light seeped through the cracks in the closed curtains, I decided to call the Ranger and try to get another copy made from the original. And try once more to get the two detectives who'd actually heard Sheila tell her story come testify.

AS SOON as I'd chased the roaches out of the shower and scrubbed my body free of the sleazy feeling from the night before, I started making phone calls. My secretary, Julie, was the only living soul I found on the planet. For Jim-Bob the lawyer and Roy the Ranger I left recorded messages designed to get their attention but not tell them much.

To my surprise, the first call back—right after I reached Perry's office at the plant—was the Ranger. He was in Houston and he'd just checked his messages. When I told him what I wanted, and that my copies of Sheila's confession and the letters he had given me were gone, he gave a perceptible groan that sounded like an extended, "Ah, shit." He'd meet me at the police chief's office in Port Oso in two hours.

Jim-Bob called and agreed to see me in his office in the afternoon, whenever I could get there. Then my secretary called and said she had searched my desk and couldn't find the tape I'd sent to the TWC hearing officer. I told her to go through the file cabinet behind my desk—and call Liz Johnson to see if I'd lent it to her. I couldn't remember. Liz had kept bugging me for a copy so she could hear the entire thing.

"Goddamn it, man, how could you let somebody steal the damn tape? *And* the letters?" The Ranger sat catty-corner to me at a small table in the conference room across from the police chief's office. The chief was still on the phone with the assistant D.A., trying to get me another copy of the tape.

216

The Ranger stretched out one blue-jean clad leg to rest a leather boot on a nearby chair. His white Stetson rested upright on the table in front of him. "Where were you, anyhow?" The Ranger's flinty green eyes drilled holes in my defenses before I could even raise them. I shrugged and looked up at the white perforated tiles in the ceiling.

"How long do you think this is gonna take?" I asked.

"You weren't with that woman, were you?"

I returned his stare with an impatient grimace. All I wanted was another copy of the tape and to get the hell out of there. The police chief's secretary was already typing up new letters from the copies Chief Henshaw had kept in his file.

"Gawd-damn! That's where you were, wasn't it?" The Ranger slapped his leg. "You can't fool me." He gave a big smile of triumph. Another mystery solved by the Texas Rangers.

"I thought she was going to divorce him and help me with the arbitration," I said and gave another shrug. "Maybe testify … She said she needed help."

"You should've kept your pecker in your pants and that damn briefcase of yours chained to your damn wrist."

Jerking the holstered pistol to one side, he shifted his bulk in the chair without dropping his boot from the seat of the other chair. He was dressed in his lawman's outfit: camel hair coat, which was hanging on the back of his chair; bolo tie with a silver slide and raised Texas Star; and white shirt that ballooned out over his ample gut and leather belt. His face and big nose were redder than ever. Flushed with irritation at my stupidity.

"Guess it was all a ruse, a trick to get me away from the room," I said. "I thought it wouldn't be too smart to carry the stuff with me when I went to meet her."

"Damn, damn, damn … So, how'd he know you'd leave it in your room?"

As I was thinking that was a good question, the door swung open and rapped against the wall behind it. The police chief charged in like an enraged bull, some loose papers held out in one hand in front of him. The thin scar on his rosy left cheek had turned a livid red.

"I can't fucking believe it," he said. "That Hastings can't find the fucking tape."

"What!" The Ranger jerked his boot off the chair and let it hit the floor with a thud.

"He got his file out and went through it while I was on the phone."

"Don't you have a copy?" I asked, not particularly worried because I felt sure the police had kept a copy somewhere.

"Fuck no." The chief was glaring at me like it was my fault. "Why you think I called him? Sent the whole damn file over to his office for the hearing ... McHugh said he wanted the originals of *every*thing."

Feeling deflated, I dropped my eyes to stare at the gold badge and nameplate on the chief's crisp white shirt.

"You didn't keep copies?" the Ranger asked. He was sitting up straight now, elbows square on the table, white-shirted belly pressed over the edge.

"Only the forms—for all they're worth. None of the detectives' notes. Or that *fucking* tape." He shook the papers at the Ranger. "You think I got a budget to make a hundred copies of all the shit I send to the D.A.'s office?"

"How about Robinson and Baggerly?" the Ranger said. "They keep copies?"

Henshaw shook his head emphatically; not a hair moved from the thick white pompadour. "Hastings took everything. No copies." Standing next to the Ranger, he held the papers out to me, over the table. "Here's the letters you wanted. Lotta good they'll do you now."

"Why don't you just sign 'em and give 'em to me," I said, my mind working. "I may have another copy of the tape in my office."

"I don't know." The chief pulled the letters back as I reached for them. "You don't have the tape we gave you and we don't know—"

The Ranger snatched the papers out of his hand and smacked them down on the table between us. "Give me a goddamn pen. We can just sign the damn things, Eric." He was looking up at the chief. "Let him worry about getting a good tape to go with 'em."

"I don't know, Roy ... This is—"

"This is nuthin but one big goddamn Aggie clusterfuck ... leastwise, if we don't do this. Now gimme your goddamn pen."

They scribbled their signatures, the chief in a tight little scrawl, the Ranger with a sweeping John Hancock. Originals and copies in hand, I gladly departed with that small part of what I needed.

First snagging a burger and fries from a MacDonald's drive-through, I sped to Jim-Bob Lloyd's office, where I gobbled down the greasy food in an empty conference room and waited for him to finish with another client. Halfway through the fries, I used the conference room phone and my credit card to call my office. Julie no sooner answered than Liz Johnson took the phone away from her.

"Daniel, I don't have your damn tape and I don't know where it is. Julie and I have been tearing your office apart looking for it."

"Where have you looked?" I kept chewing on a french fry.

"Your desk ... the file cabinet. Are you sure you didn't send it down to the file room?"

"Never! Anything I want to see again in this life I never send down there. Has to be in the office somewhere."

"Well, it isn't."

"Have you been through the boxes ... under the table?"

"Why are you such a packrat? We're just starting on the stuff on top of the table. Why would any sane person—?"

"Call me if you find anything." I gave her the number for the conference room and hung up as Jim-Bob appeared through the door.

219

"We've got to ask the arbitrator to subpoena the detectives," Jim-Bob said once I'd finished telling him about my trip to Chief Henshaw's office and showing him the new letters. "Those letters aren't enough, even if you do find the tape ... And no court 'round here will consider issuing a subpoena without you going to the arbitrator first."

"Then I've got to let Joplin know, maybe even tell him I don't have the original copy anymore."

"He may know that anyway."

"Ah-h-h," I shook my head, "not even Joplin would go along with his client stealing evidence—even for a lousy arbitration."

"Don't bet on it," Jim-Bob said. He placed his hands over his big ears, squashing them against his head and making his shock of wiry brown hair look like the topknot of a woodpecker. "Hear no evil, see no evil," he said, then dropped his hands onto the table. "Let's go ahead and fax the arbitrator, ask him to subpoena the cops ... We'll copy Joplin."

"Shit!" Then I sighed, feeling despondent. "Guess I don't have anything to lose." I raised an eyebrow at him. "But not a word about losing the tape. Keep that business to ourselves."

"You let me handle it ... Who's the arbitrator?"

"Hodson Gray. He's a professor at U.T."

"Umm ... you can always ask to postpone the hearing."

"Why? Is he pro-union or something?"

"No, sir. He's just ver-r-ry careful. He won't do anything out of the ordinary unless he has a month to think about it. We'll ask for a postponement when we send the fax."

"No! I don't want to delay this thing. Who knows what they'll do next!"

"They? You worried about this Mills character coming after you?"

"No ... Maybe a little. But that's not it." I figured the risk was the same whenever we had the hearing. But I was ready to fight this battle now. Not later. Not wait for Sheila to pay me another visit, make another plea.

Jim-Bob called his secretary and we sent off the faxes. Then I talked with Liz Johnson a couple more times. By five o'clock, Jim-Bob and I were on a conference call with the arbitrator, Tony Joplin, and Mary Albright. We made our case for the subpoenas, and Joplin reminded everyone the hearing was less than two days away.

"Moreover," he said through a buzz from one of the connections, "subpoenas will only be a waste of time, just another exercise in futility."

"They're not something that's commonly done," said the arbitrator. "Certainly not going to law enforcement officers."

"You can issue them under the Federal Arbitration Act," Jim-Bob said.

"No, you can't." Mary Albright's husky voice. "There's no power in any court to enforce a subpoena in a labor arbitration."

"Why don't we try it?" I suggested. "I'll have the subpoenas served by tomorrow morning. See what the city does. Maybe they'll—"

"They won't comply," said Joplin. "They'll just ignore it."

"That's our problem if they do," Jim-Bob said. "We can go to court to compel them to attend."

"By Thursday?" Joplin again.

"Your problem," Mary Albright said, "is that no court in this county will force *any* police officers to come testify in a private labor arbitration, *under oath*, about a criminal matter that's still the subject of an open investigation." As she spoke, I was staring at Jim-Bob over the speakerphone between us. He shrugged and mouthed the words, "She's right." She had hit it on the head, and I was stuck. But I don't give up easily.

"Why don't you issue the subpoenas and see if we can convince the city to cooperate? They may want to help us."

"Wel-l-l," said the arbitrator, "this will take some time, whatever I decide to do. Would you like to postpone the hearing, Mr. Esperson?"

Before I could answer, Joplin objected. "Nothing's going to change if you give him six days or six months, Professor Gray. This is nothing but an act of desperation because *he* knows *he* doesn't have a case. The man may have been accused of a crime, but he's never been convicted ... never even been tried ... And he never will be." I heard somebody sigh, probably the arbitrator, unless Mary Albright was rolling her eyes and sighing at her own partner.

"Maybe you ought to go for a postponement," Jim-Bob said. He had muted the speaker. Joplin was still going on about something and I missed part of it, but I distinctly heard the last line.

"—and Zack Mills deserves to have his day in court."

I unmuted the speakerphone. "His day in court is the last thing Zack Mills wants," I said.

"Do you need more time, Mr. Esperson?" The arbitrator. "Under the circumstances, though, I don't think any subpoena I sign will do you any good."

"No," I said, "we'll proceed on Thursday, as scheduled." And that ended the discussion.

What I didn't say was that I had my tape. Liz Johnson had found the return envelope from the TWC with the tape inside and phoned me ten minutes before the conference call began. It was in a box of old arbitration tapes—recordings from past hearings—under the table. I must've tossed it in there, or maybe my secretary Julie had in trying to straighten up my office. Liz was listening to it as she spoke to me. It was all there, or she thought it was, and she still couldn't believe what she was hearing. How could that woman help her husband kill a man after having an affair with him?

By the time we were finishing the conference call, Hank Greenberg was well on his way to Houston to retrieve the tape.

Chapter Twenty-eight—The Arbitration Hearing

THE HEARING WAS AT THE SANDS, in a long interior room with dark imitation pine paneling, frayed forest green carpets, and a low tile ceiling with recessed lights—from which half the fluorescent tubes were missing. It was so dark that when I entered from the hallway, I almost missed seeing Zack Mills deep in the twilight of a back corner. But I had no trouble seeing his eyes, glaring at me like a jungle predator ready to pounce on its prey.

He was sitting at the far end of the union's table, on the opposite side of the room and away from the entrance. As I opened the new briefcase I'd bought the day before and removed a legal pad and the expandable red folder with my exhibits for the hearing—and the envelope with the tape, three copies now—I watched Zack watching me, and watching what I was placing on the table.

There were actually three tables, collapsible ones covered with white tablecloths and positioned in a "U" formation, the company on one side, the union on the other, and the arbitrator at the head table. In the open space between the tables was an empty chair, facing the arbitrator. For the witness.

As I finished emptying my new briefcase, the arbitrator arrived. He was a stocky man, the victim of male-pattern baldness with a neatly trimmed brown fringe of hair and a round passive face. He introduced himself, "L. Hodson Gray," in a gruff, no-nonsense voice that I found comforting. He shook hands all around and took his place at the head table. I sat to his immediate right, then Perry, Hank, and Layton Van

Horn to my right along our table. Frank Landry, the union chairman, took the seat across from me, with the witness chair in the well between us, and Pete Reneau beside him to his left. Zack stayed in the shadows at the far end of the union table. His eyes seemed never to leave me, and while the arbitrator set up for the hearing, I stared back at the man I couldn't believe was Sheila's husband.

He was dressed in a dark plaid shirt and a lightweight tan vest, not what I would have recommended had I been his lawyer. I'd only seen him up close once before, with Sheila at her desk in the plant, and I hadn't remembered how black his hair was or how heavy his brow or how swarthy his complexion. Or maybe it was just the dim lighting in that corner of the room.

Hank Greenberg was busy setting up a tape recorder at my elbow. Using an extension cord, he plugged it into a wall socket next to a roaring motel air conditioner that blasted out damp artic air, rippling the papers on the table. Hank lowered the volume, but a second air conditioner behind Landry kept blasting away, forcing me to leave on my suit coat to keep from shivering.

The air in the room was redolent of a pungent deodorizer that irritated my contact lens but failed to suppress the insidious odor of mildew leavened with the stench of stale cigarette smoke. Despite the no-smoking signs on two walls, each table held an ashtray. But no one was smoking.

Professor Gray produced his own small tape recorder, battery operated, which he placed with the recording end pointed toward the witness chair. We were all there, except for the union's lawyers—late as usual. I looked around expecting either Tony Joplin or Mary Albright to appear at any moment.

"Let's get started," said the arbitrator. "It's already ten after."

"Where's Joplin?" I asked, looking across the well at Landry. "Don't we need to wait for him?"

"No," said Landry, shoulders back, chest out, his big face full of his own self-importance. "I'm gonna handle this one myself."

I glanced over at Zack, but he gave no reaction, just continued staring at me. Landry shifted his large frame to face the arbitrator and dipped his head, almost like he was bowing to him.

"We're ready to proceed, your honor."

The arbitrator nodded and gave a slight smile. At being addressed as your honor, I thought.

"Since this is a discharge case, he..." Landry pointed at me, "the company has to go first." Then he sneered, glaring at me, "if they have anything."

While Landry was speaking, my mind was circling around Joplin's absence. This was too big a case for the union not to have legal counsel. Why had they elected to forgo their lawyer on this one? Money? I thought they paid Joplin a flat fee for arbitrations. Or maybe it was Joplin who opted out. Or Mary Albright. But if so, why?

"Mr. Esperson, are you ready to proceed?" the arbitrator said, ending my puzzling over Joplin's absence.

"I'm ready," I said and glanced down at Zack again. His eyes were fixed on me like he was sighting down a gun barrel. The open hunting vest was thin, but it looked more appropriate for fall than the end of summer. For deer season. Was he trying to send me a message? I hoped the arbitrator noticed.

"Let me tell you about this case," I said, turning back to Professor Gray. And I told him—with a few contentious interruptions from Landry—then concluded with a statement of the issue: whether killing a supervisor was just cause for discharge.

"You gotta prove he did it," said Landry.

"That's right." The arbitrator dipped his chin in my direction. "You have the burden proof, counsel. As I understand it, the grievant has never been convicted of the crime, or even tried. Is that correct?"

"Yes sir," I said before Landry could jump in. "But he's been indicted for the murder." With a shaky hand, I marked Zack Mills' indictment as Company Exhibit One and passed two copies to the arbitrator, who gave one to Landry.

"Is that it?" Professor Gray asked as he put on half glasses to read the indictment. "You don't have the police officers we had the conference call about?"

"We have other evidence," I said. "First, though, I'd like to call Zack Mills as an adverse party."

"You can't do that," Landry growled at me. "You can't make the grievant testify in a discharge case. That's not done."

"Won't he take the Fifth Amendment, Mr. Esperson?" said the arbitrator. "It doesn't mean he's guilty under the law, but if he's been accused of a crime..."

"I didn't do it," said Zack from the other end of the union's table, "but my lawyer told me I can't testify in something like this."

"Can't we just put him under oath ... see what he says?" I gave Landry a fake smile, then looked back at the arbitrator.

"Seems like a waste of time." The arbitrator took off his reading glasses and shook his head. "It's clear to me how it'd go, and it doesn't help your case any ... so why don't you tell me what else you have."

I grabbed the manila envelope with the tape cassettes and dumped them out on the table, then reached into the red folder and extracted the new letters from the Ranger and the Port Oso police chief. Across the well, Landry was staring at the tape recorder at my elbow. So were Reneau and Zack Mills. They must've just realized it wasn't there for us to make our own recording of the hearing, as we often did—in the event we had to go to court to challenge the arbitrator's award.

"I have here," I said, holding up one of the cassettes and waving it in the air, "a tape-recorded confession that Sheila Mills, the grievant's wife, gave to the Port Oso police last January. In her confession, she says that Zack Mills gunned down company supervisor Earl Graham in cold blood."

I glanced at Zack. Even in the low light, I could tell his face was ashen.

"Where'd you get that?" Landry snapped.

"I had more copies than the ones somebody took from my room ... in this motel." I passed a copy of the tape over to Perry to place in the machine.

Landry glared at me. "We don't know anything about that. I *mean*, who gave you that tape?"

Not answering him, I handed a second cassette to the arbitrator. But I was wondering if Landry knew my first tapes had been stolen—and how he knew it. And how much he knew.

"That's exhibit two..." I handed the arbitrator two copies of each letter. "And these are exhibits three and four." The arbitrator took one copy of each and passed the others to Landry. "Those letters certify the authenticity of the tape recording," I said. I hadn't given him a cassette for Landry.

"How do we know that thing," Landry jabbed his big index finger at the tape cassette the arbitrator was holding, "hasn't been altered or tampered with somehow? You can do that you know." He pointed at me. "They have audio-visual people who can do anything they want with that kind of stuff. They even brag about it, all their research and technology. They even have a lab—"

"Oh, come on, Frank!" said Perry. "You know we wouldn't do crap like that."

"You might not, but that lawyer..." Landry shook his meaty finger at me. "He's a lawyer. That little ... he'll do anything he can get away with."

"All right, gentleman," the arbitrator said, stopping my retort. "Let's get back on track here." He frowned at me. "Is this *all* you have to show that this tape," he held it up in his fingers, "is complete and unaltered from the original? And can you establish when and how the original was made?"

"On the last," I said, "the tape will speak for itself. It was an official police investigation and the people who were there, and the venue and time, are all identified on it ... And I'll vouch for its authenticity," I pointed to the letters in front of the arbitrator, "based on those certifications—which you can see have notarized signatures and are on official stationery."

"He'll have to be sworn," said Landry. "I'm not going to sit here and let him lawyer talk that tape into being played."

"It's no good, anyway." Pete Reneau. Everyone looked at him. He waved two fingers toward the head table. "That's Zack's wife on that tape, and she can't be heard to speak against him." He had a pleased-with-himself look. I smiled at him. Pete had just helped me vouch for the tape and who was on it.

"This is a civil matter—a labor arbitration at that," I said. "The marital privilege doesn't apply."

I read the statute and cited a case from my notes, reconstituted with some quick work at the plant. The arbitrator's own tape recorder was whirring away now, taking all this down. I ended, saying, "I will give you all the legal authority you want in my post-hearing brief."

The arbitrator nodded. "Okay, we'll hold that issue until then ... How did you get the tape, Mr. Esperson? And how do you know it hasn't been altered?"

"He has to be sworn," Landry said, his hand clenched in a big fist on the white tablecloth. But he hadn't asked for a copy of the tape.

"No problem," I said. I pushed my chair back. "I'll be sworn."

"You can stay there." The arbitrator said, motioning for me to stay at my seat. "Just go on and take the oath."

I stood and raised my right hand and took the oath to tell the whole truth and nothing but the truth, "so help me God." Then I sat down and started talking.

"Professor Gray, this tape recording," I held up the black cassette, not white like the original, "was made by two detectives on the Port Oso police force, James Robinson and Sid Baggerly. They identify themselves and give the case name and the nature of their investigation at the beginning, and they identify the grievant's wife as the witness they are interviewing. The Texas Ranger who was assigned to the case, Leroy R. Rogers, obtained this recording from the Port Oso Chief of Police, Eric Henshaw, and he gave it to me for my use in this arbitration case." I tapped my finger on the copies of the letters from the Ranger and the police chief. "Just like it's says in these certifications."

"I object," said Landry. "That doesn't prove anything about the tape."

"So, you couldn't get witnesses to come testify," the arbitrator said, staring solemnly at me. "And these aren't affidavits, are they?"

"No sir, but they're as good as ... They're signed and the signatures are notarized."

"You're not challenging these letters, are you, Mr. Landry?" The arbitrator held up one of the letters.

"No, but they're not worth the paper they're written on."

Removing his reading glasses, the arbitrator rubbed his eyes. "Well, they do show how the tape recording, or this cassette of it, got here." He dropped his hand and looked at Landry. "This is an arbitration hearing, not a court proceeding, so we don't need to act like it is one." Without giving Landry a chance to respond, he turned back to me. "Mr. Esperson, to your knowledge, has this tape been altered in any way from the original?"

"No sir."

"Has it been under your custody and control since you received it from the law enforcement officers?"

"The original ... that is, my copy, was stolen from me the other night. Out of my room here at the Drifting Sands Motel. But I made this tape personally from that copy, and it's a complete copy of the original."

The arbitrator frowned at me and said, "A copy of a copy."

"See," said Landry. "It's not even the copy he got from those people."

"It's a complete copy. I can vouch for that. Everything is on this copy that was on the original."

"How do we know the original wasn't changed," Landry said, "or the cops didn't pass on a copy they'd fixed up? ... They could do something like that and we'd never know it."

"Look at the letters. They're originals, and you'd have to question the veracity of the Port Oso Chief of Police."

"And he's not here," Landry said.

The arbitrator gave an audible sigh and rubbed his hand across his bald head. He peered at Landry, then at me.

"If it's all you got," he said, "then I guess we'll have to listen to it. For what it's worth."

I had a sinking feeling at the last words. But at least he'd agreed to hear it. And he hadn't pressed me on the custody and control issue.

"Wait," said Landry. "Don't I get to cross examine him?"

"We-l-l-ll..." said the arbitrator. He looked taken aback, but I could tell he was considering it. What the hell is Landry doing, I was thinking.

"I have some questions for the lawyer," Landry said, bulling his way ahead. "We need to sort some things out here."

The arbitrator gave him a pained look. "Well, if you must."

Bracing his elbows on the table, Landry leaned forward and fixed me with a malevolent glare. Water sloshed out of a glass beside one elbow and soaked the white tablecloth, but he ignored it.

"Mis-ter Esperson, I have just a few questions for you."

"Shoot," I said, and almost choked on my saliva. I glanced down the union table at Zack. His eyes never wavered from me.

"You say it's Sheila Mills on that tape there." Landry pointed across the open well between the tables, and I dropped my gaze to the tape cassette. And then brought them back up to Landry. He had a large square face with heavy jowls that seemed to have grown heavier during the strike. His arms bulged in the blue work shirt, faded and slightly rumpled. His fists on the table looked like the pale heads of mallets, with black hairs spread across them.

"Yes," I said, nodding slowly. "The detective—Robinson was the one in charge—identifies her as the witness, and she identifies herself."

"And you know it's really her. You're sure of that?"

"I know her voice ... and Perry Comeau here can identify it, as well." I gestured toward Perry.

"That's right," Perry said, bobbing his head in agreement.

"She worked for him," I said.

"And you believe she's telling the truth?"

"Yes."

"She wouldn't lie about what happened? To protect herself?"

"Not about that." I shook my head, worried about where Landry was going with this. "You can tell she's not lying from what she says ... How she says it."

"Would you, Dan Esperson, say she has a reputation for telling the truth?"

"I wouldn't know what her reputation is." I could guess, but I wouldn't say it. "I didn't know her that well. I just know what you can tell from the tape ... She wasn't lying there."

"So, Mr. Esperson, you didn't know her that well? ... Now, if she said that you and her had an affair, would she be telling the truth about that? Or would that be a lie?"

From the far end of the company table came an audible snort of disgust, or so I took it. Layton Van Horn. Out of the corner of my eye, I could see Perry staring at me and Hank Greenberg's pen poised motionless above the pad on which he was taking notes. I watched the pen slowly sink to rest on the table. After the first shock, I brought my eyes back to Landry and tried to keep them focused on his big face. And avoiding Zack Mills.

"First," I said, "she wouldn't say that and, second, I may have met her a couple of times—the first time was at her request ... when she was trying to find out what was going on in the police investigation. The last was this week, when I was trying to get her to testify in this arbitration hearing."

"There were more than a couple times, wasn't there? A few times between the first and last, and it wasn't just to talk?"

I glared at Landry. "We met more than twice ... maybe once or twice more ... I thought she needed my help to find a lawyer ... that's what she said ... and then after her indictment, she wanted me to know what really happened. That was before I got this tape." I held up the cassette.

"Are you denying that you had a relationship with the grievant's wife?" Landry spit out the words like they were bad crawfish. "An il-legal relationship?"

He means illicit, I thought, and looked over at the arbitrator. His face was impassive, his tape recorder whirring away.

"These questions are highly improper," I said as calmly as I could, but I was shaking. "They have no bearing on this tape." I tapped the cassette on the table. "Or on this arbitration case. I object to Mr. Landry using this red herring to confuse the issues and divert attention from what's really at issue here."

"Mr. Landry, is the grievant's wife going to testify?" the arbitrator asked.

"No, sir, Mr. Arbitrator, but this lawyer is standing up for her speaking the truth on that tape—while he's denying the truth of other things she says."

"We haven't heard her *say* anything yet." The arbitrator shifted his head to one side, his mouth in a tight line, a look of impatience. He seemed to be going my way—although all of it, everything between Landry and me, had gone down on his recording.

I'd stopped shaking, and I was thinking clearly, but my gut was in turmoil. I leaned forward over the table, and more forcefully, with a show of anger now, I said, "They're just offering false gossip and innuendo to try and badger me and embarrass me and get us off the subject."

I figured Joplin must've told Landry to challenge Sheila's veracity through me. Or Mary Albright had. But why weren't they here? Either would have been more effective than Landry. Then again, he was being pretty effective—aggressive and persistent.

"Can I just ask the lawyer one more question?" he said to the arbitrator.

"Okay. Go on."

"Are you denying you met with her, Mr. Esperson?"

"No. Of course not. I've already said I met with her to—"

"And that she went with you to your house? In Houston?"

I shook my head. "I met with her to get her to tell me about Zack—"

"And that you two also met a few times in a motel room out on the interstate toward—"

"She told me that Zack Mills, the grievant there," I pointed at Zack, who was glaring bullets at me, "killed Earl Graham and—"

"That's not the question," shouted Landry. He was half out of the chair, his belly hanging over the table. I noticed that the big wet spot on the white tablecloth in front of him had spread to the exhibits the arbitrator had passed to him. An unworldly sense of calm self-possession came over me; I was merely an actor on the stage, playing a part.

"And she was there," I said, "just like she says she was on *this* tape." I kept my voice steady as I held up the cassette and shook it at Landry.

"She never said that!" Zack Mills yelled from the far end of the room—almost a primal scream. He was standing, his body rigid over the table, knuckles resting on the tabletop, like a lean hostile ape. Glaring at me. "That's just another goddamn lie that fucker's telling." For a moment, I was afraid he was going to come over the table after me.

The arbitrator raised his voice for the first time. "All right, people. Let's not get carried away here."

That stopped Landry's shouting and Zack's preparation to do whatever it was he was going to do. The arbitrator held both hands up, palms out, and motioned us back down. I noticed then that I had stood, as well, at Zack's howl of protest. Perry and Hank were still seated, gaping at us as if they had been struck dumb, while Layton and Pete Reneau had shifted forward as if they had ringside seats at a fight. Landry, Zack, and I settled back into our seats as the arbitrator spoke, now in a low, gruff voice, so low that it commanded everyone's attention.

"I think we've had quite enough theatrics ... so we can get on with listening to that tape Mr. Esperson has there." He pointed at me. "It's the best, or I should say, the better evidence."

Landry was silent, probably figuring he had done *his* best, or his worst from my viewpoint. Or perhaps concerned that he was at risk of unloosing Zack to commit acts of violence and mayhem. On me.

I handed the tape cassette to Perry, and he snapped it into the cassette player. He started it, and we heard Sheila say, ""He figured we needed to wash the car and make sure it was clean."

"Uh ... Perry, stop the tape," I said. "You need to rewind it to the beginning."

On the other side of the room, Landry gave an exasperated sigh and Pete Reneau laughed. Zack was silent.

Perry stopped the tape and pushed the rewind button. Reneau and Landry started whispering to each other, and Zack quickly huddled with them, the only time I think his eyes had left me. Irritated at the setback, I decided to get in one last shot.

"I want the record to reflect that Sheila Mills admitted to me that she participated in the murder of a company supervisor, one Earl Stanley Graham, which makes it an admission against her own interest and thus admissible in any proceeding, and that the grievant there," I pointed at Zack, once more glaring in my direction, "was the killer." Good God, I thought. What have I done?

"That's a lie," Zack Mills said, his voice quieter, but he was on his feet again. Pete Reneau reached up and put his hand on Zack's arm and pulled him back down, close beside him.

"Okay, counselor … " The arbitrator held up his hand.

"He can't give evidence," Landry said.

"I've been sworn." Which would make it even better for the D.A.

"All right, all right, everybody." The arbitrator raised his hands over his head and waved at us to be quiet. "I've heard your testimony, counselor. Now let's hear the tape."

"Perry, start the tape," I said.

"Wait!" said Landry. "We object to this tape recording as irrelevant, immaterial, lacking in proof of authenticity and completeness, and it was obtained by fraud, misrepresentation, and coercion." He was reading from a legal pad he held in one large paw, bobbing the pad up and down in sync with his bobbing head. "It wasn't admissible in a court proceeding, and it couldn't even be used against the woman who gave it, and especially it couldn't be used against her lawful husband."

It sounded like something Pete Reneau and he must have come up with from various television shows and perhaps some discussions with Tony Joplin. But while he may have garbled the legalese, the objection worried me.

"This is a civil proceeding," I said. "A private matter to which criminal protections do not apply."

The arbitrator nodded slightly, but he gave me a look of exasperation. He pointed at the tape player. Before he could speak, Landry slid two documents toward him across the head table.

"This is our exhibit," Landry said. "The order from the criminal court judge throwing out the so-called confession on that tape for all the reasons I said in my objection, and dismissing the case against Mrs. Mills."

"Okay, let me see it," said the arbitrator. He picked up the paper and adjusted his half glasses on his nose and began reading.

"That doesn't..." I started, but he held up his hand.

"Just give me a minute to read this." He did, and we waited.

We had been at this for over two hours now. I looked at Perry, and he smiled and winked back at me. Hank gave me a thumbs up. His pad was mostly covered with elaborate blue-ink filigree. From beyond him, Layton glared at me with almost as much malice as Zack Mills.

The arbitrator cleared his throat. "This is Union Exhibit One. I will take it under consideration ... " He held up his hand as I started to renew my protest. "You can address the issue in your brief, Mr. Esperson. Right now, I want to hear that tape recording. We don't have all day here ... just waste more time arguing about all this."

"Go ahead, Perry," I said, and Perry started the tape player. Detective James Robinson's voice came on first, with the preliminaries, and then Sheila's voice, identifying herself.

"Pause that a moment," said the arbitrator. Perry hit the stop button.

"Is that the voice of the grievant's spouse?" asked the arbitrator. He was looking at Zack, but Zack didn't answer.

"That's Sheila Mills," said Perry. "Zack's wife."

"Well?" said the arbitrator, still staring in Zack's direction. Zack mumbled something inaudible.

"That's her," Landry said, his mouth drawn in a tight, unhappy line.

"Are you still married?" the arbitrator asked. To Zack.

"Yes, sir." Zack's voice was quiet, subdued. Resigned.

"Let's move on." The arbitrator said, pointing to Perry. Perry restarted the tape player.

We listened to the entire tape, all the way to when it clicked off after Sheila refused to sign a written statement. I watched Zack almost the whole time. He glared back at me at first, then after a while, when Sheila was describing the trip out to the StarLite Drive-in Theater, he looked at his hands, the wall, the ashtray on the table in front of Reneau. At one point—I think it was when Sheila was telling about washing their car—he put his head in his hands and left it there almost to the end of the tape.

What's he thinking, I wondered. I found out one thing he was thinking when he brushed past me after the hearing was over, on his way out of the conference room.

When the taped clicked off, Landry restated his objection but offered no rebuttal testimony or any other evidence. The arbitrator gave us thirty days to mail post-hearing briefs to him, both at the same time. When I started to make a point about the tape and Sheila's confession, he stopped me and told me to address any issues in the brief. He'd take a copy of the tape, he said, but he didn't think he needed to listen to it again. Then we all packed up and left.

Somehow—maybe he maneuvered it that way—Zack came close to me as he went around the company's table to go out the door. I felt his arm touching, rubbing lightly against mine as I was loading my briefcase, and his voice came to me in a low whisper. A whisper no one else could hear above the growl of the air conditioning. Or would have understood had they heard it.

"The air's not good in here," he said, his mouth twisted in a grim smile. "It needs clearing." I drew back and stared after him as he hurried on past and out the door behind Landry and Reneau.

"What did he say?" asked Hank. He was collecting the tape player close by where I was standing.

"Nothing," I said. "Just some nonsense about the air in here." But I was remembering what Sheila said on the tape, and what she had told me. Before they moved into their new house, Zack had told her they needed to clear the air between them. Before he killed Billy Graham. To clear the air.

Chapter Twenty-nine—Deconstruction Begins

IT WAS LATE AFTERNOON BEFORE I started back to Houston. Right after the hearing, Perry, Hank, and I went for a late lunch at Mi Casita Bonita, where I downed a couple of beers under Perry's disapproving Baptist eye. The good thing about Perry was that his disapproval extended only to the sin and not to the sinner, and never lasted for long.

"You did a great job, Dan, absolutely great," he said for about the tenth time, the latest over his wiped-clean plate. "I think the arbitrator's leaning our way. I really do."

"Yeah, I hope so," I replied and took another swallow of Tecate. "But you never can tell." After every hearing, Perry always said something glowingly positive about how it had gone, and I hated it. Bad luck.

"Don't you worry about Layton," he said, "and all that business Frank Landry was going on about." Layton had zipped off without a word to me, and he hadn't joined us for lunch.

"Why should I worry about Layton?" Of course, I should worry about Layton. He was probably off plotting my demise as we spoke. Him and Zack Mills. At least Layton only wanted to get me fired.

"You know," Perry said, "all that garbage about you and Sheila. Trying to get you to say she was lying, so he could get the arbitrator to think she was lying on that tape ... You handled it like a champ." He reached across the corner of the table and patted me on the shoulder.

"Yeah, I did, didn't I." I nodded and glanced over at Hank. He was studying the lemon in the bottom of his iced-tea glass. Looking up, he signaled to a server carrying around pitchers of tea and water and held up the glass.

"Had to be tough," Perry was saying, "sitting there and taking that kind of guff from him. Not losing your cool and calling her a liar."

"Yeah, it was tough." I took another swallow of the beer.

"What I liked," Hank said as the server refilled his glass, "was your telling the arbitrator Sheila admitted to *you* that she and Zack killed Graham." He paused, giving me a quizzical look. "She really say that?"

"She really said that ... Well, she told me Zack killed him and she was there. Not to the extent she said it on the tape, though."

I was praying that all this didn't get back to the D.A. If it did, I might become a key witness in a revived murder case against Sheila, maybe even Zack. Like a regular jailhouse snitch.

"That should just about do it, shouldn't it?" Hank was staring at me while he stirred packets of Sweet'NLow into his iced tea.

I started and forced myself back to the present. "Not that easy," I said. "Technically, what Sheila told me, and the cops, is all hearsay—subject to an exception, we hope, and I'll argue that in the brief. And the tape is suspect in a lot of ways. Our biggest problem may be that Zack didn't get to confront the only witness against him."

"Aside from you," Hank said.

"I'm just repeating what she told me."

I stopped the waiter as he went past and asked for the check. We still had to go tell Derek about the hearing, and I wanted to get back to Houston before midnight.

"I've got to argue all those issues in the brief," I said when the waiter had gone, "then show how the murder was related to his work, Zack's work, at the plant. Like in Sheila's unemployment comp case."

"We won that one," Perry said. "The work-related part should be easy."

"Doesn't mean we'll win this one."

Perry shook his head. "That arbitrator's nobody's fool. He'll never make us put Zack Mills back to work. If he does, Derek Frazier won't ... Here, let me get that." He snatched the check out of my hand and reached for his wallet.

Leaving the restaurant, Hank walked with me out to the parking lot. Perry had already headed back to the plant for our meeting with Derek.

"Dan, Perry's right," Hank said. "You don't need to worry about Layton."

I stopped behind my pool car. "Doesn't do me any good to worry ... nothing I can do about it ... What's done's done."

"No." Hank shook his head. "Derek likes you, and he despises Layton. Especially after what I've heard about that blowup Monday in Derek's office ... Layton may try writing a memo, but he'll never be able to send it anywhere—Houston, New York, anywhere outside the plant, without Derek approving it. That's the way it works here. And I can promise you that between Derek and Perry ... You heard him, didn't you? How he views what Frank Landry said?"

I nodded. "Yeah. I like his take on it." I jiggled the keys in my pocket, then pulled the keys out and looked down at them.

Hank's voice was quiet, and kind, a tone I wasn't used to hearing in this job. "Between Derek and Perry," he said, "no one in Houston or New York will ever hear a peep about ... about what Landry said ... about you and Sheila."

I looked at him. Stared into dark eyes that seemed bemused at what they saw, but also held understanding and sympathy, and I knew he had no illusions about what had happened. Not like Perry's fantasy. And he didn't care.

I stuck my hand out, and he took it. "You're a quick study," I said. "It's been a real pleasure working with you ... whatever happens."

"Same here." He grinned at me, then turned away to go to his car.

Back at the plant, we reported in to Derek. The chair by the window was empty, but I could tell that Layton Van Horn had already been there. And poisoned the well. Throughout Perry's glowing report, Derek said little, and then he eyed me coldly as I outlined the issues I had to address in the brief. The riding crop tapped steadily on the edge of his desk the entire time. As we rose to leave, he gave us only a vague wave of dismissal. By the time I was out the door, the warm glow of Hank's words had dissipated under a dark cloud of gloom.

Chapter Thirty—Life in the Rearview Mirror

LEAVING THE ADMIN BUILDING and driving down the road to the main gate, I wondered if I'd ever be back here—amid the interlaced web of steel pipes and cracking towers, the rising clouds of vapor, the belching fire and black smoke from the giant flare, the acrid smell of tar and creosote and sulfur. The waiting and watching for something to go wrong. The dull-eyed days of routine activity, day-after-day, years on end, punctuated by the inevitable cataclysm that would bring death, destruction, and injury by fire or heat or force. For all the risk, the passing days would deliver most of those working here only into internal rot or fading old age, their mornings spent weaving and tottering about the golf course.

At the main gate, I waved to the guard as I slid past and pointed my old Plymouth pool car back toward Houston. A hundred and twenty-five thousand miles it had on the odometer, most in crisscrossed straight lines, back and forth across the Texas Gulf coast. Both the car and I knew the way home, without thought or guidance or reason. A good thing, too, because my mind was elsewhere.

Crossing the Alligator Bayou Bridge, I had a despairing fear that my career was really over, done for good. Not even Liz Johnson in all her good-hearted benevolence could save me.

Then my outlook brightened a bit, and not only because of the westering sun, still white and hot in the pale sky. I didn't care that my career was over—although some things about it I would miss. Liz and

Hank Greenberg and Jim-Bob Lloyd, I sincerely liked, and I enjoyed the work when it was with them. And Perry, with his quirks and lapdog fawning over Derek—I was even fond of Perry. And Derek I didn't dislike. I had a grudging, if wary, admiration for Derek, who lived by a moral code and a set of rules that placed us in the same universe, even if we orbited different suns light-years apart.

And I liked being a lawyer. I loved it. It wasn't the money, though that was a pleasant byproduct. It was the contest of wits and words. The warp and woof of *The Law*. The thrill and excitement of battle. The fight to win. Especially the winning. Calculating, maneuvering, manipulating, and taking risks. To win.

I wanted to win this case against Zack Mills, the murderer. Like every case, but this one I wanted to win even more.

The air conditioning labored in the afternoon heat. I turned it up a notch and adjusted the vent to hit my face. We, the old car and I, had traveled beyond the green rice paddies on Highway 73 and past the Winnie cutoff, where the new Pizza Hut was aging and decaying and advancing toward its ultimate doom like every mortal and temporal thing. Like me. Like even the sun, on a cosmic scale.

The radio, my usual diversion, I'd neglected I was so deep in thought. I turned it on and found only static-tinged violins on a classical station and a stream of ads everywhere else, except for the religious networks. After listening briefly, I turned it off, leaving no distractions from the tired scenery and booming traffic on Interstate 10.

Due to a thirty-year construction project, the traffic going toward Beaumont had settled into a crawl, but going my way, to Houston, cars and pickups and semis were moving fast, much faster than the fifty-five mile-per-hour speed limit set by law to save gas, reduce oil imports, and stop the stranglehold of foreign oil—from which we the people in this state, or many of us, derived our wealth and livelihood, with no intention of ever abandoning it. Black gold.

Ever law abiding, or almost, I set my speed at fifty-nine, then paid no more attention to it, while everything but plodding RVs or eighty-year-olds in land yachts sailed past me.

Despite the Christmas tree deodorizer hanging from the mirror, the car reeked of stale cigarette smoke and mildew—worse than the hearing room in the morning. Bringing back Zack Mills' parting shot: "need to clear the air," or something like that.

Maybe it was best if I never went back to Port Oso. Or Beaumont or Port Arthur or anywhere else in the Golden Triangle. Of course, now that his criminal case had been dismissed, Zack roamed freely and widely, and he could come after me even in Houston, if he wanted to. He could seek me out anywhere.

I glanced in my rearview mirror. Coming up behind was a semi, a Confederate flag emblazoned on its grill. It was rapidly narrowing the gap and bearing down on my bumper. The windows of the cab revealed no driver, only two bright shimmering mirrors in the slanted sun.

Or maybe Zack could get a friend to help him out. Like J.C. Ledbetter.

The semi drew closer as I glanced back and forth between it and the road in front, until all I could see in the rearview mirror was the Confederate flag and two large red fenders and round headlights. On the left, and in my side mirror, was a line of cars and pickups whooshing past and hemming me in with the truck. I sped up. The colossus behind me accelerated at the same rate. I must've dropped to fifty during my wandering thoughts, but now the speedometer showed fifty-five, sixty, sixty-five, seventy, and the other vehicles were no longer passing us—but the semi was still on my bumper and I was blocked in by a Texaco tank truck in front.

We were approaching an exit, leading off to Liberty on the right. One-half mile said the sign.

I could get off the highway there, take my chances he wouldn't follow. But he might, and then we'd be on a back road, two lanes, maybe narrow with no escape. I decided to stick with the interstate.

I looked in my rearview mirror again; he was falling back, slowing. Speeding past the exit and onto the overpass, I watched in my mirrors as the big semi—only a tractor, no trailer attached—peeled off and braked down the off-ramp. He disappeared as I went over to the other side of the bridge.

I slowed to sixty-five and took a deep breath, then looked over my right shoulder to make sure he hadn't come back up the other side of the overpass. He hadn't. But the rest of the way to Houston, I kept watching in my mirrors for the big grill with the Confederate flag.

I knew, at least after I'd slowed down to fifty-nine and returned to my senses, that the driver of the semi-tractor hadn't been a friend of Zack's. No one could engineer something like that to look like an accident—force me off the road or whatever, here on a busy interstate highway. No, they'd wait until a dark night, on a back road. Or they'd make it look like a botched robbery in a downtown parking garage.

How stupid, I thought. I was being paranoid. Irrational. Was I going to spend the rest of my life looking over my shoulder, checking all the cars around me before I parked, keeping a .38 by my bed?

Really now. I wasn't especially afraid that Zack would try something ... but you never knew. He was probably looking over his own shoulder, watching for George Graham or one of Billy's friends or relatives to do justice to him.

Still, if he hadn't known about Sheila and me before, he certainly did now, after today. And he'd kill for her in a New York minute. He had killed Billy Graham because of her—and she helped him do it.

What was it Sheila told me on our first dinner date together? Zack had been charged with something in a hunting accident. I wondered if that was the consequence of another of Sheila's outside activities. Why did she take up with these other men—Billy Graham ... me? Was she trying to get Zack's attention, make him kill for her? What was it between them?

Had she cared anything at all for Graham? And what about me?

It was like one of those comic-strip light bulbs coming on in my head, or an alarm clock jolting me awake. An eighteen-wheeler, this one sleek and black with a long trailer behind it, blasted its horn and zoomed past. I had slowed down to forty-five while I was thinking, and I had to gun the engine to avoid being run over by a sluggish Lincoln Towncar pulling a silver Airstream trailer. But the realization of what was true remained stuck in my mind.

Sheila had been using me all along.

Okay, I'd always suspected she was using me, and buried it deep in my subconscious, but I knew for sure after Pleasure Island. What I'd just figured out was that she'd done it for Zack. All for Zack. Or for her and Zack to stay together.

On Pleasure Island, she had told me the truth. She would stick with him no matter how many men he killed. And he *would kill* for her.

My God, what a twisted relationship.

She was protecting Zack—maybe herself, as well—but protecting Zack in everything she did. Even in her confession.

Had Zack known what was going on when she set out to seduce me? Use me? He damn well knew now. So, what would he do—now?

Had it been worth it, for me? Even if *I* meant nothing to her? I sighed and gripped the steering wheel tighter. Did she mean anything to me, now, in the end?

Remembering what I had considered the too-short nights with her, and thinking about them—her smooth, taut body, her fingers clawing at my back, panting against my neck, urging me on—I decided it was worth it, every minute of it. Whatever the consequences.

I was moving with the traffic now, trying to pay attention to my driving on the narrow bridge high above the Trinity River. In the distance, I could see the silvery waters of the Old and Lost Rivers spreading out to the Gulf of Mexico and the first jagged lines of

Houston faintly marking the horizon, and not too far above it, a dull yellow sun cushioned by feathery clouds. The flow of cars and trucks of which I was a part had gathered into a surging flume from which they would gush out, into and around the city, that massive obstacle of concrete, steel, and glass piled high by human hands on the green coastal plain.

Could I, I was wondering, place myself in her shoes? A woman's high heels or flats? Probably not. But in Zack's shoes? I could understand Zack's emotion, the anger, the bitterness, the feelings of betrayal and mistrust. I'd been there and felt that. But I couldn't understand his actions: the planning, the tracking, the trapping, the killing.

And Sheila. What would happen to her now? Living with Zack, both of them still faced with the threat of prosecution and under the cloud of legal action by Graham's relatives. Of vengeance. And the house she and Zack had built and moved into. After clearing the air between them.

Of all the women I'd known, none had ever seemed so loyal to anyone as Sheila. Not to me. To Zack. She would lie, cheat, and condone murder to protect her mate. And snuggle up with any old company lawyer, even if she loathed him, to save Zack. Or maybe she didn't loathe me and that part of it she enjoyed. I'd never know.

There was no line she would *not* cross to keep him safe. That's what she had told me. Goddamn me and my blind stupidity.

Was that the meaning of love: that she would stick by Zack no matter what? I shook my head and speeded up again, passing a truck that had just passed me. There had to be something about Zack she wouldn't tolerate. I couldn't imagine how the two dealt with each other. What did they talk about? Could they even fuck without their crime perching on the headboard above them on their conjugal bed? Did Zack ever forget Billy Graham's dead body, the wounds and the blood when he took the wallet from Billy's pocket? Did she?

I wondered if there was anything, anything at all, that could ever make them divorce—and make Sheila a witness against him. Would they stay together, through sickness and health, until death only do they part? Prisoners of each other against the world. A marriage made in hell.

Why do men and women *ever* stay together? After the initial attraction of sex, and of companionship and they grow old and their relationship perhaps becomes boring and banal, and after the ephemeral promise of something called "romance" fades to nothing? Why do we stay together?

Sheila was sticking with Zack, and Zack was sticking with Sheila. Was that kind of loyalty—that emotion, that connection—was that what preserved the species? Protect the mate, the children, the family. At all costs. Maybe even the tribe, but always the family and the mate first. Use whatever device, deception, trick, or weapon. Isn't that how the human race survived? Isn't that what the Ranger said? Twist whatever truth, morality, and reality to fit that end?

"The Law" was just a thin patina of regulation over the instinctive hard core of human nature. A frail web holding together the larger society, a porous sponge buffering individuals and families and cliques struggling against each other.

Then there was Dana and me. The doppelganger lurking in the shadows behind and just beyond my thoughts of Sheila and Zack Mills. What would Dana think of all this? Could she, would she have done what Sheila did for Zack?

No, I didn't think so. She had moral standards and ethical principles she would neither violate nor bend for me or anyone else. Or had she? She was a woman, and I had decided that I didn't know anything at all about women. Like the Ranger—who, for all his rant about Eve, probably knew and understood even less than I did.

But why had Dana gotten involved with that jerk? Familiarity should breed contempt, not sex. But I knew better, and I knew it had, or so it seemed.

Or maybe it hadn't. Yet she had been involved with him in some way, caring for him, kissing him like that at the Christmas party. And the counseling had been about telling me something I didn't want to hear, trying to get me to understand something about who she was and what she wanted. A plea of some kind. Well, that was over, whatever it was she had with the jerk. He divorced his wife, abandoned his child, and absconded to Mexico with the few hundred dollars his string ensemble entrusted to him. Whatever feeling—sympathy, love, passion—she may have had for him would have vanished into the nether reaches of space. I knew that much about her. Dana would be appalled, disgusted, no matter what she'd felt for him.

Another thought struck me like a bolt of lightning. What if he hadn't been a jerk, but a nice guy, a decent human being? How would she have handled that one? Where would that twist have left me? But then, of course, a truly decent man wouldn't have abandoned his sick wife and his kid and fled to Mexico.

My stomach was in knots, my eyes burning from the sun, now a bright red disk, halved by the horizon. Then it was gone, leaving only a brilliant halo to dim slowly into twilight. It was a beautiful sunset—rose clouds fading into grays with swatches of blue, like a crumpled blanket spread out over the uneven battlements of the city and its long shadows on the dappled plain. With the final dissolution of red and gold into deepening hues of gray, a calming sadness spread over me.

In the end it wasn't about Sheila or Zack or Dana. It was about me. How I reacted and what I did and said. Other people—no matter how close they came to my orbit—what *they* did and said I couldn't control, even if I understood some modicum of truth about them. And I understood something about Sheila and Zack and their relationship. And maybe, if I thought about it and reasoned about it enough, I could understand what had happened with Dana and me and how we had ended up where we were.

She was frustrated with her life, her work, while I was absorbed in my own work, and myself. And Susan leaving—her only child gone and the house empty except for me, and me only some of the time. She had been seeking something more than what she had, to find herself and who she was, to be young again, perhaps. Maybe she had made a mistake, and realized it and tried to tell me. Or maybe I was the one who had made a mistake ... was mistaken.

I certainly couldn't change the past, and I couldn't change her, but I could do something about myself. I could learn how to forgive, and maybe I needed to take a lesson from Sheila—though not from how she acted. A lesson of loyalty. Or was it love? Could I be as loyal to Dana as Sheila was to Zack? Love Dana as much as Sheila seemed to love Zack?

No. Participating in murder and lying and deceiving everyone around me I couldn't do. But I could do better than I had done.

Again, the question—why do men and women stay together, year after year? Despite the conflicts, the self-absorption, the dueling egos? It must be based on some deep, deep mutual need. Or perhaps just the comfort of routine, or a presence, like an old hat or a pair of comfortable old shoes. Or was it a fierce instinctive loyalty, one for the other, that seeds and gestates and grows and matures until the two of us are eternally linked. Or mortally linked? Maybe that's love. One more thing in life I didn't understand.

I swung the car off the freeway and up an exit ramp. I was going home now and leaving Zack and Sheila, and my work, far behind me. Leaving all that in a separate compartment in my mind. Leaving behind the doubts and worries and fears. I was going home to another contest. Another struggle. A quest. A quest to win Dana back. And I intended to do it. Whatever sacrifices I had to make.

Part V

Chapter Thirty-one—More Than Time Passes

THE END OF OCTOBER, HALLOWEEN to be exact, and there I was again on my way to Port Oso. I still had a job, but this trip wasn't going to be any more enjoyable than the last one.

The day before, six in the morning, I had run into Liz Johnson, getting on the elevator in our Houston offices. The elevator was half full, everyone in a daze with their eyes straight ahead. Standing next to Liz, I touched her arm.

"Congratulations," I said close to her ear. She'd just been promoted to General Manager of Public Relations. In New York. The press release had hit my desk the previous day, but I hadn't had a chance to call her.

She turned slightly and grimaced at me. "Thanks … You going over to Port Oso this week?"

"Yeah, later in the week. I've got a couple of things to deal with and the Ledbetter arbitration's next week."

The door opened at her floor. "Come talk to me a moment, will you?" She grabbed my arm and pulled me off the elevator before I could answer. But I always had time for Liz. Well, usually. Today it was mostly her talking to me.

"That promotion," she said, starting down the hall, me close by her side and her looking sideways at me, still holding my arm, "I'm being kicked upstairs. A female-friendly position in PR. Shits didn't even make me a VP and I'll still be reporting to Dawson. That fucker, he's the one who's good at PR … Zigged and zagged all over the fucking place during the strike." She swung to the right and then the left, hitting me in the leg with her briefcase. "First hardnosed as hell *and* belligerent, then neurotic and conciliatory." She turned into her office and I followed. Her secretary was already at her desk and biting into a croissant.

"Linda, any messages?" Liz asked.

"Couple by your phone," Linda said, swallowing fast. "Can I get you some coffee, Liz? And you, Mr. Esperson?"

"No, thanks," Liz said. "We can get our own." She swept into her office and dropped her briefcase on the floor by her desk. I followed her in and placed my briefcase in a chair, then stood beside it and watched her fume as she stripped off her suit coat and carried it past me to the door.

"He turned tail and ran from making any of the hard decisions." She jerked a hanger off the back of the door and hung her coat on it. "Naturally, he's been promoted. Anointed, I should say ... Senior Vice President over both HR and PR ... I still have to report to the bastard." She went back to her desk and picked up the pink message slips, more than a couple, then dropped them after a quick glance and looked at me for the first time since we'd reached her office.

"I make the tough decisions and he receives the credit." She shook her index finger at me. "I was the one for staying the course and settling the strike without reinstating that shit who took a shot at Layton Van Horn ... I'm the one who said we'd only agree to arbitrate." She tapped her chest with her finger, no nail polish today. "I'm the one ... Well, that's fine with me ... There are still a few people around here who know the difference between beefsteak and bullshit ... Right, Dan?" She smiled at me, and I smiled back.

"Right, Liz."

"I'll tell you one damn thing, I'm gonna outlast the bastard, professionally and biologically." She jerked her chair out from the desk and sat down. "You heard anything from the arbitrator on the Mills' case?"

"Not a thing." I didn't know if that was good or bad. The briefs had gone in on time. Mine was over forty pages and the union's less than ten, but I knew the weight of the paper never determined the outcome. Except for my waiting on the award, Zack and Sheila seemed to have moved on, out of my life.

"I'm sorry to unload on you, Dan ... I just heard about Dawson's promotion, and I'm on a slow burn." More like a short fuse, I thought. "You like some coffee?" She bounced up again and started past me.

"Sure," I said and trailed after her, across the hall to a coffee bar, where we poured a dark substance of unknown composition out of a glass beaker.

"Would you mind going with me to meet with Perry ... tomorrow?" she said, as I mixed a white powder into my corporate coffee. "We're giving the union their sixty-day notice in the afternoon. Almost a third of their people are out the door and I don't want any fuck-ups."

"Perry should be able to handle it," I said. "He's an old hand." We started back across the hall.

"Not at this. He's never been through a layoff this big, and we're offering the hourly people a voluntary plan first. I want it done right and I don't want any confusion. Most of all, I don't want a wildcat strike."

"It would violate the contract. We could go to court to stop it."

"Be a lot better if we didn't have any more fights like that." She closed her office door behind us and we both sat down with our coffee. "You say the arbitration on J.C. Ledbetter's discharge is next week?"

"Next Monday. I don't know how I got stuck with a Monday. Have to prepare most of the witnesses this week and Van Horn's coming in on Sunday."

"It'll be my last visit to the plant ... in this job." She sipped at her coffee, eyeing me for a few seconds, then said, "You ought to know,

Hank Greenberg's coming to Houston. He'll be the new benefits supervisor. It's a nice promotion for him—thanks to Perry and a few good words from you."

"Hey, that's great," I said. "He's sharp." And he knows when to keep his mouth shut, I told myself.

There were a lot of changes taking place now. The one I liked best was the departure of Layton Van Horn. Within days of Zack Mills' arbitration, Layton had been transferred to the Bayonne Terminal. Assistant manager of something or other. Not quite Siberia, but any threat he posed to me had gone with him to Bayonne, which, despite the geography, was about as far away from New York as you could get in this company.

"He'll be working for Al," Liz said, still talking about Hank. Albert Boyd was her successor. "He's not a bad guy and Hank can help you deal with him."

What Liz didn't say, and probably wouldn't, since she liked Albert almost as much as she liked me, was that Albert had gotten the job by golfing and backslapping his way through the good ol' boy network.

"Okay," I said, as she started looking through her phone slips, "I'll meet you at Perry's office. What time?"

"Eleven ... I've got things to do here."

"Eleven's fine, but I may go over earlier; I want another shot at Derek ... on the supervisors." I grimaced; the coffee or something was giving me heartburn. Even with Layton gone, Derek was still following the original plans, Layton's plans, to lay off almost all the black foremen. Derek needed convincing, and it would take both Perry and me to do it.

"I'll help if I can, but on those selections," Liz shook her head, "it's his ballgame."

"I've been talking with Perry on how to handle it ... Does Derek know you're coming over?"

"No, and don't tell him. He might call Dawson to stop me. He doesn't want Houston involved in the layoffs—or in Perry telling the union."

"Ah, the might of a plant manager."

"How are you and Dana doing?" Liz picked up one of pink message slips.

"Great," I said, "Just great." My signal to leave.

IT HADN'T been easy, but after my last trip to Port Oso—the one for Zack Mills' arbitration—I managed to get Dana to meet me for dinner, once then twice, and one thing led to another, and after one of those dinners, we found ourselves back in the big marital bed at our home for the first time in almost a year. Over one long rainy weekend, I helped her clear out her apartment and move back home, and now I was trying to adjust to the new life she had made for herself: not going to work in a law office anymore but practicing her violin at home, five hours a day, almost every day—preparing for auditions, then playing nights with a community orchestra or a quartet she'd joined. But I guessed she was having to adjust to me, too. It was a good thing I had my own life—all of it at work except for an occasional trip to the gym or to church on Sundays—and I'd honed my cooking skills over the last few months. Fortunately, I'd found a good maid service, better than the once-a-week, out-in-a-jiffy gang we had before.

There was no discussion about what had happened—with her and Tim Oakes or between the two of us. Or about Sheila. There were no questions, no answers. No clearing the air. I had come to understand that life is filled with ambiguities, and that our relationship, the connection between us, the love—if that's what it was—was more important than almost anything outside our little two-person cocoon. I couldn't change Dana; I couldn't rewrite the past; but I could change myself and how I reacted to the world around me. By doing that, I could redirect the future. Or my future.

Our future. That all seemed so obvious now. But maybe it wasn't that easy to do.

All this, and more, I went over in my mind on the drive down I-10 and past the rice paddies on highway 73 to Port Oso. It was another warm fall day and the night would bring out trick-or-treaters by the scores in our neighborhood. I wouldn't be home, but Dana would—handing out candy, laughing and oohing and aahing over the costumes and congratulating the kids or their parents on how great they looked, as she'd done every year since Susan was small. I wished I could be there. Crossing the Alligator Bayou bridge to confront the bleak prospects of layoffs and J.C. Ledbetter's arbitration, I felt a warm glow of contentment, if not outright happiness. More than at any time in months.

The greeting I received from Perry only served to make me happier.

"Dan, we did it," he shouted. Waving a stapled sheaf of papers, he came charging out of his office, into the anteroom, as if he had been watching for me.

"We won. We won." Seizing my arm, he danced a small circle around me.

Dropping my briefcase onto a chair, I stood and grinned at him as he did his dance, his marble bust of a head and fringe of white hair, bobbing and bouncing. I knew he had the arbitration award.

"Let me see that," I said and reached for the document as he went past.

"We need to go tell Derek." He started out the door, but I managed to grab the award from him before he made it into the hallway. I flipped to the last page. "All grievances are denied" appeared right above the arbitrator's signature.

"Just give me a second to read this, will you?" But Perry was already down the hall, so I followed him, skimming the award as I went.

Chapter Thirty-two—Derek

"GOOD WORK, DAN."

Derek had only glanced at the last page after Perry handed him the award. We remained standing in front of the desk.

"I never doubted the result," Derek added. Giving me a thin, fleeting smile, he tossed the award back across his desk to Perry.

"Yes sir," Perry said, "I always knew Dan could do it." He patted me on the arm and ended with a friendly squeeze. Then uninvited, he took one of the leather chairs facing the desk and gave me a push toward the other one.

"There's something else—"

"Only way it could've come out," Derek said and snatched up his riding crop as if he were afraid of losing it. "An arbitrator would have to be crazy to do anything else." He smacked the palm of his hand with the riding crop.

I knew better than to disagree. "Yeah," I said, settling into the chair beside Perry, "good thing we got a sane one."

The chair by the window was empty. The new assistant manager was out in the plant with Hank, getting a facility tour. I glanced at Perry, expecting him to raise the issue I'd asked him to bring up with Derek.

"We still have a problem," Perry said. "Security called not ten minutes ago. They saw Zack Mills coming in the contractors' gate over on the west side this morning."

"What!" Derek's riding crop stopped in midair. Surprised, I

forgot about the layoffs for the moment. I didn't say anything, but I was paying close attention.

"Autry checked it out, he ... he went over and talked to the contractor's rep." Jack Autry was the head of security. "They had to make a few calls. Zack's doing welding on new construction over there."

"You mean he's working in the plant?" Derek asked. The riding crop hadn't moved.

"For a subcontractor—Belleau Brothers, he said."

"Tell 'em to fire his ass. I don't want him anywhere near this place."

"I wouldn't tell 'em to fire him, Mr. Frazier." I hurried up at Derek's ominous scowl. "He's working for them and it's up to them to decide who they employ. They have a lot of business up and down the coast here, and—"

"I sure as hell don't have to put up with him in *my* plant. I'll kick the damn Belleau Brothers out of here first." Derek was forward in his chair, leaning with his elbows on his desk, and still glaring at me. Which made me think he'd kick me out along with the Belleau Brothers.

"You can't do that," Perry said. "They're too big and—"

"You don't have to," I said. "Just tell 'em Zack Mills isn't allowed on our property. That way you haven't interfered with anybody's contract, and they can work him anywhere else they want, just not here."

"Hmm," Derek said and settled back in the chair. He began tapping his palm with the riding crop. Slowly. A good sign.

"Makes sense," he said finally, "even if it is all lawyer mumbo-jumbo ... So do it, Perry." He looked from Perry back to me. "Why can't you come up with a way to keep J.C. Ledbetter out of here ... that easily?" His eyes were narrowed and I could tell he was needling me. But he *was* irritated.

"You can after we win the arbitration."

"Layton coming back to testify?"

"Yes sir," Perry said. "It was his car—"

"Bet you aren't looking forward to that, Esperson." Derek's eyes had shifted to me again, and he gave me a slight smile.

I shrugged. "Part of my job."

"We expect you to win that one, too." To my surprise, his smile became almost ingratiating. "You will, won't you Dan?" Before I could answer, his face grew stern again. "It's a no-brainer. Shooting ball bearings at an assistant plant manager ... even if he was a shit. My God, we had one manager gunned down, and with the layoffs coming up, there may be people gunning for me." He tapped his desk above the center drawer. "I won't be that easy ... anybody wants to try it."

I listened, keeping my face impassive. Perry had told me the first time I came over here that Derek kept a .38 in his desk drawer. He was certainly better prepared for an adversary than I was. I wondered if he carried it with him out in the plant, and outside the plant ... if he was always checking behind him, ready for an attack. Then again, I'd never seen Derek out of his office more than once or twice, and never coming or going through the gate. During the strike I'd started to wonder if he slept here.

Perry was nodding his head, obsequious as ever. I was waiting for him to launch into the reason I was here today, but he didn't get the chance. Derek seemed driven to talk by some bottled-up anxieties. He'd always been guarded in his speech when Layton was perched by the window. That was it, I thought. He had to watch his back with Layton. The all-powerful plant manager wasn't as invincible as he seemed.

"What day did you say the Ledbetter arbitration is?" he asked Perry.

"Next Monday, Mr. Frazier. Dan's going to stay over and review the videotapes from the gate and talk with the security people tomorrow."

Derek waved the tip of the riding crop at me. "I don't want that man back in this plant ... no more than Zack Mills. Those two are just alike. Two peas in a pod ... I've seen 'em together."

"That's right," Perry said. "Asshole buddies ... go huntin' and fishin' together all the time. Sheila said the four of 'em, J.C.'s wife and her, too, used to go out to their deer lease, go shootin' out there—even when it wasn't season. You know, Dan," he turned toward me, "they went out there together right after Billy Graham was killed. Remember ... she said that on the tape."

"That's right."

Derek was still, his brow furrowed as he examined the riding crop balanced between his two hands in the crooks of his thumbs. Lowering it, he asked, "Whatever happened to Sheila?" He was pointedly looking at Perry and not me. "She still living with that murdering so and so?"

"Far as I know," said Perry. "Saw her last week over at the K-Mart. She was working one of the check-out counters."

K-Mart? That's one place I won't be going, I thought.

Derek shook his head. "A sad case, that woman. For the life of me, I'll never understand how she got involved in all that. Always thought she had a good head on her shoulders, a really fine secretary. Didn't you, Perry?"

"Yes sir," Perry said. Derek still wasn't looking at me.

"Professional, neat and tidy in her appearance, and always friendly to everyone," Derek said. "And nice looking, too." He glanced at me, and I looked away, over at Perry, who was nodding enthusiastically. Perry started to say something, but Derek still had more on his mind.

"But George Graham told me she was some sort of witch ... a sorceress, he called her. Claims she cast a spell on his brother. Couldn't understand why a good family man like Billy would get himself tied up with a white woman like that, and get himself shot."

"Nobody understands it, boss," Perry said.

I was feeling hot and flushed. My face must have been as red as my tie. I wanted to get off this subject before it got personal to me.

"What did you finally decide on George Graham?" I asked. "Is there a foreman's job for him?"

Perry had told me that Layton lost the battle on laying off George, but I didn't know what Derek had planned for him, and this would let me segue into the subject I wanted to talk about.

"George will be just fine," said Derek, hitting his palm with the riding crop.

"There could be some resentment," Perry said. He was giving me a worried look, so I gathered this echoed a conversation the two had before I arrived.

"We'll pull him out of the plant for a while," Derek said, "make sure he gets the training he needs." He pointed the riding crop toward the closed door and the outer office where his secretary sat. There was an empty desk there, kitty-cornered to hers. "He's going to work as my assistant for six months, then we'll put him back out in the field."

"I helped him map out a career path," Perry said, nodding his head.

"He actually thinks he can have my job someday." Derek laughed. "Even go to New York, be a vice president or something." He was grinning in delight, whether at having set this subversive plot in motion or at the ludicrousness he saw in George's expectations—I couldn't tell which. But I could see why he never grinned. His teeth were all there, but they were stained and crooked. I figured he hadn't come to this office by birth or money.

"I think you're doing the right thing, Derek ... sir." And I did, even though I felt his motives were a little off.

Because of Billy's murder and George's direct appeals to him, Derek had taken on George as his personal responsibility, almost like a pet or foster child, or a project to be developed like a new refinery system. But I knew it was more than Derek becoming his mentor, and I suspected that the demands and expectations would prove a heavy burden for George Graham. I just hoped he could survive Derek's assistance. If he did, he might lead the way for others in this Byzantine corporate empire—which was my main concern at the moment.

"Derek ... Mr. Frazier," I said, "there are only eight black foremen in the refinery. Saving one isn't enough to keep us from having legal problems."

"Either in court or with the OFCCP," Perry said, right on cue.

"Layton assured me the rankings were based on performance." Derek no longer looked so pleased. His riding crop was still.

"I wouldn't trust Layton's evaluations," Perry said, shaking his head. "All the blacks are flat at the bottom of the list."

"Your rating system may be validated," I said, "but in the end, it's still subjective."

"And every one of the rate-*ers* is white," Perry added, leaning forward in his chair. "And most of 'em worked for Layton in Operations." He was following the script I'd given him.

"Blacks haven't been out of the labor gang all that long, Dan," Derek said, his brow knitted. He shook his head slowly. "We can't fix a problem like that in a day, no matter how it came about."

"Based on the spreadsheets Perry sent me," I said, "you'll be laying off roughly ninety percent of your black foremen and other supervisors versus twenty percent of whites in the same positions. They can't go back to union jobs, not with their breaks in seniority ... so they're all out the door."

I explained how a lawsuit using statistics would work, either for a group of discrimination plaintiffs or in a class action. Derek listened closely, his riding crop resting loosely in his hand. An engineer by background, anything dealing with numbers and probability was a language he understood.

"But, Dan," he said when I finished, "I can't take jobs away from white foremen just to make the numbers right. Those men are doing a good job," he was shaking his head at me, "and they have far more years of experience. I can't lay them off and keep blacks, who I honestly and truly believe are not as good—even if they're not *bad* performers, and they're doing okay, and they might even get better over the years ... You know what I mean?"

I knew what he meant. He was as much a prisoner of history and social custom as the black workers were victims of a system that not only separated them from whites, but also degraded them as individuals and denied them, or most of them, the education and environment that would allow them to succeed in a white world.

Leaning forward on his desk, Derek gripped the riding crop with both hands flat on the blotter, his eyes fixed on me, his face screwed up in a pained expression. I felt like he was sincere in his feelings and deeply troubled by this quandary. But I had a solution—if he was willing to make a leap of faith and break free of our shared history and corporate culture.

"Why don't you keep a few more black supervisors on the payroll—like supernumeraries, redshirt 'em or something?" I asked "Make your layoff list a little shorter. Do it in the name of affirmative action, diversity ... community relations, whatever you want to call it."

"We ... we can't do that," Perry said from beside me.

I glanced over at him. His head and shoulders were swaying, his feet moving under his chair. He had told me yesterday he didn't agree with this; my proposition didn't fit into the company's plans or in any playbook he'd ever seen.

"H-Houston has given you ... us the numbers we ... we have to get ... get rid ... reduce," he said, his words close to a stammer. "How many we can keep and all ... We can't just up and say we're gonna add a half-dozen bodies. They ... they're not in the budget. We can't—"

"The hell I can't," Derek said. The riding crop smacked the desk with a "thwack." "I sure as hell can."

Both Perry and I stared at him. Perry had reacted like I thought he would—and the result was as predictable as bluebonnets in the spring.

"This is *my* plant, and I can *make* it work. Don't you worry about the budget." Still leaning forward, Derek paused and frowned at Perry, then at me, then back to Perry. "No one's going to tell me ... not here, not over in Houston ... how to run my plant. They can move me, they can fire me, but as long as I'm here, I make the personnel decisions." The emperor, having made his pronouncement, sat back in his chair with the scepter resting in his hands.

"I can talk with Liz Johnson," I said quickly. It was time to cement the deal. "She'll support keeping more African-Americans up as supervisors." But Liz had told me there was a condition. "It might not hurt, though," I said, giving Perry a sideways look, "if you also found a female promotion somewhere."

"We ... we don't have any w-women in the pi-pipeline to ... to be su-su-supervisors," Perry said, a note of despair in his voice.

Derek was grinning at me. "I'll have one up in a line position in about six months. Miss Johnson's already mentioned it to me—four or five times. But you tell her she'll have to get me a good replacement. A Chem-E. Some reason they don't like transferring down here to the Golden Triangle."

"She has a few more weeks before she leaves for New York," I said. Derek was looking at his watch.

"I've got another meeting." He jumped up from his chair, and we quickly followed. "Perry, have you taken care of that Jarvis fellow?"

"Yes, sir," Perry said. He was finally back in his comfort zone. "Told the union this morning. Hank'll give him the letter at shift change and have him clean out his locker." Perry looked at me and shrugged. "The man's missed half the days since the strike and the doc says it's not job-related."

"I knew he was in the program," I said, referring to the absentee-control program. "But it's just one more fight. We'll have to arbitrate it."

"You'll handle it for us, I'm sure," Derek said and came around the desk. He held out his hand to me. I was so surprised I hesitated before I took it.

"Dan," he said, squeezing my hand and shaking it slowly. He nodded, his nose a good five inches from mine, and looked me squarely in the eyes. "We appreciate all you've done for us ... That was a fine win on the Mills thing."

I knew then that whatever Layton Van Horn had told him, Hank was right. Nothing about Sheila and me would ever leave the plant. So, I was safe from my own foibles, so long as Liz Johnson kept quiet, and I knew she would.

"Thank you, sir." I nodded and smiled back, feeling more than a little flustered, and grateful. "I'll talk with Ms. Johnson tonight ... at dinner ... about the supervisors." Uh, oh. I'd blown Liz's surprise visit.

Derek's hand was gnarled and bony, and I thought of the contrast with Mary Albright's as I wondered when he was going to let go.

He did and tapped me on the shoulder with the riding crop, like I was being knighted. "I know she's coming over to meet with Perry," he said and tapped me again. "Not much goes on in this place I don't know about."

He looked past me and I could've sworn he winked at Perry.

Chapter Thirty-three—Paths Crossed

FRANK LANDRY AND THE WORKERS' Committee were stunned by the size of the layoffs, Perry said. Almost one-third of their members. They knew it was coming, but not anything this big. When Perry briefed us, he looked weary, saddened, not his usual ebullient self.

Before the meeting with the union, Perry, Liz, and I had met in Perry's office to go over the layoff plans. It was nearly lunchtime, so Perry's secretary ordered in sandwiches. We sat around the small conference table, sandwich wrappers and canned soft drinks interspersed with pages from a notebook Liz's staff had assembled: timelines, Q&A's, talking points, a press release. For the first time ever, the company was offering the union a voluntary separation plan, with the level of benefits based on years of service to induce some older workers to take early retirement and save jobs for those further down the seniority pecking order.

Perry listened attentively and answered Liz's questions quietly and succinctly, as she walked him through what he could tell the union. Her basic point: stick to the script. There were no quips or sidetracks and none of the exuberance Perry usually displayed before going into battle with Frank Landry and the Committee. His mood was more like he was headed to the funeral of a long-time friend. And in a way, he was. I knew he would miss the old days—sparring with Landry, each testing the other's limits. In the end, they were wary companions, if not friends, and they had grown old together in this place. They had studied each other, and they understood each other, probably better than most married people did. Certainly, better than Dana and I did.

As Liz talked, and Perry nodded his reluctant agreement, I was remembering what he'd once told me: he had started in the union, even been on the Committee—a vice chairman and strike leader, like Pete Reneau. And like Perry, Pete Reneau would be promoted to supervisor by the end of the year—after the dust settled from the strike and the layoff notice. Reneau was smart and aggressive, and management preferred him on their side. He could turn it down, but he wouldn't. It meant more money and status and an opportunity for further advancement. His stripes will change so fast, he'll be my good friend by this time next year, I was thinking as the buzzer on Perry's phone sounded.

"I need to get this," he said to Liz. He hurried behind his desk and picked up the receiver. For his secretary to use the buzzer when he was in a meeting, it had to be an emergency. The whistle had sounded; a short blast for noon, not the long wail for the fire teams. Through the window beyond his shoulder, I could see gray piping and a couple of towers and the usual clouds of white steam against the blue sky. No stray puffs or trails of black smoke or glow of fire. Not even the flare was going today.

Perry listened to the voice on the phone and his face grew redder and redder. "What the devil!" he shouted.

"What's going on?" Liz asked.

Perry shook his head and held up a hand. "Hold on a moment," he said, finally, and covered the mouthpiece with his palm. "Gene Jarvis is at the infirmary. He fell down the steps from the maintenance trailer. Hurt his shoulder."

"He the one you're firing today?" Liz said. "The malingerer?"

"We were ... wait." He uncovered the mouthpiece and held up his hand. I could hear a voice still coming over the receiver. After a minute, he pressed the phone against his stomach. "Another industrial accident, dammit. What do we do? Wait til he comes back to work?"

"Hell no!" Liz said, waving an index finger back and forth in front of her.

"Can he walk?" I asked.

Perry talked to the man on the other end, probably a general foreman, then inverted the mouthpiece over his head. "They just put his arm in a sling. Doc says it's a sprained wrist. He's on his way out, headed up to his locker."

Liz and I looked at each other. That was where Hank would be waiting with the discharge letter.

"You don't have a problem, right Dan?" Liz said, telling me I better not.

"Well ... only that now we'll have a lawsuit—for retaliation, as well as an arbitration. But we'd probably had one anyway."

"I'll take the risk," Liz said.

"Hank's already out there with the letter," I said, "so we might win, even with a Beaumont jury."

"That's why we have you and your friend Jim-Bob." Liz gave me a smile that was too wide to be sincere.

"We told the union first thing this morning," Perry said. "I bet they told him, damn their hides."

"Well, *you* can tell Hank to go ahead," Liz said. "And tell that fucking Landry whatever he was trying to pull didn't work."

I was going to miss Liz. She always said what she thought. But she turned me down for dinner. She left right after Perry briefed us on his meeting with the union. She wasn't going to spend one more minute than she had to "in this fucking hole, Golden Triangle or not." And spend the night in a roach-infested motel? You had to be kidding.

Perry begged off for dinner, as well. Instead, Hank Greenberg and I ended up sharing a nice meal at Caprice's in Beaumont. A pleasant evening with pleasant company, which I enjoyed immensely—once Sheila's ghost stopped staring at me in the mirror beyond Hank's shoulder.

Crossing the highway bridge coming into Port Arthur—the

refineries blanketing the land before me—I was thinking of Dana, of calling her, telling her how much I missed her. The dash clock showed 10:40pm. She would be home from rehearsal by now and getting ready for bed.

With no other vehicles behind me on the bridge, I slowed the car so I could take in the panorama, from east to west, all the way to the Gulf of Mexico, a landscape like an inchoate pointillist painting—a Rorschach test of light and dark for those crossing the River Styx. Aided by most of a bottle of red wine, I tried to discern in that ragged tableau what the future held, as if it were hidden in the twinkling lights and belching flares, the billowing steam and roiling black smoke—all of it soon to be subsumed in an opaque fog rolling in off the Gulf. Red lights blinked from the highest towers to warn off any who might stray near.

I would stick it out for a while longer. See how things went with us, Dana and me. Maybe I'd leave this job in a few years—if they'd give me a separation package like the one at the refinery, buy-outs to get older employees to leave without drawing a ton of lawsuits. If they'll pay me to leave, I'll go gladly, I decided as I came off the bridge and the refinery lights faded from view.

My mouth was dry and my stomach hurting. It had started after Dana left and gotten worse during the strike. It seemed these days that I travelled with a bottle of Maalox in my briefcase. Better that than seeing doctors.

In front of me, the highway curved for a short distance above shrouded suburbs before dipping down among pecans and live oaks shading the small neighborhoods. In the lowering sky beyond the trees and houses was the steady glow of the refineries, and at the center, throbbing and angry, the reflection of a giant flare, the heartbeat of this place, a living presence bigger and mightier than all the human flesh it sustained—or threatened to devour.

I needed something for my stomach, a Coke, a Sprite, anything fizzy, and I didn't have change for the machines at the motel. Rather than go hunt for the desk clerk when I got there, I swung off the highway and down an unfamiliar exit several miles before my usual way to the Sands—and went searching for a convenience store.

Not more than two blocks off the highway, I found a 7-Eleven that was still lit up. Next door was a self-serve car wash with lights on all around it and a pickup truck in one of the bays.

Turning off the street and crossing the parking lot of the 7-Eleven to reach a space by the front door, I didn't notice the Oldsmobile Cutlass at the gas pumps. Oh, I saw a car there, but it didn't register until I started to open the door to go inside and found Sheila Mills facing me on the other side of the glass. I backed up and held the door open for her.

"Hey, Dan. What ya doin' out here? Not your usual stompin' grounds, is it? And this late?"

She was carrying her wallet in one hand and in the other a small paper sack with two longneck beers nestled up against her body. Her straw yellow hair was pulled back from her face and ears and was clipped with a barrette at the back of her head. Her clothes were what I'd expect her to wear for yard work or hiking in the woods: a hooded sweatshirt, dark gray, the hood down, and blue jeans tucked into worn leather boots. Her cheeks were flushed and she looked nice, very nice, alluring as ever.

"It is late, isn't it?" I looked at my watch. "Good thing they haven't closed yet." I gestured at the door.

Slipping the wallet into the pocket of her sweatshirt, she glanced to one side, then the other. Holding the paper bag cradled in the crook of her arm against her chest, she grabbed my arm and pulled me away from the entrance and over toward the ice machine, into the shadows. I was surprised, but I didn't resist going with her. When she stopped, we were so close that her hand and the bag with the longnecks pressed up against my shirt. A set of keys dangling from her fingers made an uncomfortable indentation in my stomach, but I ignored it.

"You've made my life difficult," she said, her voice level, her eyes narrowed and fixed on mine. No hint of a smile.

"Sheila, I did my job."

My back was to the entrance and the inside lights, and her face was only a couple of inches away from mine. I could see her pupils, small dots within luminous irises surrounded by white sclera, darting back and forth at me.

"I saved your butt ... Do you know that?" She spoke in a hoarse whisper, a tone I'd never heard her use before. Her hand was still gripping my arm.

"Saved my butt?" I drew back from her hand and the paper bag against my shirt. "What do you mean, saved my butt?"

Lifting the paper sack, she rattled the keys at me. "I locked Zack in the trunk. Took the keys out of the lock ... You owe me," she said in a hiss. "You know that? You fucking owe me."

"What the fuck are you talking about, Sheila?" But the full significance was sinking in. "Oh, my God."

She shook the keys at me again, bouncing the bag with the longnecks against her breast. She gave a choked laugh.

"I saved you, and what did I get for it? Huh? What did I get?" Glaring at me, she shook her head and started to slip past me. I seized her by the arm and stopped her.

"You mean out there ... on Pleasure Island? You—"

"It wasn't Zack who got into your room."

"That's ridiculous ... I don't believe it ... He couldn't get away with it."

"You don't think so?" She tried to pull free, but I held her tight. "He and J.C. were working at Fina. The chemical plant ... They have an acid tank, you know." She gave a strangled laugh, or maybe it was a sob, and her face contorted into a grimace, or a smirk. I couldn't read it. "Right there by the fence." She struggled to pull her arm out of my grip. "Let me go," she hissed. "I gotta go."

The two longnecks in the bag clinked against each other, and their significance ripped into my dulled consciousness for the first time.

"Where's Zack?" I said and glanced around, then back over my shoulder. Twisting deeper into the shadows by the ice machine, I relaxed my grip, and Sheila broke free. She moved backward off the curb and into the light shining on the empty parking spaces next to my car.

"Next door," she said, jerking her head toward the car wash. "Washing his truck."

I stared at her. She smiled back at me, her face once more smooth and pleasant, as I remembered it being when I used to meet her.

"Bye, Dan." She passed the keys from the hand clutching the paper sack to her free hand and gave me a little wave with it, the keys dangling from her fingers. "I'll see you around." She smiled brightly at me. "Maybe we'll see you and Dana over in Houston sometime. Okay?"

I didn't answer. She turned away from me and hurried to the Cutlass by the gas pumps. I watched as she got into it and scratched gravel out of the parking lot. Making a wide arc through the street, she whipped into the car wash drive next door.

My stomach was still churning—even more now, but I had no interest in buying anything to try to settle it. Getting into my own car, I backed out of the space and drove through the lot, past the pumps, and out into the street. Slowly. Watching the car wash.

There were three drive-through bays. The pick-up truck was still in one. A man in a short jacket was spraying water into the bed of the truck. I couldn't tell anything about him, his hair or his features or build, but I knew it was Zack.

Sheila had parked her car off to one side and was walking toward him. In each hand was one of the longneck beers. I didn't wait to see if she pointed toward my car or if he looked my way. I drove off in the opposite direction.

Chapter Thirty-four—J.C. Ledbetter

THE NEXT MORNING, WHEN I FINALLY reached the plant, I found Perry's door open and him sitting at his desk, gazing at the picture of the refinery rookery on his back wall. His chin rested on a steeple made with his fingers. It was already after eleven, since I had to make a trip up to Beaumont on a new lawsuit. I'd spent a fitful night, for once wishing I had Derek's .38 under my pillow. But no one followed me to the Sands, and no one bothered me once I was there.

"You'll never guess who I saw last night," I said, dumping my briefcase on Perry's conference table.

"You'll never guess what L-Landry just told me," Perry said and dropped his hands onto the desk. "The arbitration's ca-cancelled ... I just got off the phone with him."

"Oh? Why's that?"

"We ... we don't have to worry about J.C. Ledbetter anymore. He ... he went fishing last night and di-didn't come back."

"You're kiddin'!"

"They found his boat over in the marshes off Pleasure Island."

I felt a cold chill run down my spine, and my legs grew weak. Pulling out a chair, I eased into it and stared across the desk at him.

"Found it this morning, Landry said. Two ... two life jackets were there ... fishing gear, cooler ... but no J.C." He was shaking his head as I stared open-mouthed at him. I was trying to work my mind around this, what it meant. "You know," Perry was saying, "before the strike, that crazy-ass J.C. was up here all the time ... to see Sheila ... All the time ... You don't reckon?" His face was screwed up in a puzzled look.

I continued to stare, not speaking.

"No, no ... couldn't be," he said after a moment. "But it makes you wonder." I was wondering, too.

"That's who I saw last night," I said, taking a deep breath. "Sheila ... over at some 7-Eleven. I'm not sure where it is exactly, the street, I mean."

"Wha-a-a-t?" He shifted forward over his desk.

"She was coming out of the store ... with a couple of beers. Zack was next door, at one of those do-it-yourself car washes. Washing his pickup."

Now Perry was staring at me with as much incredulity as I had exhibited at his news. He sat without moving, his lips pursed.

"Hmm," he said finally. Then he started rocking in his chair while we both contemplated all this.

"Cynthia, honey," he called to his secretary after a minute, "would you bring us some coffee? Two cups ... Black okay with you, Dan?"

"Just some cream."

"You get that, Cynthia?"

"Sure thing," Cynthia called back. I could hear her bustling around next door. Andrea had returned to Houston and Cynthia was Perry's new secretary. Or the new title, Administrative Assistant.

"So, what do you think, Dan?"

"No sign of him at all?" I asked.

"Not a thing. He left his house about four yesterday afternoon ... that's what his wife said. She's usually asleep before he gets back, she said. When she got up this morning ... that was at five this morning, he wasn't there, so she called everybody she could think of. Couple of Landry's people who knew him pretty well ... Pete Reneau and some others, they went out looking for him and found his boat … That was around eight this morning. His truck was locked up in the parking lot over at the marina."

"Did he go out by himself? No one see him put his boat in?"

"They're still asking around over there, but it's not a real busy place in the afternoons … Wife says he told her he was goin' fishin'—that's all. She wasn't home when he left, but sometimes he went out by himself. She said."

"Here's the coffee, Mr. Comeau." Cynthia came in carrying two cups, moving slowly and carefully watching them to make sure they didn't spill. Secretaries are getting younger all the time, I thought, following her with my eyes. And more innocent looking. Nothing like Sheila. The only similarity was the gray slacks and white shirt. She handed me a cup, accompanied by a nice smile. A pleasant, friendly face. A smooth café au lait complexion and dark brown eyes.

I smiled back and said, "Thanks."

"Would you close the door on the way out," Perry said as she placed the second cup on his desk. After she had gone, Perry asked me again what I thought.

"Guess that solves your J.C. Ledbetter problem," I said, "and it saves me an arbitration." I shrugged, but I was feeling a deep sadness, thinking of Sheila and her eyes darting back and forth at me in the shadows by the ice machine at the 7-Eleven.

"Yeah, guess it does." Perry sighed and rocked in his chair. "I guess it does." He stopped rocking. "Do you really think Zack could've done it? … Could have—"

"Well, it was close to eleven when he was washing his truck."

"Yeah, and most people don't go washing a car that late at night … unless they're on a late shift and just got off." Perry picked up his coffee, took a sip, and stared at me over the cup.

"Was he?" I asked. "I mean working for the contractor, Belleau or whoever they are?"

"Let me check." He picked up the phone and made a call while I drank my coffee and tried to think. But mostly it was just a swirl of confused images: Sheila, Zack, Pleasure Island, Sheila's Oldsmobile Cutlass. While Perry waited on someone on the other end and then talked some more, he stared out the window behind his desk, and I stared out past his head and shoulders. It was a nice day, blue sky, gleaming latticework of refinery pipes and towers, white clouds of steam. The unit with the flare had been shut down, Perry told me yesterday. Because of its perpetual upsets, it was a casualty of the cutbacks, so there was no column of black smoke to mar the sky. Maybe never again.

Perry turned away from the window and hung up. "Zack left out of there at shift change yesterday, the day shift. They told him not to come back. Like we told 'em to."

"Maybe I should call the Ranger," I said, sounding tentative even to myself—but thinking he might also be interested in what Sheila told me about locking Zack in the trunk of her car when she met me on Pleasure Island. But I couldn't see me telling him that.

"They don't have a body or anything," Perry said. "Sometimes people drown out in that lake and they never show up ... get carried out to the Gulf with the tide or something."

I wasn't sure what the "or something" was. "Or maybe somebody's given them cement overshoes," I said.

"It happens," Perry said, and we were silent a long moment, each of us staring off as if seeking an answer from a distant oracle and lost in our own thoughts.

"I'll give the Ranger a call," I said, sitting up and putting my empty cup down on the table. "Let him know about my running into Sheila and Zack last night ... But I doubt he'll be investigating J.C.'s disappearance."

"No. Not even a criminal matter at this point," Perry said. "Certainly, nuthin there for the state, and Derek won't call the governor on this one."

I stood up. "Guess there's no need in my staying over here now.

Unless you have something else ... or you need me to go with you to see Derek."

"No." He shook his head. "Nothing here we need a lawyer on. All routine now ... 'Cept they're all pissed off about Jarvis, so you'll be hearing some more on that one."

"Yeah," I said and shrugged. "Reckon I will." I picked up my briefcase. "Keep me posted on J.C. and whether they find anything. I'll wait a couple of days to call the Ranger ... after I get back to Houston."

"What are you gonna tell him?"

"Just what I saw—Zack washing his truck."

So, I went home, the long drive past the still-green rice paddies and through the swarm of traffic on I-10. I didn't mind the drive. I was going home. This time, Dana would be waiting there for me. I had talked with her after I got back to the motel last night, told her what had happened, and to make sure the doors were locked—and that I loved her. She told me to be careful. And that she loved me. Nothing else mattered. I was going home to Dana.

Afterword

THIS NOVEL WAS INSPIRED BY a true crime that occurred in Port Arthur, Texas, in 1979. A husband and wife, both white, were accused of murdering the first African-American supervisor in the small Texaco refinery where the three worked. The wife confessed that the husband killed the supervisor—with whom she had had an affair—but her confession could not be used against the husband so long as the two remained married. And they did.

In the end, she was convicted of being an accomplice to the crime. Her conviction was sustained by the Texas Court of Criminal Appeals many years later, in 1990. There is no record of the husband, who pulled the trigger, ever being convicted of anything. While this outcome, with the husband going free, seems an injustice that cannot be corrected, what continues to intrigue the author is the psychological aspects of the case: the motives of the people involved and the nature of their relationships. *What Seems True* uses a similar fictional murder and situation to examine those relationships and motives—which may not be as clear cut as they seem at first blush.

The legal technicalities described in the novel are accurate, based on the law at that time and the context of the crime. The characters, the plot, and the relationships described in *What Seems True* are entirely fictitious and a product of the author's imagination.

Made in the USA
Middletown, DE
07 December 2024